Monika Maron

FLIGHT OF ASHES

translated by
David Newton Marinelli

readers international

The title of this book in German is *Flugasche*, first published in 1981 in West Germany by S. Fischer Verlag (Frankfurt am Main).
Copyright © S. Fischer Verlag GmbH, 1981

First published in English by Readers International, Inc., London and New York, whose editorial branch is at 8 Strathray Gardens, London NW3 4NY England. US/Canadian inquiries to Subscriber Service Department, P.O. Box 959, Columbia, Louisiana 71418 USA.

English translation copyright © Readers International, Inc. 1986

Cover illustration, "Die Gedanken sind frei" (Thoughts Are Free) by Klaus Staeck, by permission of Edition Staeck, Heidelberg
Design by Jan Brychta

Typesetting by Grassroots Typeset, London NW6
Printed and bound in Great Britain by Richard Clay
(The Chaucer Press), Bungay, Suffolk

ISBN 0—930523—22—9 hardcover
ISBN 0—930523—23—7 softcover

David Newton Marinelli has translated works by Thomas Bernhard, Hermann Kant and Guido Gozzano. He obtained a Bachelor of Arts degree in history at Ohio State Universtiy and Master of Arts at Rutgers University (New Jersey, USA). Since 1981 he has lived in Vienna, where he is completing his doctoral dissertation on the comic opera librettos of Carlo Goldoni.

PART ONE

I

My grandmother Josefa died a month before I was born. A year before that they had driven her husband, grandfather Pawel, into a Polish cornfield. When Grandfather and the other Jews got to the middle of the cornfield, they set fire to it from every side. I am unable to think of grandmother Josefa without imagining a long braid, a blue sky, a green meadow, twins, a cow and the Vatican. In the photo that hangs on the wall in my room my grandmother is washing dishes in a white enameled pan with a black rim. There is a heavy knot of hair at the back of her head rolled together from a braid. My grandmother is thickset with sturdy forearms and black hair.

My mother used to describe my grandmother's childhood as a warning whenever I didn't want to straighten up my room or pretended to have a sore throat to keep from going to school. Your grandmother would have been glad to have been able to go to school, my mother would say; then she would tell the story of six-year-old Josefa, who wasn't allowed to learn how to read and write because she had to watch out for the twins and the cow. I had to admit that I was better off than my poor grandmother, who had to sign her name with three Xs until the day she died. I wouldn't even admit to myself that I envied poor Josefa. But I must have, because the picture that my imagination painted of the enviable farm girl was bright and happy. The child Josefa sat under a blue sky on a green meadow covered with buttercups. A lean cow chewed dully on her cud. The twins lay next to each other asleep on the grass. Josefa had pulled her broad-striped skirt over her knees, played with her long braids and talked to the cow. She was barefoot and didn't have to go to school.

Later on—when my grandmother moved with her husband from Kurów near Łódż to Berlin, and had given birth to four children, of whom my mother was the youngest—they said she cooked sauerkraut for every meal, with bacon, onions and browned flour, simmered it a long while until it was soft and dark. To this day my mother and my Aunt Ida refuse to cook sauerkraut any different from the recipe my grandmother used.

I don't really know why I also think of the word Vatican in connection with my grandmother. The religious circumstances in our family were chaotic for respectable Prussia. My grandfather was a Jew, my grandmother was baptized a Catholic at birth and later joined a Baptist sect; the children were Baptists. I hear that my grandmother used to inveigh against the Vatican. They say she was an intelligent woman, though illiterate.

Although I envied my grandmother for her childhood on the green meadow and was very satisfied with her cooking as it had been handed down to me, I decided one day towards the end of my childhood that I had inherited my most important personality traits from her husband, my grandfather Pawel. I didn't consider my paternal grandparents in my genetic makeup. He was an upright school custodian; she was an honest cleaning woman. Both of them had, as far as I could tell from what I'd heard about them, little to offer in the way of qualities worth emulating.

But grandfather Pawel had the sort of character that opened up for me a wealth of possible traits useful for my future. As his heir I felt I could come to terms with my own nature. My grandfather was a dreamer: restless, spontaneous, hot-tempered. He didn't get up when the cat sat on his lap; every morning he made what each of his children wanted to drink for breakfast: tea, milk, coffee or hot chocolate, and he is said to have been a bit mad, now that I think of it. My mother always talked about my grandfather's constant restlessness, about his wanting to emigrate to Russia one minute and America the next; all that kept him from doing it was my grandmother's peasant inertia. Whenever my grandfather and grandmother had an argument, my grandfather always threatened to take to the road once and for all. But Momma never packs my clothes for me, he usually added, and stayed on. When he really had to go one day, he didn't do so willingly, and my grandmother went with him. But before that happened his passion for travel was limited to Sundays. On Sunday Grandfather got on his bicycle and visited friends. If it was summer and his friends had a garden, he would bring my grandmother flowers in the evening.

My grandfather's madness was enticing. Crazy people seemed freer to me than normal ones. They escaped the irritating value judgements of other people, who quickly gave up trying to understand madmen. They're crazy, they said, and left them in peace. Soon after I decided that I had inherited my grandfather's madness, I was already able to observe the symptoms in myself, which I knew from the stories my mother and Aunt Ida told. I became restless, hot-tempered, a dreamer. How I relished my success the first time I heard Ida whisper to my mother: "She must have gotten it from Papa."

I even found charming the poverty that my mother's family had lived in. It was a poverty different from the one my father talked about when he gave me a bicycle for my birthday, saying that I really ought not to get a bike for my tenth birthday because it would turn me into a spoiled brat. He had had to work to get his bike. He had had to earn his suit for confirmation, too. He had to deliver newspapers after school and he could count himself lucky that he didn't have to hand over the money he earned to his parents. I would let these sermons go in one ear and out the other without contradicting him and calmly wait for my mother's objections, usually signalled by an ironic smile while she was listening to my father. She didn't understand, she began innocently, how that could happen in a family with two children where both father and mother were working. After all, there were four children in her family, father worked at home making clothes and the brothers were unemployed. But she didn't have to earn money as a child and had a bike when she was ten, old to be sure, but a bike, an old camera at twelve; and when she went with her class on a skiing trip, one brother managed to find skis, the other boots, Father knit a pair of pants at night, Mother unknit her cardigan and knit her a sweater from it. Her brothers took her to the train station and they could boast afterwards that their sister was the prettiest girl in the class. We were much poorer than you were, my mother said, but we weren't Prussians.

Without ever knowing what was Prussian about the Prussians, I developed a contempt for all things Prussian, regarding grandfather Pawel as their antithesis. Prussians weren't crazy, that

3

much was for sure. They had to earn the money for their first bicycles themselves, spent the whole day washing their hands and were always performing their duty. I didn't like being Prussian. Since I considered myself my grandfather's sole heir, I doubled my portion of Jewish blood and I said I was half Jewish. A quarter Jewish didn't sound convincing to me. Every chance I got I brought up my Polish extraction. Not that I wanted to be considered a Pole— I can never remember having felt proud of belonging to a national group—but I didn't want to be German. It seems to me today that my distaste for all things Prussian was part of a fear of growing up, when I would once and for all be subject to all the social norms. Appealing to my heritage was the simplest way of getting out of threatening constraints.

Grandfather Pawel was dead, burned to death in a cornfield. He belonged to me. There was nothing he said or thought that I didn't like. I lent him all the qualities I thought important in a person. My grandfather was clever, poetic, gay, generous, frightened. There was no denying that fear must have inhabited him, and it took a long time before I could come to terms with it. If it hadn't been for the photo I found showing my grandfather in front of a small farmhouse in Poland, he would have remained a courageous man for me. My grandfather is thin and grey-haired in the picture, his mouth is twisted in an uncertain smile, there is a frightened look in his eyes. The picture was taken in 1942 in the village where grandmother Josefa was born and where my grandfather lived after he had been deported from Germany and before they shipped him to the ghetto. My grandfather's fear depressed me. Once I had discovered it, I found it in the older pictures as well, which go back to Berlin when Grandfather still worked as a tailor and visited friends on Sundays. His skeptical, vigilant gaze, almost identical in all the photos, awoke the impression that Grandfather was avoiding the eyes of the viewer. When I discovered my grandfather's fear, I had no fears myself except math homework and dark basements. The books that I read at the time dealt more with courage than fear: the courage of resistance fighters, of heroic farmers, of Soviet partisans. Fear wasn't a likeable quality, and I tried to suppress it as best I could.

4

I later recognized being related to my grandfather in fear as well. When Mohnhaupt didn't want to accept me into the Party because—his words—he would be afraid that I'd shoot him in the back, I was afraid of him. I'm afraid of every doorman who snaps at me because a page is loose in my identity card. I'm scared of old women who chase children away from a meadow with their crutches so that their dogs can shit there undisturbed. The thirst for power in primitive souls makes me tremble. Since my grandfather was hot-tempered, I believe his fear followed the noise in his ears, a noise which fills up your head and drives out all thoughts except for the thought of fear. Fear grows, grows larger than myself, wants to break out. It revolts and stretches out until it becomes rage and I burst. Then I scream at the doorman until he creeps back into his booth with a grumble. I even went so far as to threaten an old hag and her fat dachshund with a beating if she didn't immediately let go of the child she had grabbed by the forearm. And the other fear, the sudden, black one that tears a huge dark hole all around me in which I float weightless. Every attempt to get my footing is in vain. Whatever I touch becomes detached from where it belongs and like me floats in the abyss. When I think about death. When I search for the incomprehensible meaning of my life. My grandfather was afraid of the cornfield they drove him into. What do I have to fear? The bed I'll die in. The life that I'm not living. The monotony unto death and thereafter.

II

I'm going to B. tomorrow. I haven't seen this town yet, only know that it's considered a stroke of bad luck to be born in B. Planned: on-the-scene report. A charming way of putting it. If it read instead, portrait of worker so-and-so, followed in parentheses: awarded the "Banner of Labor" on October 7th, I wouldn't have to go to B. I could look up a similar article from a few years back, call up and find out age, hair color, color of eyes, distinguishing marks, and I could start. Colleague so-and-so from B. is a modest (or:

lively) man in his forties (or: thirties or fifties) who looked at me with his blue (or: brown) eyes, as he talked seriously (or: cheerfully) about his work. Etc. and so forth. Not that Colleague so-and-so hadn't earned his medal and wasn't an exemplary human being. But he wouldn't have many other possibilities to behave differently once his name got in the papers.

Either he receives me with a condescending smile, not arrogant, but sympathetic and amused, because I'm the sixth or seventh and because he knows, whatever I find out about him, I'll write only good things. But Colleague so-and-so is a friendly person, who spares me these qualms, tells me about his good collective, his good foreman, his good marriage—and goes back to work.

Or he's become a victim of my colleagues in the meantime. So he'll tell me how he's read about himself, accepts the legend of his past and is afraid to use his own words for fear of not doing justice to the unfamiliar honor of being a celebrity.

Any other attitude would be awkward: an ingrate who thinks he deserves the medal instead of having been granted it as a gift; someone who could do just as well without it because he already has a high opinion of his work.

I'm going to B. tomorrow. "Look around. Do something," Luise said in her broad Berlin dialect. I'm never sure in cases like these whether she just didn't want to bother her head about me or whether she regards all agreements today as pointless anyway. Or else she trusts me in moments like these automatically.

She gave me a heartening, almost loving look. I was once again astonished by her child's blue eyes in a face crossed by wrinkles large and small. "Go. Do something."

I pack my bag as I've been doing once a month for six years. Two pairs of jeans, four blouses, underwear, books. The indispensable phone call to my mother, yes, she's going to pick up my son from kindergarten tomorrow; 'til Wednesday then. Yes, I'll also pack a sweater he can change into.

I ought to go down to the basement to get coal. When I come back on Thursday, the apartment will be cold and I'll be tired. But the basement light doesn't work and I'm scared now and again. An indefinable fear, goosebumps from childhood that make my heart beat faster, and my shoulders get a cramp, which makes me pull in my head. A long way 'til Thursday; let it stay cold.

I ought to eat something.

Business trips make me homesick even before I leave. Three or four days in a strange town full of doors with strange people behind them. "Hello, my name is Josefa Nadler; I'm from the *Illustrated Weekly*"... Experiences, impressions... bewilderment and no one to share it with. After a day at most, I begin to envy all the people on the street who apparently know one another. Perhaps they don't like each other, but at least they know each other.

I look greedily into all the windows behind which families are eating their dinner, behind which their mouths move while they talk and look like people on television with the sound turned off.

I watch with increasing sadness as bipeds melt into quadrupeds in front of movie theaters, laugh and smoke. I'd like to smoke too, but a woman by herself with a cigarette? Perhaps in Hungary or Paris.

Sometimes I ask directions or the time simply to talk.

The monuments, the stony, the famous dead of the town become my most intimate allies, the only voices besides mine. My last salvation: intensify my loneliness to a pleasure, climb the highest rung of solitude, me the most forlorn among humans.

I should make use of the fact that I'm home. The telephone stands conveniently in front of me on the table within easy reach. I pick up the receiver in order to check whether the artificial heart of our communications is really beating. But evidently no one wants to talk to me. I turn the filter of my cigarette between my index finger and thumb, study the structure of the fibers, flick off the ashes that aren't there.

This doubly damned waiting around. For what?

For the famous fairy tale prince who rings the doorbell: Hello, lovely lady, you are going to B. tomorrow and are afraid of being alone. Please do me a great honor; I am at your service.

The escape for the inconsolable remains. I take my bed out of the chest, change the linen, place a vase with a wilted rose next to it, put on my nicest and longest nightgown—a sensual birthday present from my dear momma to her thirty-year-old daughter. I look fresh for someone who is suffering. I make up my skin to an appropriate pallor, make up my eyelids a bit darker, use up the rest of my best perfume and look at myself in the mirror, complacent, suspicious, full of malice for princes and others. One day that will all be over and they won't have seen it. I pour myself a glass of wine, place it carefully next to the rose like a poisoned draught and lie down in bed like Snow White in her coffin.

Ah, Luise, you always were clever. You knew why you bolstered me up with optimism and pleasure in my work before you sent me to this wretched dump. These smoke stacks like cannon barrels aimed at the sky shooting their charges of filth at the town day in day out and night after night: not with a roar, no, but quietly, like snow that falls slowly and gently, that stops up drainpipes, covers roofs where the wind blows without waves. In summer it swirls through the air, dry black dust that flies into your eyes because you are a stranger here, too, as I am, Luise. Only strangers stand still and rub the soot from their eyes. The population of B. walks through the town with squinting eyes; you'd think they were smiling.

And these fumes could serve as road signs. Please go straight ahead to the ammonia, then turn left at the nitric acid. When you feel a stabbing pain in your throat and bronchial tubes, turn around and call the doctor, that was sulphur dioxide.

And the way people clean their windows. Every week, better still every day. Everywhere clean windows in this god-awful filth. They wear white shirts, the children, white stockings. You have to imagine it: going through the black, greasy rainwater with white stockings. The salesgirl said that white sweaters sell best here. Go, look around—I'm staring my eyeballs out of my head: everywhere this filth. When you meet the dwarfs from the kindergarten who walk in rank and file down the streets, you have to think how many of them must have bronchitis. You wonder about every tree that hasn't died. What am I doing here, Luise, if I can't change anything? Every word that I hear, every face that I see is transformed by my pity. And by my shame. I'm ashamed because I knew that this town existed and I was stingy with my imagination, which I'm so proud of. No doubt I've taken gondolas through

Venice in my imagination, or been scared to death in New York, or picked oranges from the trees in Morocco. But I didn't let it into this B., which I could have entered all the while.

The little man behind the desk examined me with his sad owl's eyes behind thick glasses when I told him that I wanted to write about the filth in B. and about the people who live in it. Alfred Thal is the Director's press agent. A nondescript little man, slick hair combed in strands to the back of his neck, thin drooping shoulders. He holds his hand in front of his mouth when he laughs because of his bad teeth.

If I asked for Colleague so-and-so, the medal winner, he certainly wouldn't have been surprised. It happens to him every day when my colleagues from the press, television and radio turn up in his little room full of nooks and crannies. Colleague so-and-so is just the right one for you. When did you ever hear of a worker receiving a medal from the government, going to the capital? He has been given an honor the ruling class deserves. Besides that, his father died at forty of an occupational disease. Colleague so-and-so is treated free of charge at the works outpatient clinic. His mother didn't get to see the ocean until she retired. Colleague so-and-so's children now go every year to summer camp by the sea. Luise, don't think I didn't see that or appreciate it! But I can imagine how Colleague so-and-so goes to buy a black suit with his wife, not too expensive, what does he need it for, but not too inexpensive either, after all he is going to pin his medal on this jacket. His old black shoes won't do any longer either, especially not with his new suit. Then Colleague so-and-so travels to Berlin. He's even permitted to use the Director's big black car. When his name is called under the letter S, loudly, it will resound throughout the entire hall: Colleague so-and-so from the chemical works in B., he could almost cry. Perhaps he will think of his father who died of an occupational disease, who got his name in the papers only once—when he died. Perhaps at that moment he'll even forgive them the freight loads of filth that fall on his head every day. He'll hesitantly walk along the buffet at the banquet. He won't take any chicken. He's afraid all the excitement will make him clumsy and

9

that the animal would land on his suit; he doesn't want to make a fool of himself. Most of all he'll put very little on his plate because he doesn't want to be greedy. And when he's back home he'll tell everyone what a once-in-a-lifetime experience it was—the reception, the buffet: mushrooms, champagne. There was everything! And how the Minister shook his hand. Someone will ask whether the Minister remembered the hot summer day when he visited their shop floor, was shown the hottest part, recorded at 70°C, how he ordered that a few crates of orange juice be brought and then disappeared. Everyone will laugh as if it was a good joke. Needless to say, Colleague so-and-so didn't have anything to say about it to the Minister, just as none of them would have talked about it.

No, I'll spare Colleague so-and-so.

Alfred Thal is shaking his head. He looks sad even when he smiles. "You can go into the old power plant. Look, behind there, the fourth smoke stack, that's it. That's where the filth comes from. We should have gotten a new one a long time ago, but between one thing and another the funds were never available. And if they were available, a power plant broke down somewhere else. So they got the new one and we kept our old one. Now that we're finally going to get it, it runs on natural gas." A cynical tone lingers in Thal's voice.

"When?" I ask.

"It's supposed to be ready in six months, but who knows. Haven't you seen the construction site? The big, light blue building?" Thal chuckles. "Light blue was recommended by the landscape architect. Since we don't have a blue sky to begin with, they're at least going to build a sky-blue power plant."

"And will that stop the soot?"

Thal laughs without baring his stumpy yellow teeth, but laughter isn't really the right expression for his pointed mouth and for the ironic glimmer in his eyes. He savors his advantage, waits until I show impatience.

"That stays," Thal says, puckers up his mouth again and is happy that I'm surprised. There's a challenge in his grinning silence. I'm supposed to ask more questions; he doesn't tell anything willingly.

10

"Why?" I ask.

"The old one is going to be used in spite of it."

"Who says so?"

Thal's grin grows wider. He makes a fist, points skywards with his thumb and looks at the ceiling, which must mean: someone all the way up top.

The street that runs from the power plant to the hotel is empty now. The second shift began an hour ago. Only a few trucks and construction vehicles are going over the bridge past the plant walls making a racket that echoes back harshly from the other side of the road, where it reverberates far across the level building site and gradually becomes lost in the sand and distance. You can hear hissing and booming behind the walls; steam rises, the sound of dull rhythmic pounding.

Like a Golem, I think, a weird giant who has been tamed but is ready to break loose at any moment, break out and burn down everything that gets in the way of its glowing green eyes.

I walk faster. Get out of here, away from the stench, the filth, away from the bent-over people in the ash chambers, from the gentle heroism with which they shovel coal into the wide-open fiery jaws. Away from my pity, which sloshes around in me like lukewarm water, which goes to my throat and eyes, away from Hodriwitzka without whom the power plant would have fallen apart long ago, as the engineer said.

So that's why Thal smiled when he suggested that I visit the power plant. That's why he said no journalist had ever been able to take more than two or three hours of it. Built 1890 or '95, what difference do five years make anyway? It was new then, now it's worn out; twenty years ago a fireman stoked two furnaces, now he stokes four and in the meantime most firemen are women. In return they're now in a socialist collective. Is that progress, Luise? Is that where our higher justice, juster distribution of wealth, of work, of the air, lies? And who dares to decide that this monster isn't shut down, although the new power plant will soon be completed? Who has the right to make people work in last century's conditions because they need a synthetic sweater or a certain kind

11

of bug killer? I don't dare to do so, I don't want the right and I won't be able to look at a fabric softener anymore without thinking of these brittle walls, of grey shops where women have to put up old sheet metal to keep the wind from whistling. And of the ash chambers, the heat and the clods of coal. And why didn't I know all about this? Every week there's something in the paper about B., about a new product, about an event at the Palace of Culture, about production plans filled early, about the medal for Colleague so-and-so. Nothing about the power plant, not a single word about the ash chambers, which are the worst there are. Why shouldn't the housewives, who are so obsessed with their wash that they do a whole load for as little as two shirts, know who pays for their laudable sense of cleanliness? Why shouldn't the active home gardeners think about whose health is ruined by their well-fertilized rose beds? Maybe they don't even want to know, or maybe they would be more careful about how they treated other people.

My train leaves in two hours, and I'm glad to be able to leave B. I feel as if I had been struck on the forehead: I'm dizzy now, I have to rest and reflect, most of all, reflect. I feel embarrassed at the thought of Thal's smile when I say goodbye to him. He will dismiss me like my colleagues who were here before, who left more or less as perplexed and shocked as I am. Thal thinks he knows what I'll write, and he will smile.

I'm sitting in my armchair with a cigarette between my numb fingers; I've got my coat on. There is still no light in the cellar, the flowers are wilted, the butter rancid.

I want to live by myself. As if this postulate would warm me up. Good God, unbelievable, to come home to a heated apartment, to a set table. Oh darling, you're finally here, he'd say. I let him take me in his arms. It was awful, he pours me a cognac, pull yourself together first, you're all pale. After a while I'm floating on a cloud of good cheer. With warm feet and cognac in the stomach you think quite differently about B. Sure, it's really bad, but the people there have gotten used to it, and things don't happen all at once: historical necessities and all that. Would you pour me another one, dear? I'll be all right soon.

But my feet aren't warm and B. has gotten under my tired, frozen skin and I'd have to pour myself.

I'm forgetting slowly what it was like when someone was waiting for me. It does take an effort to remember details over five years. An indulgent transfiguration suffuses it, sometimes there is even the thought that it really couldn't have been that bad after all, as if it had only been three years ago that I had taken the vow to live by myself. I only know that I didn't want to be asked all that any more: whadyathink, wheryacominfrom, whereyagoin, whenyacominagain, whyyalaughin? I didn't want to be a Siamese twin who can only think with two heads, dance with four feet, decide with two voices and feel with one heart. But emancipated women don't shiver, much less scream, and they cross the word "longing" from their vocabulary. I shiver, I scream, I feel longing. I leaf through my notebook to see who I can expect to put up with my groggy feelings and my tear-stained eyes. Indisputable virtue of a man of mine: he has to, whether he wants to or not. G-Grellmann, Christian.

My mother always called him a nice boy and Aunt Ida, a faithful soul. Ida still maintains wistfully to this day that I would have long since been a happy woman if I had only married this handsome nice Christian. I ask her in return how she would wish so much spite on this dear, handsome Christian. And then Ida has tears in her light blue eyes when she thinks of me growing old alone. I decided that I would never marry Christian on the day we both finished school and were celebrating this tremendous, long-awaited event. I loved handsome Hartmut at the time, the best sportsman in the school, on top of being in a successful jazz band. But Hartmut loved a lot of girls, among them a palefaced blonde with a white lace blouse and a black taffeta skirt, whom he held victoriously in his arms that night. I sat in a corner and howled. Christian took me home. It was light already, the subway reverberated in the distance, somewhere a milk truck stopped on the other side of the street. I loved the milk trucks, which put their rattling crates in front of the stores while we were still asleep. They radiated the security of the big city and were for me the epitome of romance.

I had stopped crying, I simply felt inconsolable and miserable in my first love. Suddenly, not far from our houses, Christian, who had been silent up 'til then, caressed my head rather confusedly and said: "Don't be sad, I still love you."

Christian as a substitute for Hartmut. This thought made my misery complete, intensified it almost to catastrophe. I ran home, didn't eat anything for three days and then went on vacation.

I never saw Hartmut again. And since then it was decided that Aunt Ida's fondest wish would never be fulfilled. Christian went to school in Halle. After a year I received letters again; then he came in person. One day with a girl. She had short dark hair, broad, somewhat square shoulders, grey eyes. She seemed strong though thin, and everyone said she looked like me. Later on they married, a while later they divorced: she left and Christian didn't try to stop her. Since then he lives alone in a one-room apartment— old building, outside toilet. No marriage, no apartment, the woman at the housing office said. We've never talked about the morning of the milk truck.

Christian's apartment has a calming effect on me. The initial impression is one of chaos: book shelves stuffed to the ceiling, magazines and card catalogues in the corners, pictures along every bit of wall, a huge solid plank as desk illuminated by a glaring lamp, an old plush sofa and two chairs close to the brown tile stove. On closer inspection it turns out that the books are pedantically ordered; the corners are tidy and free of dust; every inch of the room is utilized. Chaos has a system.

As long as I can remember I have envied people with an ability to spread harmony and warmth, to translate their mental balance to rooms. All my attempts at creating domesticity have failed. I have always created the same coolness, disharmony and imperfection, although I tried to make up for my incompetence by imitating others.

The footwarmer is shining on my feet, which are cozy inside big felt slippers. I am spooning goulash soup out of a can, talking about sad Alfred Thal, about the white knee socks and about the power plant.

"What do you want to write?" Christian asks.

"I don't know."

"Then write two versions. The first like it is, and a second one which can be printed."

"That's crazy," I say. Schizophrenia as an aid to living—as if refined double dealing were less horrible than the vulgar kind. A cynical abandonment of the truth. Intellectual perversion.

Christian makes a sign of refusal. "Stop making such a fuss." The corner of his mouth twitches for an instant—the notorious Grellmann scorn: gentle and arrogant. "It's better at any rate than your self-censorship: pen in the right hand, red pencil in the left!"

Next thing he'll tell me simply to forget the newspaper when I write, not to destroy my logic by anticipating objections from the Editor-in-Chief, watching me the whole time to see if the sting has finally taken effect. And at the first sign of uncertainty he'll withdraw his suggestion or even accuse me of incompetence. And the trap will already have snapped shut. I'll suddenly advocate his ideas and he'll play the sceptic. Sooner or later I'll say. all right, I'll try it, and Christian will have a hard time hiding his triumph. No, my dear, not today. What good is your truth to me if no one finds out about it? And what's supposed to be left over for the false imitation? I remain quiet, stubbornly bend a paper clip until it finally snaps.

Christian yawns; he's annoyed at his failure. "Go to sleep," he says, "you look like a chicken."

I feel like a chicken, too, a dead chicken: cold, plucked and headless.

So it's not Snow White in her coffin today, but a chicken in the freezer.

Christian is making his bed on the sofa. He carefully smooths out the sheets until there are no wrinkles left. I curl up, warm my hands on my stomach, one leg over the other. The bed clothes are cool. It's silly to sleep in two beds when you're shivering.

"Two beds are silly," I say.

Christian looks up for an instant. He then continues pulling on the sheet which is long since smooth over the sofa.

"Be glad you have a bed. Chickens sleep on a perch, you know."

15

''But I'm a dead chicken without wings to keep warm.''

''Dead chickens don't shiver.''

I turn towards the wall. He's right. We are neuter to each other since a milk truck morning a hundred years ago. Not even the temperature outside can change that.

And then a warm current flows from my right shoulder into my arm and neck. Christian is lying next to me and I'm seized by a paralyzing fear. This isn't Christian any more, this is a man, strange, like the others. His hands will soon be probing my flesh, if it meets with his general standards he'll wait for the best; if it doesn't I'll be classified as frigid. Nothing is left of me except the piece of woman lying under the covers tense with cold and strain.

Christian lights a cigarette, puts it in my mouth, slides his arm under my neck, laughs quietly to himself. ''You looked something like this when you had to go to the board in math.''

May well be. The stabbing feeling in the pit of my stomach when my name was called, hands behind my back, blue with excitement, Blessin's pleasant voice: ''Well, Miss Nadler, hasn't the coin dropped yet?'' Nothing in my head except a painful pressure. When I sat down the flesh on both fingernails was torn and bleeding. But I'm not standing at the board. All I have to do is reach out my hand and touch Christian's warm skin. I wouldn't even have to do what I don't want to. Instead I feel violated before I am touched.

The monotonous voices of drunks come through the open window; the bar on the corner is closing. ''You—pull up your pant leg,'' someone stutters. ''I said pull up your pant leg so I can piss on you.''

We laugh, probably louder than the thing deserves, and I stretch out my arm. I read in Robert Merle that the Haitians call playing what we call sleeping together. Playing is nicer. It makes you think of meadows and flowers, of fun and laughter, not of stuffy bedrooms, sentimental oaths or of a tired reach next to you just before you go to sleep. Come, Christian, we'll play, forget B. and Blessin, and you too, Luise. Don't think about life, feel life until it hurts, feel all thoughts away, just be leg and stomach and mouth and skin.

16

The hairdresser is just raising his Venetian blinds, stands in the doorway like a well-groomed model with a nightclub smile beneath his little blonde beard. No, no, I'm no customer. I also smile instead of sticking out my head. Hazy, sunny yellow hangs in the air, tired wind rocks wilted leaves on the trees and tassles on the plane trees. The end of the world didn't happen, or I slept through it. If the tram leaves, I'll walk. The market is on the promenade between church and city hall. Plump, puffed-up women are standing in their booths, shift their weight from one leg to the other. A white carriage is waiting in front of the church and a taxi decorated with flowers is parked in front of city hall: a wedding. Someone calls: "First class fish, fine fish" and "Mrs, ya got corns, I can see 'em from 'ere." A cloud of various smells floats above the square: oranges, fish, spices, flowers and curry sausage, all of it very close, and the people shove against each other and push others aside to feel material and apples. The vegetable co-op is right across the street, almost empty. But it's only at the market that you can feel and choose. After that you go to the pharmacy on the corner to stock up on the week's supply of pills. The pharmacy is always over-crowded on market days. I buy three bouquets of the last Michaelmas daisies: violet, white and yellow.

The cardboard strip on my door has been torn again—these brats. Josefa left, Nadler right: each part of the name hanging from a thumbtack. The sight tempts me to symbolic interpretations. But none of that today; today there's more humble work on the agenda. And I'll finally call the plumber on Monday. "You have so many friends," Aunt Ida always says, "and in spite of that everything in your place always needs to be fixed." Right, Ida, I'll probably never learn. I even have to fetch coal myself. And Rickert's door opens promptly. "Miss Nadler," she says. The very fact that she says that. Thirty years old, mother of a five-year-old, divorced and "Miss". "Miss Nadler, the house committee is building a small fence around the garden out front." Could I maybe help out with the painting? No, I can't, I don't want to either. I don't need any little fence. Why these people go on building fences around this little garden and that little courtyard; why not around every little tree? "I live alone with a child," I say, confine myself to

17

benign inconsistency and the Rickert woman puckers up her face so that she looks like a goat. "A man rang your doorbell yesterday at about 5:00 in the afternoon, but it wasn't the dark one with the beard," she says and disappears again behind her door. I hear her put up the chain.

And she'll lock the house door punctually at 8:00 p.m. And after 8:00 p.m. you can't talk to us any more. That's when we lock ourselves up in our dens and lock others out of human society. It's no use knocking, dear friend, or calling either; you can't outyell the traffic. Go home. Order is essential.

I go into the kindergarten once my breath has stopped turning into clouds of steam.

"Mommy!" A violent assault against my body; firm, warm, soft flesh; the intoxicating feeling of being irreplaceable, the dearest; you can't imagine her not being there; the other's great joy. I know that the disappointment comes quickly. "What did you bring me?" But I've taken care of that, don't want to spoil the fun, not his or mine. I place the red tractor on the sacred altar of our love and am rewarded with a shrill cry of joy: "Mommy, you're sweet."

When we're on the street I ask: "Well, shall we go for a beer?"

A brief look of agreement, an answer in his deepest voice: "Yes, I'll drink a great big beer." A passerby turns around, my son giggles: "That man must really think I drink beer."

We order ice cream and coffee.

"Andreas hit me."

"So hit him back."

"But he's bigger."

"So what. Maybe he's weak."

"No, but he can't run as fast. I'd just as soon run away."

"But it's better to hit back."

"But I'm scared."

"Make him scared, too. Look, when you're all worked up you can spit fire."

My son is excited, shows how he's going to spit fire, instead he spits ice cream on the table.

At night he asks in bed: "Can I really spit fire?"

18

"Yes, when you're in a big rage, no doubt about it."

"And you?"

Me? No, I'm sorry. I can't help you out with magical powers, I can only talk about them. Poor kid.

"Yeah, me too," I say.

That uneasy, blank calm hangs in the room while my son is asleep, it spreads anxiety, it provokes: disjointed life. I put on a record. Czech baroque music, feel no affinity today; try Chopin, but the uneasy feeling remains that somewhere, something is going on—there's life, that life is passing me by. I'm missing people, events, days. And yet I'm well aware of how things end if I do violence to a day, if I am unable to come to terms with its normal, planned course, and instead of seeking my life look for another, strange one, if I suddenly leave my apartment, dead tired, go to some bar where I suspect friends are and come back home an hour later not richer for the experience but twenty Marks poorer for the taxi fare.

One day I'll set up my building, a large apartment building where only mutual friends live. Not the sort of artificial house-community that does nothing more than build little fences all the time and where everyone window dresses. Eight or nine tenants, each has his own apartment, you can be alone but don't have to be. The doors all have plates, red on one side, green on the other. You can ring when it's green; red means do not disturb. For Christmas and birthdays each apartment cooks a course. The floor will be a playground for the children. No one has to return from a business trip to a cold apartment. And when someone wants to write a book, he can stop working and the others will pay him a sabbatical for a year. If everyone chips in fifty Marks, he can have a month's stipend. In return he'll look after the children now and then. And when his book is finished, he can write our names inside thanking us all. If no one wants to print it, that's all right too, then he'll read it out loud to the others.

I would have turned my plate to the green side today.

The white winter sun, dimmed by the uncleaned window panes, is caught in my coffee spoon. I stare into the captive sun, play

19

with it, as I swing the spoon back and forth, then I put a white sheet of paper into the typewriter, look alternately at the sun and the paper, search for a first sentence on B. In front of me on the round table—analyses and tables of dust emissions, my notes, newspaper clippings, disorganized, on top and underneath each other, next to which lies the coffee cup: gentle transition from breakfast to work. For heaven's sake, no writing desk, no square spaces in front of me, no well-ordered pencils and loose-leaf notebooks?

An empty white sheet full of possibilities, resolutions, responsibilities to oneself: this time it will be completely different from before. Avoid old mistakes: there will be new mistakes. But the chance still exists that I'll get past the cliffs in one piece. No obstacles as yet in sight. B. still lies before me—facts and experiences smooth as still water.

I'm sitting legs pulled up close in my big, hard, old chair looking at the maple tree in front of the window, I let the image blur, imagine the path from the train station in B. to the collective combine, my first horror at this town, think of Alfred Thal, who said, "B. is the dirtiest town in Europe." That should be the first sentence; that's how I have to begin. But even Luise would cross that out. The dirtiest town in Europe in a socialist state of all places. If we can afford this sad fact, we ought at least not to worry about making it public. Possible variation: B. is a filthy town. Rubbish, everyone knows that already.

If not the whole truth, then at least a nice sentence. Well: the only people who get off the train in B. are those who have to get off there, those who live there or work there or have something else to do there. This is my first sentence. I'm satisfied.

The sky. What a feeling that was when I saw it sink down on me, took the yellow grey poisonous fog into my consciousness, counted the high funnels that it spewed out of, hanging over the town like a ceiling. I was stunned or terrified, I was afraid of the thought of all that poison. I smoked less in B. Fear is out of the question. We don't write to frighten people, nor to horrify them. Bewilderment—still too strong. Perplexity, that will do. "Strangers look perplexed at the sky over the town..." etc.

20

After two hours I have written two sentences. It takes a real effort. Too much effort. I'm looking for a word, *the* word, the apt one, the only one. In order to throw it out as soon as I've found it, to exchange it for a milder variant, not too mild, the closest nuance, the one they can print. Whatever isn't printable isn't thought through. It's only a short path from unprintable to unthinkable as soon as you agree to measure reality by this standard: whatever lies in between doesn't exist. I've almost gotten out of the habit of talking about alternatives in public, of expressing thoughts whose unprintability I can measure. And why? I know in advance what they will tell me, and I can't take it any more: you give your opponents the arguments to use against you. You can write everything as long as you put it in the proper order, then everything has its unassailable order and nothing can be other than what it is. And this constant: you're right, girl, but we simply couldn't right now...there were other more important things...don't you think we know the problems? This Comrade "We". They put up their unshakeable "We" against my pitiful "I saw" and already I'm the griper, the loner who swims against the stream, unwilling to listen to reason, arrogant, autocratic. They shore themselves up in their "We", make themselves invisible, invulnerable. But woe unto me if I enter into their grammar of majesty and call them "you" and "them". I am then pelted with their stern questions: Who are "they"? What do you really mean? Why do you say "you" and not "we"? Whom are you trying to distance yourself from?

I'll say this once and for all: whoever speaks of himself in the plural has to allow me to address him in the plural. Anyone who is a "we" also has to be a "you" or a "they". And if they make their opinions into mine without asking permission, I'll say "me" to me and "them" to them.

Perhaps only a few years separate me from them, years during which the mechanism of *"un"* finally meshes and the *un*printable, *in*effable, *un*thinkable become *un*truths because I've been unable to put up any more than the others with not writing the most exciting and moving stories, not to say, not to hesitate. Then I'll say "we": "we" were unable, because *I* was unable, and I'll reject someone

21

new who says "I" again and for whom I am "them".

I'm not all that far from them now. I'm already uncertain whether they are right or not, the Strutzers and Mesekes. The people have settled in, have gotten used to being citizens of B. and to being sprinkled with filth. Perhaps it's simply coarse and heartless to tell them: you've been forgotten, sacrificed for something more important, and I can't change anything.

But what is more important, Luise? Every sibling in B. pays his tribute to our well-being. A small power plant would suffice for that, a mere 160 megawatts.

But I write "perplexed" instead of "horrified" and hide the truth behind nice sentences.

When Colleague so-and-so reads the article (maybe he'll read it because it concerns his town), he'll put the paper aside contemptuously, turn on the TV and tell his wife these people really ought to live here for a while, they'd learn to forget their sanctimonious blab. Besides, the one who wrote it was all pale when she left the power plant. "But paper is patient," he'll add, and his wife will agree with him.

What good are white lies to anyone, Luise? Do you think that Colleague so-and-so would let us talk him into believing his town wasn't all that bad after all? Do you believe he doesn't think about the uncompleted power plant and rejected plans because we don't talk about them?

Or does someone believe that 180 tons of flue ash weigh more on newsprint than on their own skin?

Imagine, Luise, that Christian's trap snaps shut and I write two articles: one like it really was and one that could be printed. And you would have to decide. Of course you'd be hopping mad about the sentences that I write only so you'd have to cross them out. You always found them and you always liked them and you were mad because I forced you into the role of censor. But if I forced you to pick the worse of two reports, Luise, I don't know where you'd aim your wrath. Perhaps against me since I created the situation. But perhaps against others as well who don't permit us to display the filth of a town in the paper. You could pass the blame onto Rudi Goldammer, too. Then you'd have gotten rid of your role as bouncer and you wouldn't need to be afraid of a scandal either, because you can depend on Rudi Goldammer's timidity.

I am unfair; I don't leave her an honorable possibility, and she doesn't deserve that. Luise doesn't pull herself out of problems. And it's pointless to try to guess Luise's reaction. My certain expectations of her behavior have too often turned out to have been wrong. Not that she has always reacted more tolerantly or kindly than I had assumed, not at all, but differently than I had thought in all my speculations. Meanwhile it's almost become a game to think up possible reactions, the worst one first and then discard them all. Because, as I said: Luise is not predictable, which doesn't mean that she's unpredictable. I've never been wrong so far on one thing: Luise is honest.

That much I know but nothing more; and I just don't know what Luise would in fact do if I were to carry out Christian's idiotic suggestion.

I have two sentences, still only two sentences. Can't do anything with my facts and experiences smooth as glass. Cliff upon cliff instead.

It's gotten dark in the room. The sun has disappeared behind a uniform grey-white blanket of cloud that hangs over the streets like a huge flat ceiling. The forecast says snow, the first snow of the year. Sentences are forming themselves in my head, meaningless sentences that uncontrollably put words together: ...We have worked on it with the utmost exertion...we have no other choice under the circumstances...we present our heartfelt greetings on...

Confused, incoherent nonsense, rhetorical embellishments that have a place somewhere in the back of my head and that come out of it now unsummoned. There's no point. I can't stumble from one sentence to the next without knowing what I want to write. But what ought I want to write? This castrated truth, perhaps, these compromises that we're always so proud of when we dare to talk about them in public, to say that shift work is hard, that somewhere a school lunch doesn't taste quite right, or that there are subjective problems now and then with a few officials. My God, what times are we living in where such insignificant statements are enough

23

to get one called a critical mind and a combative personality?

I roll a fresh sheet into the typewriter and write: B. is the filthiest town in Europe.

Only this sentence, no more, not today.

III

For the first time in fifteen years I'm afraid to knock on Christian's door. What happened to make us afraid of each other? We were a bit closer than usual, infinitely closer. Nothing to fear. And yet the oppressive feeling: it will be different from before. Fear of expectations, his and mine, of a new vulnerability that no longer allows familiar tones. My own uncertainty, as well, as to which Christian I'm looking for here—the old reliable friend or this new Christian with powerful warm hands. Or I've known it for a long time and don't admit it because I could be disappointed. Perhaps Christian's feelings are still for a sexless lifelong friend, who had to be cheered up when she was shivering, when words were no longer enough, when she wanted to feel that she was alive. It's hard to suspect oneself of dishonesty. But I couldn't avoid asking myself whether it wasn't vulgar and quite simply unbearable for me to have left nothing behind except a pleasant memory or the possibility of forgetting.

Sometimes I'm shocked at how little I know about myself, how perfectly practised my self-deception is, just how difficult it is to separate lies and truth and shame about lies.

The desperation with which I still invoke an honorable motive every now and then when I've long since seen through myself, when I've already found myself trying to please my vanity or passion. And if I just don't want to admit the truth, I'll look for an acceptable explanation, encourage understanding in myself before I give up, if at all, look down into the abyss and find what is most horrifying of all: that I'm no different from the others.

There's music coming from Christian's apartment, "...Why don't we do it in the road... ." A door opens a floor below, it smells like sauerkraut. "But don't hang the laundry on Schreiber's

24

line again or they'll get upset," a woman's voice calls. Someone is shuffling up the stairs in slippers.

I knock.

Before Christian can even say hello, I tell him something or other about a nearby fabric shop where I happened to have been just now. Ask if I'm bothering him, don't wait for an answer because I don't see a strange coat in the clothes closet, bitch about the boring selection of fabric. I see Christian smiling. "All right, just stop talking," he says and kisses me on the cheek as always. Or not as always. He pushes the cigarettes across the table.

"Tea or coffee?"

"Hard stuff."

"How's the report going?"

"You won; I'm writing version number one."

Christian sinks a bit deeper into his chair, puts one leg over the next, his flinty eyes light up for just a moment and not in triumph, simply happy. He looks tired. As long as we've known each other, Christian was the reasonable one who was always a few years more grown up. I was used to leaving the larger part of the responsibility for our friendship to him. I had a bad conscience every so often because I knew Christian wouldn't defend himself even if I made excessive demands on him. But I accepted him as something secure and beautiful that was always there for me. Comparable to a mother or to a big brother. At the beginning of our friendship I felt this security from him only indirectly. I was fascinated by the intellectual, cultivated atmosphere of the Grellmann household. And I respected Christian's father, a feeling that I've kept for Werner Grellmann to this day. He was forty the first time I met him. At that time a forty-year-old seemed older to me than a fifty-five-year-old seems to me today, as I hadn't yet taken ageing into my own consciousness.

That was towards the end of the 50s. As recently as two years before that Professor Werner Grellmann had still held lectures in the Philosophy Department that were always overcrowded, although the majority of the students understood only half of what he was saying when he dissected Sartre and Kirkegaard from the Marxist point of view with the elegant rudeness of a practised

25

surgeon, but not without the unavoidable respect of the scholar for someone else's intellectual feats.

It was probably the same respect for the thoughts of others that moved him not to raise his hand in agreement when a young colleague was expelled from the Party on the grounds that his constant reading of Western literature had shown him to have considerable ideological weakness. Werner Grellmann wasn't expelled from the Party because of this, but he was judged incompetent to train young scholars. He was promoted from Professor of Philosophy to Mayor of Wetzin, a muddy village in the Oderbruch region, which he was supposed to turn into a model village. His wife and three sons—Christian was the eldest—remained in Berlin. Ruth Grellmann interrupted her dissertation to feed her family by clerical work, as the five hundred Marks that Werner Grellmann earned as mayor weren't enough for two households.

I'm trying to remember if there were traces of bitterness in Werner Grellmann when I first met him. I don't think so. He is wearing the same expression of a wise clown in the photos from that time on his fine, sensitive face with grey eyes.

One of the weekends I spent with the Grellmanns, Werner Grellmann told us how he had gotten the streets of Wetzin paved. We sat around the large round table in leather high-backed chairs. It was a cold, humid day just before Christmas, a Hanukkah candelabrum provided the only light in the room and stood on the small bookshelf on the right-hand side of the doorway. The candelabrum was the only thing which Ruth Grellmann, *née* Katzenheimer, had brought to the marriage. Werner Grellmann— who wouldn't tolerate a Christmas tree, who considered all this dubious since it was based on superstition, who raised his eyebrows sceptically as soon as the person next to him mentioned the word God—Werner Grellmann had an attachment to this object which I haven't been able to explain to this day.

Ruth brewed the third or fourth pot of tea while Werner Grellmann told Christian and me the story of the paving of Wetzin. He had noticed that spring the difficulty his Wetziners had in getting their boots and bicycles out of the mud produced by days and days of rain. The roadway was paved with rough cobblestones,

26

that was true, but the sidewalks were nothing more than trampled-down clay, and the rainwater stood there for days after a cloudburst. Werner Grellmann, a passionate pedestrian and bike-rider, was concerned most of all, however, with the rights of the majority, and decided that the sidewalks in Wetzin must be paved. He simply lacked the needed money. A few days after his decision, he told us, he walked through the village cemetery by accident, an event which was to make a decisive change in Wetzin's public life. I was certain that this walk to the cemetery was no accident. Werner Grellmann hated cemeteries as much as he did Christmas trees and once startled us with the question, after we had defended graveyard idylls against his mocking, irreverent attacks, of where Friedrich Engels' grave was located. In London, we guessed. And Werner Grellmann let loose a cheerful and sly laugh and blew an imaginary something from the palm of his hand with his puckered-up mouth, saying: "Here it is—in the wind." So I'm certain that he didn't go to the cemetery by accident but knew what he was looking for and found it, too. He had counted on rural traditionalism and the farmers' lethargy, which was made manifest in the Wetzin cemetery in the form of valuable old marble headstones. Werner Grellmann found out from the village tax collector, a sly man you couldn't put anything over on, that the right to a funeral plot ran out after thirty years. Werner Grellmann's next step depended on the avarice of his Wetziners, who had been poor as long as anyone could remember. He placed a notice in the local newspaper: "Whosoever wishes to lay claim to a continuation of his family plot, please pay the rent for the next thirty years before the end of the month. Otherwise the burial ground will be levelled. Relatives are responsible for the removal of headstones. Should they not fulfil their duty, the village will find itself compelled to assume removal of the headstone(s) itself. Signed: the Mayor." If the Mayor doesn't want the headstones, then he ought to have them taken away himself, the farmers must have thought; and Werner Grellmann took another walk through the graveyard accompanied this time by the village stonecutter, who was supposed to estimate the value of the stones. A disbelieving Werner Grellmann went with the estimate to the district seat and invited the stonecutter there to take a walk in the cemetery. He doubled the offer. Werner Grellmann then told this sum in turn to the Wetzin stonecutter, and I don't know how many other stonecutters he showed the cemetery to before he deemed the offer adequate. In any case Wetzin got its paved sidewalks, which have since become for me the epitome of useful, aesthetic monuments. I recall this gloomy pre-Christmas afternoon at the Grellmanns' more clearly than all the others. I became aware that day that I envied Christian his family, even though this feeling was mixed with gratitude in being allowed to participate in a community that had more than a mere sense of family as I knew it.

Later on, when Werner Grellmann was once again allowed to work in his field, the family moved to Halle. I've seen Werner and Ruth Grellmann only once since then. But my friendship with Christian has always remained linked to the feeling of intellectual security that I came to know in his parents' house.

Christian is silent. He is playing with a sheet of paper, folds it ingeniously, smooths it out again, creases it slowly. No, it's not like it used to be between us and it isn't different either. Only anxious uncertainty instead of carefree familiarity. Perhaps a sentence would be enough to find the old tone again, or a new one. "Are you going to stay here?" Christian is looking at me, pale and tired, grey eyes under narrow brows, not a trace of mockery in them.

I'm afraid that whatever I answer will be wrong. What am I looking for here, and who? Suddenly the closeness is inconceivable again, despite the desire to stay here where I know I don't have to keep explaining myself. Then again the fear of being a quadruped, the thought of the morning of the milk truck, of the evening with Werner Grellman when he told his Wetzin stories, childhood memories, Christian, my brother.

"No, I don't know, not today."

I want to go home.

Seating order is strictly observed during editorial staff meetings, and although I've come too late, my seat next to Luise is still empty. On her right sits Günter Rassow, a thin, sickly man who walks bent over like an old man, though he's only a little beyond forty.

He moves along with small awkward steps as if he were about to fall over from one foot to the next. Now and then he is endowed with the bizarre humor of an old Englishman. Günter Rassow pushes the newspaper across to Luise with two columns underlined in red pencil while fat Elli Meseke is just beginning to struggle to assess the newest issue of the *Illustrated Weekly* with her motherly voice. "Have you read it?" he asks softly, straining audibly to suppress his anger. It reads: "How Frankfurt railroad workers oversalt the snow." Günter suffers almost physically from such abuses of language. Siegfried Strutzer, being the only representative of the Editor-in-Chief, is sitting at the table of the Executive Committee and taps vigorously with his pencil on the table. Luise lowers her grey-haired head with a guilty conscience, like a schoolgirl who has been caught talking. "Where is Rudi?"— "Rudi has a toothache; he's not coming," Luise whispers and makes a grimace as if she had to suppress a loud laugh.

Rudi Goldammer is known for his whining, most smile at it, few take it amiss. When I heard Rudi Goldammer's story, I could hardly imagine how this fragile man with the soft face, sad eyes and careworn mouth could have survived eleven years in a concentration camp. He was nineteen when he was arrested; when he returned home at thirty, he had a weak heart, a sick stomach and couldn't sleep. He had fallen in love at seventeen with a girl he knew from the Workers' Social Movement. Two years after he was arrested she married an SA man; after the war she got a divorce, came to Rudi Goldammer with her daughter, and Rudi married her as if he had suddenly awakened and was looking for the youth he had lost behind barbed wire. It became a curiously quiet marriage; and Luise, who visits Rudi Goldammer every so often, always talks about his wife with a trace of sympathetic revulsion.

Rudi has managed to retain a sensitive understanding for others in the face of the catastrophes of his life and a goodness that often crosses the border into weakness. It is as if he had had enough pain and evil for one lifetime and was incapable of inflicting any more. These are all reasons to love Rudi, but fatal qualities for the Editor-in-Chief of the *Illustrated Weekly*; and Rudi Goldammer tries to escape the consequences again and again with stomach cramps or toothaches.

A dull whispering emanates from the assembly. Apparently no one agrees with Elli Meseke's satisfied statement that the articles in this issue are especially considerate of the readers, as is appropriate for the *Illustrated Weekly,* and that it does us all credit. Rhetorical phrases that are heard without fail at every meeting. I'm constantly amazed at how someone can still utter them without laughing, well, without smiling at least.

"We'll get to the discussion later," Siegfried Strutzer taps with his pencil. Whenever Rudi Goldammer suffers a toothache or stomach pains, Siegfried Strutzer presides, and he almost always moves into the Editor-in-Chief's office. Supposedly because someone has to watch the phone. A hypocritical excuse, as both Rudi and Siegfried Strutzer's lines go through the same secretary's office, and Rudi uses his private phone only for private calls.

"Watch out, it's your turn," Luise whispers.

"...Report by Josefa Nadler," I hear Elli Meseke's motherly voice, and I wince as I always do when my name is called out loud, an ingrained feeling from my school days when I used to be terrified of my own name. Josefa Nadler, don't gab!...Josefa Nadler, don't tip your chair! Josefa Nadler, why did you come so late?

"Josefa Nadler gives a precise description of the atmosphere of the capital in her article on the Berlin city center," Elli Meseke says and stresses the importance of her words by speaking slowly and broadly, as if she had to think of every word at that moment. She was pleased at the heartwarming realism, Elli said, although—oho, now it's coming, would be surprised if it weren't—this realism sometimes goes too far. Luise grins at me with the twisted corner of her mouth and rolls her eyes.

"I'm thinking specifically of the business with the tunnel and similar allusions. I think that it goes too far," Elli says with the gentle sternness of a schoolteacher.

I had written an article about Alexanderplatz and had developed my anger at the drafty, bleak pedestrian tunnels for ten lines, I thought harmlessly. I would willingly have left out a description of our future below an armored city, although I considered my vision worthy of passing on as soon as I closed my eyes and gave the theme of cities and cars over to my imagination. Tripledecker trams on the ground that intricately run over and under one another, zigzag roads around skyscrapers, parking lots in corridors, automatically locking gates, auto elevators, airfilters in the windows of old apartment buildings instead of glass sheets, the new houses without windows, pitiful trees in tall stone pots alongside the roadways and the concrete balustrades. Trees are changed every week; they don't live any longer. Along the eight-lane roadbeds, one-man autos in the shape of beetles with an attachment for fastening children—a new model developed to ease the horrendous parking crisis, statistics in the last two years showing a sharp increase in the number of deaths resulting from fights over parking spaces. Because of the one-seater, the old four-seater is never used except for official purposes and as taxis. Children are allowed to ride only in cars painted bright red for warning. Children under eight are strictly prohibited from driving cars. Underground, the pedestrian catacombs. The walls are sun yellow, the ceilings, sky blue, the pavement, grass green; you can smell the paint. Everywhere road signs on manholes, store tunnels, doctor's offices, large restaurants that are housed in old subway stations. Children rush along the tunnels in toy cars, the small children have scooters, the larger ones, battery-operated. Grownups walk slowly, very slowly, they creep; some wear support rails, others prop themselves up with crutches, many have bent backs and bulging stomachs. An elevator every hundred meters goes to one of the parking garages. A hastily written slogan in red paint on the yellow wall: We demand public transportation!

Elli smiles at me gently: "Josefa, escalators would certainly have been nicer. But can you really talk about an inhuman plan in this context?" Escalators, who is talking about escalators? With people crawling from one side of the street to the other like maggots so they won't have to dodge the cars with their expensive radial tires—and all Elli Meseke wants to think about is how they can be transported more easily into the creep holes.

Luise mumbles to herself: "It wouldn't hurt her to climb a few stairs with that fat behind of hers."

The "inhuman plan" had already brought Luise a short but memorable telephone conversation, though that is hardly the right word for what went on, between the one talking and the other listening. I happened to be in Luise's room when the phone rang.

"Regional administration," Luise whispered to me. An expression of intense concentration spread over her face and deepened wrinkles large and small. "Speaking," she said.

I didn't hear anything from the other end; the comrade was obviously speaking softly. But long. I watched Luise's face: the tension was slowly replaced by a reluctant smile.

"All right, Comrade...all right, we'll think it over."

She slowly placed the receiver back on the hook with her finger tips, turned around to me on her imitation leather chair with the metal swivel and said with a broad smile: "Comrade Kunze is outraged by your inhuman tunnel."

"But I didn't build it."

"Now don't get excited," Luise said as if she were trying to calm herself down, "it's been printed, that's the main thing."

Luise can calculate like a business woman. She weighs precisely what something will bring, weighs the chances for profit, calculates the risk, insures the settlement in advance. She's scheduled an interview with the city architect for next week's edition, which will certainly calm down the excited Comrade Kunze and convince him of our understanding.

Luise got up and returned with a cellophane bag with licorice from her pocketbook, put a piece in her mouth after she had looked at it lovingly and offered the bag to me, a special favor, as Luise is stingy with her licorice.

Elli Meseke states forgivingly that she thought my article a success despite this one reservation and Luise says softly: "There, ya see."

This could mean: There, ya see, now we've got that behind us; or: There, ya see, it works after all, you just have to believe in yourself, or: There, ya see, the fat woman isn't all that bad after all... Heaven knows all the things Luise can conceal behind her Thereyasees. But, at any rate, she's satisfied.

It was really nothing more than a sigh I let out over the

32

pedestrians' underworld. Imagine, Luise, if I had written about my encounter with the Stoker Hodriwitzka in B. But I haven't even told you about that yet, only Christian. He laughed and asked whether or not I was really sure if I understood correctly the principles of Socialist Democracy.

Stoker Hodriwitzka is a short, broad-shouldered man who looks like a square at first glance. His squat, massive body; his large, angular skull on his broad shoulders; even his hands with their short fingers look square. The soft lines in his round face are all the more astonishing for that. Friendly, naive eyes, which he never squints when he looks at you; a small, bulbous nose; broad lips, which aren't fat. He is over forty but you can just imagine what he looked like as a child, when he was still living in the Sudeten Mountains with his parents. I met Stoker Hodriwitzka when the chief engineer took me on a tour of the power plant. We hadn't met him on our rounds, but the engineer said that if I didn't meet Hodriwitzka, I couldn't understand why the power plant hadn't fallen apart yet. I considered this empty phrase a poor joke by the chief engineer. I couldn't prevent the engineer from trying to locate Hodriwitzka by phone and having him brought to his office. I found this embarrassing because he had summoned him as though I were a superior or an official and as though it seemed that Stoker Hodriwitzka wanted to talk to me and not the other way round. He came five minutes later, face and hands black from coal still damp from the mines that they used to fire the furnaces. He wiped his right hand on his dark blue uniform before he held it out to me with an apologetic smile. I would have liked to have been invisible that very instant, I was so ashamed. Luise, I suddenly looked at my right hand. I had glanced secretly, almost accidentally, at my right hand. Not because I would have been disgusted by the dirt. It was fresh, clean coal dust, not the invisible dust on an office hand. No, I looked more out of curiosity, to see whether Stoker Hodriwitzka's hand had left its imprint. I tried to hide my gesture by busying myself with my blouse sleeve, said something stupid about it being too tight, felt my face flush. Hodriwitzka had placed his cracked black hands on the desk. He withdrew them hesitantly and held onto the corners of his chair so that you could no longer see his hands.

"Well, Colleague Hodriwitzka," the engineer said, who seemed not to have noticed our embarrassment, "this is a colleague from the *Illustrated Weekly* in Berlin, and we've asked you here so that you can tell our colleague from the newspaper about your work here in the power plant. Not glossed over. The way it really is."

"It's dirty," Hodriwitzka said and smiled at me with his shiny brown eyes.

What should I have asked him, Luise? What I had seen was enough for me—ancient equipment, drafty shops, heavy, dirty work, men stooped in the ash chambers where only a midget could stand up straight, women with five-meter pokers in front of the furnaces. What could I have asked Stoker Hodriwitzka?

"Do you like living in B.?" I asked.

Hodriwitzka sat tense and clumsy in his chair, shrugged his shoulders, smiled helplessly. He looked at me like a polite Chinaman whom someone had just tried to talk to in Turkish. I must have asked him a particularly stupid question.

Well, what can a body say to these innocent journalist questions? What could I answer if someone asked me whether I liked living in this country or not?

"My wife's folks just left us their little place," Hodriwitzka said, and this seemed to him to be the answer to the question of whether or not he liked living in B.

And then, Luise, I had enough of this embarrassing, concocted worker-journalist game. The former knows what the latter is going to ask, and the latter knows what the former will answer; and the former knows that the latter knows it. This stiff, pointless circus performance in which each one gapes at the other and both think that he's in the cage."

"Why don't you fight back?" I asked. "You are the ruling class after all." Hodriwitzka, who could not have sensed my spontaneous inner protest against the part of journalist that I was playing, must have found my question abrupt. He looked up in surprise.

"Fight back? Against what?"

"Against the old power plant. Why don't you demand that it be shut down?"

34

The expression in Hodriwitzka's round brown eyes oscillated between disbelief, amusement and interest. "The General Director would have to do that. He's even supposed to have sent a letter already," he said and looked around for the engineer, who was standing obliquely behind him leaning against a cabinet, and who confirmed the information with a nod.

"I'm only small fry here," Hodriwitzka added without malice or bitterness, a statement of fact, modest and objective. "But there are a thousand power plant workers in the collective combine."

Don't be shocked, Luise, I didn't want to proclaim a strike. But Hodriwitzka's imperturbability provoked me and excited me; I only understood later how little this apparent indifference had to do with imperturbability. "And just what do you think this kind of protest would be like?" Hodriwitzka asked with a smile.

"You have to demand an explanation," I said, "why they have to continue using an unsafe, filth-spewing power plant when a new one is being built. And if the works manager can't give you an answer, you'll have to ask the General Director. And if he doesn't know anything either, you should invite the Minister here to B."

Hodriwitzka moved his chair closer to the desk and rested his head on his black hands. "You just don't know all the complications," he said pensively. "If they're not going to shut it down it must be because they can't. They sure wouldn't keep us sitting in this muck on purpose."

"But someone has to explain that to them," I tried to convince him, "you have to demand that. Please understand, that's not forbidden, it has nothing to do with a strike. On the contrary, if you don't try it, you'll destroy the whole democratic system."

Hodriwitzka couldn't help laughing, and I assured him what a serious matter it was. The Minister could put things straight with the General Director in a few words—a phone call or a letter and then everything would be quiet. What else can a general director do if he wants to stay general director? "And what do you have to do to stay stoker?" I asked Hodriwitzka. I had expected him to have an ironic answer to this question, hint at his stupidity at risking his life in a ramshackle building like this. But he looked at me attentively, almost with curiosity, and said softly: "But I

35

have to stay here. They just can't find anybody to do the work. Way things are every fourth job goes begging.''

"Do you think the Minister doesn't know that? And do you think he would dare not to come here if a thousand power plant workers from B. wanted to talk to him about their future?''

Hodriwitzka didn't answer. He looked puzzled at his hands, suddenly lifted his head, said more to himself than to me: "Without the power plant nothing runs in the whole works.'' He then let out a brief laugh, shook his angular head and said, still half in disbelief: "He might even come; you never can tell.'' He seemed to find the idea amusing. Maybe he imagined all the workers from the power plant sitting in the large culture hall in their blue uniforms with dirty hands and faces, just the way you look after you've left the job for an hour or two. The Minister would drive up in his big black car, wouldn't take a seat on the rostrum because they wouldn't have set one up. He would sit down at the table like all the rest of them and answer their questions. The Minister would leave out the world political situation this time, his tribute to their successes, too. He would only explain to them what defect in state planning prevented them from shutting down their unsafe power plant. If the Minister found an adequate reason they would be ready to talk. They understood something about power supply; he wouldn't be able to talk nonsense to them.

Hodriwitzka's cheeks turned red, his eyes shone making him look even more like a child. "But one of us can't just sit down and write to the Minister,'' he said. I didn't know myself how Hodriwitzka should go about what I had proposed in my anger at this dirty town without having him fall under the suspicion of counter-revolutionary activities. I was simply convinced it was possible. So I said that the union would have to send an invitation to the Minister.

"I see,'' Hodriwitzka said, sober again. You could tell from his face that he had left the large culture hall without rostrum and returned to the bare office chair in the engineer's room. "I see,'' he said again. "Well, then nothin'll happen. Our delegate doesn't have the guts.''

It was the same old story. They elect the stupidest or the most cowardly because he can get elected and then when he becomes a stupid or cowardly delegate, they gripe about all union officials being stupid or cowardly.

I ask why they elected him.

"The other one didn't want to any more," Hodriwitzka said. They had had one with freckles and red hair. "He was a real anarchist," Hodriwitzka said. "He got something done: warm food at night, renovated wash rooms and dressing rooms. But they were always taking pot shots at him. 'Til he got fed up."

Hodriwitzka looked at the clock. He had to go now, he said; he stood up slowly, put the chair back where it belonged, stood in the room undecided. "Well, I guess I'll go now." He's had enough of my public speech by now, I thought. I felt ridiculous. What could have gotten into me, I came out of my fully airconditioned open-plan office into this cave and wanted to teach people how they should live. "Or you'll destroy the whole democratic system!" You just couldn't get any stupider. As if Hodriwitzka or his redheaded anarchist would ruin democracy. If I only hadn't come on like an itinerant preacher who had come to bring word of the Resurrection.

Hodriwitzka offered me his heavy, square hand. "Goodbye," he said and added suddenly with what seemed to be great effort: "I'd like to thank you." I felt a choked-up sensation of joy and embarrassment. "You don't see some things any more," Hodriwitzka said, "when you do the same things every day." I had gotten him to thinking about a few things. I could have screamed or embraced or kissed him. He had understood what I meant. Didn't suspect me of being crazy, a smart-aleck or a wacky do-gooder.

"Thanks," I said. Then Hodriwitzka quickly left the room.

The engineer stood by the cabinet quietly smiling. "Do you believe now that the power plant would have broken down a long time ago without Hodriwitzka?" I was irritated by the cynicism hidden behind this comment.

Just think what would happen, Luise, if Elli Meseke and Siegfried Strutzer were to find out something about my talk with Stoker Hodriwitzka. What is an inhuman tunnel compared to a letter from a thousand power plant workers to a minister? Or would that be going too far even for you? No, of course not. I'll tell you the story right after the meeting when Strutzer has finally hammered his last remarks on work discipline into our tired, bored heads.

IV

I hate all that: whistling tea kettles, smoke-filled kitchens, sticky plates, sugar-encrusted cups, beads of fat in the dishwater, leftovers, forgotten sausage casings that slide through your fingers. And before you've gotten rid of one mountain, another starts to build up. Sisyphus Nadler. There they are climbing around on the moon, profoundly sorry that they haven't gotten to Saturn yet, and here I am in a cold, unheated kitchen, two sweaters on, slippers on my feet, scraping egg yolk from my plates with soggy fingernails. You just have to wash dishes regularly, Ida always says, at least once a day, so that you'll have only half the work. What a bunch of baloney; then I'd be disgusted every day. As things are I only feel that way twice a week.

The phone. Michael Timm, chief layout man for the *Illustrated Weekly*, his voice sounds suspiciously cheerful as does the noise in the background. They're at Reni's. Reni's is a dark bar on a side street behind the publishing house, which spontaneously became a hangout for almost all the editorial staff soon after we moved into the new building. They have excellent knackwurst, you sit on wooden chairs instead of the plastic and steel tubing kind, and you rarely have to fear a sudden appearance by the boss in this gloomy pub.

"You can wash your dishes tomorrow, too, you know," Michael says, "Come on over, we're having a party."

I'm standing deaf and dumb between thick smoke and beer fumes and inarticulate noise. Three silhouettes slowly appear out of the stinking fumes at the counter directly next to the entrance; they look as if their elbows were nailed to the table top, which is holding them up. They stare at me with bleary eyes.

38

"Hi, babe," one growls, wrenches his arm from the tabletop to grab me, knocks over his glass in the process and looks on sadly as beer spills from the bar onto his stomach, which swells under a brown nylon parka.

I see three or four arms raised in the left corner of the front tap room. I recognize Michael Timm from his light blue shirt. He wears only light blue shirts of coarse linen. Some people say that he owns only one, but once when I was at his place there were seven light blue shirts hanging in the bathroom alone. He was wearing the eighth. Pretty Ulrike Kuwiak from the Letters to the Editor Department is sitting next to him. Günter Rassow gets a chair from the next table and pushes it between Hans Schütz and Eva Sommer. Eva Sommer with her smoky voice is just trying to buttonhole Fred Müller; he is staring into his beer glass and is mechanically sloshing the dregs back and forth. Fred Müller is considered a serious drinker. Some say he hasn't gotten over his divorce, others claim they noticed this tendency before that. When sober or slightly drunk he is reserved, tending to melancholy. Hans Schütz pushes his glass over to me: "Go ahead and drink or else you won't be able to put up with the bullshit they're talking."

I really can't understand why Michael Timm and Günter Rassow are arguing with such determination, but it looks frightening. They yell at each other, bang on the table with their fists until the glasses jump, constantly interrupting each other. Günter Rassow tries to drown out Michael's penetrating voice by articulating with pedantic clarity.

"But that's just it," Michael shouts and looks fiercely at Günter Rassow. Hans Schütz grins with relish as he looks closely at the two. "The funny thing is," he says, "that they agree with each other all the while."

Suddenly Eva Sommer's smoky voice drones in my ear: "So, listen, where are we going now?"

The evening runs its natural course. At some point someone always asks this question and the whole thing ends in a drinking bout. One shot and another shot, they rub the goose bumps from their arms and keep on drinking. Sometimes they are afraid, cheer themselves up with forced jokes when they talk about their livers,

39

which, thank God, aren't swollen yet, carry on dead serious discussions about the borderline between an alcoholic and a social drinker. After which they all say with a sigh of relief that there is no way they could be considered alcoholics. The uncertainty remains, however, of slowly and imperceptibly crossing the line from the social tippler to the compulsive, lonely and secretive drunk. Maybe they aren't there yet in the medical sense, but are compulsive in the need for the lightheadedness, the floating sensation, the chidlike state that can be achieved only artificially. They wash away whatever inhibits them with 150 grams of double shots. They forget the day to come, the pending aggravation of missed deadlines, the unspoken thoughts, the children's shoes that they couldn't find in the right size again, the line waiting for them in the morning at the post office. They even forget the daily anger over the drafty, chalk-white room with the sounds of rattling, gabbing, clattering. They rinse their souls in forty percent spirits until they are innocent through oblivion.

It was agreed to move to Hans Schütz' apartment. Hans Schütz' wife is an actress in a provincial theater and is seldom home. Hans says that this is the only way, if there is one, to be married, and that an engagement in Berlin would mean divorce for sure.

Twenty minutes by foot to Hans Schütz' apartment.

"At least they can sober up there," says Hans, who scarcely drinks anymore since he had a liver-related ailment. He helps me into my coat. I don't like being helped into my coat. Most men make me go through gymnastics by holding the sleeves as high as my head.

It is quiet on the street, the air cold and humid, snow is predicted for tonight. We walk one behind the other along the narrow sidewalk, a mere half-meter wide due to the cars parked up over the curb. Ulrike Kuwiak suddenly stands still so that I step on her heels, looks lovingly at the totally starless sky. "I love winter nights like this," she says, "when you see how transient everything is." She sighs and goes on.

Hans Schütz cleans his spectacles as he walks, checks them in the glare of the street light and asks without looking at me: "Which version of B. are you on?"

"The only one."

"That's sensible."

"But I'm not writing the sensible one."

Han Schütz remains quiet. A passing car lights up his face for a few seconds. He chews pensively on his pipe, his skin is gently flushed from the damp air. With the collar of his unfashionably plain leather jacket up, his neck pulled in, he looks like a turtle in its shell. "Wasn't there a Council resolution on this subject?" he asks.

"What of it?"

"I hope you're not biting off more than you can chew."

"I just have to try. It may just be an article like this that will be the grain of sand that tips the scales. Just imagine this in the paper: In spite of the new power plant in B. the old one hasn't been shut down. Five times as much bronchitis as elsewhere, trees that lose their branches overnight as if they had been swept away by black magic or just a gust of sulphur dioxide, a power plant where you don't dare to mention the word *safety*, but it isn't shut down. And two million people read that; it just has to have some effect."

"Maybe," says Hans Schütz. "But they won't read it because it won't be in the paper."

"Well, then it won't. But that isn't my decision. I'm writing what I found, Luise shouldn't have been allowed to send me to B., then. I can't write about a town and keep quiet about the most important thing. The most important things in B. are the new power plant and the filth from the old."

Schütz seems to be unimpressed by my determination. "You've been in the business long enough to figure out the trouble there's going to be."

"Can be, doesn't have to be."

"You're an incorrigible optimist," says Schütz. He puts his arm on my shoulder. "Are you cold?" he asks.

"A little."

We buy liquor and cigarettes at the train station. Ulrike insists on salted peanuts.

The room Hans takes us to is warm and disconcertingly well-

41

kept. Of course there is hardly a chance to create disorder. Nothing in the large room except book cases up to the ceiling, an oval table about two meters long, whose size goes well with the six very old thick leather chairs and a few stools that are placed around it. Dark green cord velvet curtains. And that's all.

Ulrike pulls a stool right up to my chair and takes a long look at me with her alcohol-glazed eyes.

"Tell me, Josefa, why don't you get married again?"

Good heavens, the same old tune.

"Because I can't hear while someone next to me is chewing on an apple."

Ulrike smiles, but obviously disapproves of the mocking way in which I talk about her holy of holies.

"Don't you ever think how you're going to be living in twenty years?" she asks, concerned.

"How do you know how you're going to be living in twenty years? Maybe your husband will divorce you or have a heart attack at forty-five and die."

Ulrike looks at me horrified. "You're cynical." All true believers like Ulrike have fanatical marriages. They feel personally offended the moment someone doesn't share their faith. The very thought is unbearable. They ruthlessly attack the convictions of others with their dogmas and confessions, paint in the gloomiest of colors all that can happen when you don't believe. The one threatens with purgatory, the other with sectarianism; Ulrike threatens with lonely old age. Like Aunt Ida, with tears in her light blue eyes.

Ulrike can talk the purest nonsense, and every man will overlook it because her narrow-shouldered, soft appearance immediately awakens the guardian in them; and even if it's only to protect Ulrike from her own stupidity. There's not the slightest doubt that she didn't have to fetch coal from the basement by herself when she was divorced. Ulrike can describe a leaky faucet with such incomparable helplessness that before long her listeners are convinced she will surely end up in a psycho ward if the steady dripping doesn't stop pounding in her tender little head. They feel genuine sympathy even if they have been scraping the mold behind the wallpaper for ten years and sit every Tuesday at the housing authority. But tender creatures like Ulrike need a sheltered place in life. I'm sure that women with narrow shoulders have an easier life. And although broad shoulders are fashionable again, I can't come to terms with my anatomy.

Ulrike smiles blissfully to herself. "You know, men treat you better when you're married, too. They simply have more respect for a married woman."

Warm snow is gently falling through my head. Another shot and I'll feel a rippling throughout my body down to my toes. Sure, she's right, but she ought to leave me alone now with her attempts at conversion. I really don't have anything against marriage. And if I drink another three shots, I'll get engaged to Hans Schütz or Michael or Günter Rassow on the spot. It really doesn't make any difference who with, right, Ulrike? The main thing: get married. I'd marry again right away if I had narrow shoulders like Ulrike. Then I would have fallen apart like she did as an unmarried woman. Fallen apart or come apart. Nothing of Ulrike's appearance stayed the way it was. She made herself up like an operetta singer, got a permanent wave, wore loud colors of imitation leather. We watched this sudden, frightening transformation with bewilderment and disgust. Even her voice was different. Her former girlish timbre was drowned out by a shrill, artificial cheerfulness that exploded every so often in high warbling. Ulrike was frightening as a new personality. She wore out her forced attempts at emancipation in glaring superficiality and demonstrative bar-hopping. Then she entrusted her daughter to her husband. She indulged herself at every opportunity, really too often, beyond the drive for freedom which anyone naturally wants to know and enjoy. Her excursions usually ended with horrible wine cramps. I was along twice at Reni's when Ulrike suddenly fell to the table, face down, and screamed. She didn't know exactly why she had screamed, probably the role she had decided to play was too much of a strain and too painful. She lived completely against her nature. Her condition lasted a whole year until she found another man, whom she married within three months. Now she looks happy again, flirts with her marital dignity and seems to be happy, although she told me once that the new husband wasn't her great love. But it's probably marriage not love that makes Ulrike happy.

If I weren't saddled with my broad shoulders, which apparently encourage others to pat them in as friendly a manner as they do when we exchange experiences on the hardships of hauling coal, I could escape responsibility for myself through marriage like Ulrike. Here you've got her, I'd say to the man of my dreams. And if after ten years I wasn't happy or hadn't gotten trained in a profession, I would say that he was to blame, he had betrayed my trust and hadn't sufficiently met his responsibilities. But as things are, I, poor creature that I am, have to see to my happiness by myself, have to accept my limitations as such. I'm not allowed to point with a faint sigh and sugary memories at all the things I could have become if I hadn't supported the man of my dreams in his studies with such sacrifice and devotion. I am the only one responsible for my incompetencies. It's these broad shoulders.

Just now Günter Rassow is telling the witty story of an Editor-in-Chief who shut himself up in a clothes closet on the 17th of June while the screaming mob of construction workers was in revolt, raising hell in front of the publishing house. Günter Rassow, who was a volunteer in '53 with the district paper, only went through an hour of the 17th of June in person, after which he was hit in the back of the head with a metal hook.

"Yeah, just think of it, he hid in the closet. But please: this remains between us."

The story always ends with this solemn appeal. Not a word; of course, we promise, also as always.

Fred Müller, who had been listening to us up until now with an absent smile, suddenly doubles over as if sick, then arches his back and bangs on the table with his closed fist. A glass tips over. Then he says softly and thickly: "I've had it with all this shit. These assholes. Snot-shitting insects. All asses and empty eggheads, brainsuckers!"

He roars these last words. Then he collapses, wipes the spit from his lower lip with the back of his hand and stares into space. Everyone is stunned and quiet. Eva Sommer and Michael stop dancing. Hans Schütz puts down his glass, pours a shot and pushes it over to Fred Müller. "Here, drink one and calm down," he says to Fred, who is slumped over dead drunk in his chair. He lets his head fall onto the tabletop with a dull thud and falls asleep.

And tomorrow he'll get into the elevator punctually at 7:45. He'll follow the floor numbers with apathetic, bloodshot eyes. He won't dare to exhale for fear of getting looks of disapproval and disgust from those riding with him, what with his foul smell of undigested spirits. He gets off at the sixteenth floor, disappears behind the door with the number 16 007, happy that he hasn't met anyone in the hallway. He hangs his coat in the closet. He feels sick and is overcome by a faintness that makes his legs and hands shake. He gets the half-bottle of vodka out of its hiding place, quickly downs a glass, pours a second to the brim and puts it inside his office desk. He then opens the window, cold air and street noise rush in, reaching the sixteenth floor as a diffuse roar that can no longer be differentiated into its component parts. Newspapers and manuscripts that he has to edit or approve lie on the desk, but he continues to find a way of escaping the disgust that comes over him the instant he feels paper between his fingers and has to read the first sentences. Another five minutes delay. He goes to the toilet, washes his hands, dries them under the air dryer, stands still until the machine shuts itself off. The toilet is a safe place to be alone in the morning. You come from home when you've already taken care of all your needs; the toilet is still clean in the morning. He combs his hair in front of the mirror, avoids looking at his face. He knows what he looks like in the morning after an all-night binge. He shoves a peppermint candy into his mouth, slowly goes back to 16 007. Twice three meters.

He puts the IN mail in order. There's nothing more to do after that. He sits down at his desk. Gulps at the disgust that rises up in his throat every morning. He reaches for the glass in the desk, drinks the liquor in a single draught. The nervously twitching musculature of his stomach and esophagus relaxes, the disgust subsides. Another glass of alcohol and he feels calm, after that he can let the sentences flow through his dull brain indifferently as if they were mathematical formulae.

Increasingly efficient completion of complex methods of

competition, the Mayor's constantly open ear, the constantly newer innovative methods: all this he frees of the crudest grammatical and syntactical nonsense. Whatever linguistic absurdities remain follow their own laws of formulaic language and can't be edited out.

This is how he spends his working day until 5 p.m., interrupted by meetings, alcohol, discussions. This or something like it.

Hans Schütz takes Fred Müller into an adjoining room. Günter Rassow looks after them with guilt on his face. Too bad about the nice evening, he says, it was so cosy just now.

"Oh, you", I say more sharply than I had intended, "as if you were any different. You all live after the fall, you know. You keep wanting to stow away in a paradise for innocents. You're a long way along on the trip to hell, too. Don't you hear the hot and cold whistling in your ears?"

Günter lets out a hysterical laugh. "Our angel Josefa is the only one who sits on a snow-white cloud high above. Just give yourself another ten years in this profession, girl, and you'll be able to spare yourself the clever speeches. Nothing personal, Josefa; we know, we get the point. I'm right, aren't I?"

I want to go home to my dirty glasses. I'll dream about my future in red and gold before I fall asleep. Close my eyes and wait to see what turns up. The strangest things happen, too. The black and white goat that always stands on its head. It walks silently through the woods with its legs stretched out in the air. Sometimes there's a marble desk elephant with a little white needlework lid on its back, and I sit on it dressed in a glittering circus costume. Or I walk through sand-colored ruins again. The city must lie far to the south, in Spain or Italy, perhaps even in Africa, as it's incredibly hot there. And the sky is blue, as blue as it is over the sea. It shines uniformly through the empty windows of the ruins as if someone had placed a blue backdrop behind the walls. The streets are narrow, steep steps of yellow sandstone, as the city lies on a hill. I'm always there alone, but that doesn't bother me. I slowly climb the steps to the highest point on the hill because I want to view the city from there. Every time. But every time I've gotten to the top and turned around, the image flies apart or shrinks to nothing, and I find myself again on a step that is halfway up the hill and I start climbing again.

The taxi driver is speeding along the Schönhaus highway. He says he only drives at night because of the quiet. Because a person who works at night needs his rest during the day. He made that clear to his wife. And you make more dough at night, too, he says. He bought a parrot for himself last week for four thousand Marks.

"Are there parrots that cost four thousand Marks?"

"Sure," the taxidriver says.

Of course he's fibbing. Why should anyone pay four thousand Marks for a parrot?

"Five Marks forty pfennig," the taxidriver says.

I count out the exact amount, make my excuses for not giving him a tip. But that's silly, isn't it, fifty pfennig and a parrot for four thousand Marks.

"Forget it, Miss. No way I could pay for it with your fifty pfennig," the taxidriver says and laughs indulgently.

Lights flicker behind my closed eyelids like red and pale blue flames. Try not to think, it'll run like a film then.

I see a broad grey street that is bordered on the other side by an orange barrier. The street is empty. I alone am walking in the middle of the street towards the barrier. There are gutters on both sides containing red and blue scraps of paper and crumpled waxed paper flowers. I don't hear my steps. I suddenly notice that the orange line is slowly moving towards me. I keep on going. When I'm very close to it, the line dissolves into single orange-colored monstrous vehicles that are moving next to each other. The vehicles remind me of street sweepers. The streets are clean behind them, and the scraps of paper have disappeared from the gutters. I keep on going. I'm afraid. I don't want to keep on going but I do. I walk faster, silently. The mute monsters approach silently. Another thirty meters between me and them, or only twenty. I want to run away sideways, but I put one foot in front of the next in the direction of the monsters. I know: this is the threat I've been afraid of for a long time. They approach at a walking pace. I can't get out of their way. The wind goes along with me. We are walking together. Now I know: I've waited for this. Another ten meters. There are no people inside the vehicles. They won't stop. No one

47

sees me. I'm no longer afraid. I have to keep on going, have to...

Luise wasn't in her room when I came. I had been typing the manuscript for two days without a break, from morning 'til night, although I still had a week before the deadline. But I wanted to have time left for the second version in case I began to have doubts myself about whether my undiluted description of my experiences in B. made sense.

It was only after I had written the last sentences that I knew I couldn't write any more or any other way about B. I would first of all have had to leave half the truth in order to be inspired for the whole. But after I had written what seemed the whole truth, I was incapable of finding a reasonable and credible measure of untruth. I wanted to finish it as fast as possible, didn't want to leave any room for petty brooding on a decision that I regarded as final.

I went to the editorial department at 8:00 a.m. the next morning, and when I arrived Luise wasn't there. Only her purse stood next to the chair and the small brown teapot on her desk. I put the manuscript down next to it and wrote a note: "Will be back in two hours and am prepared for everything. Please be prepared for the same before you read. J."

I got my coat out of the large room and decided to go for a walk. Under no circumstances did I want to sit in the open-plan office and stare at Günter's Rassow's back at the desk in front of mine. I knew Günter's thin back in every detail, every movement of muscles when he extends his arms to pick up the phone, the shoulder blades that stick out when he puts his head in his hands and the pointed vertebrae that become visible under his shirt when he leans forward.

During the three years in which, except for Saturdays and Sundays and the days I'm on the road, I've stared at Günter Rassow's back, I've developed a separate relationship to it. There are days when its sickly leanness almost moves me to pity. On other days I despise this puny, always slightly arched back, with its paucity developed a separate relationship to it. There are days when its sickly leanness almost moves me to pity. On other days I despise this puny, always slightly arched back, with its paucity of expression,

48

which barely feels the need to stretch and expand. On days like that the back awakens my slumbering aggression, and I have to keep from throwing a pencil at it.

It also happens, seldom of course, that I don't even perceive the back, that I'm completely indifferent to it. There are numerous nuances in-between these three possibilities through which my relationship with Günter Rassow's back moves. But I wouldn't have been able to bear it today.

Without expecting her to believe me, I tell the secretary that I have to go to the press room in the Ministry of Coal and Energy, and leave the building.

The department store on Alexanderplatz was still closed. A biting wind blew across the square, assaulted the pedestrians at irregular intervals and bit them in the face with sharp teeth. A bockwurst stand was besieged by hungry people. The poor souls. What horrible fate could have befallen them that they have to eat bockwurst so early in the morning in this cold. The sun stood still, seemed undecided whether to go to work or to stay behind its bed of clouds, throwing emergency light on the earth with the squint of a half-open eye.

I walked fast, as if I had a particular destination, through the commuter train underpass in the direction of the City Hall passage, wound my shawl tighter around my neck and forgot why I usually hated the northwest wind. I smiled at myself with a dumb and blissful expression from the show window of the shoe store where I had stopped unintentionally, out of routine. Again it was this feeling I once equated with happiness that now spread through me, both playful and solemn.

I was in my second semester at that time and had been agonizing for three days over a Shakespeare report. I had just turned nineteen, lived in the right wing of a rundown apartment block in Prenzlauer Berg. Outside toilet, water pipes in the stairwell, small room and kitchen. For me attributes of demonstrative emancipation from parents, guardianship and a predetermined path through life. Cold or lack of money was considered welcome proof of my independence and wasn't felt to be an inconvenience. The word *work* replaced *study*. Study—those were school days. I was grown up.

49

Three days of torture over Shakespeare and Tadeus, whom I loved, loved more than anyone before him and most who came after, and whom I didn't allow to see me for three days, because I used to think, still believed when I started my career, that serious work doesn't leave room for love. I know better now or just wasn't able to put up with the crushing consequences of a postulate like that.

I must have been able to put up with them when I was nineteen, because I can clearly remember how I went to a phone booth to call Tadeus only after the visible result lay bunched together on my black desk.

A sunny evening in late spring. Mild, dusty air that slowly warmed me as I walked along the promenade, tired, exhausted, satisfied with myself. The dragon-killer after a battle won. The fading light, the unaccustomed warmth, the scent of the linden trees separated me from the rest of the world. But not from Tadeus. I wasn't conscious of myself as I walked, floated above the sandy ground, sank into it as if it were cotton, dissolved into the warm, dense air. This is happiness, I thought, happiness is like this. After five minutes on the promenade my happiness had shape, odor and color. Happiness is the evening sun in late spring, blossoming linden trees, Shakespeare, exhaustion, liquification.

My "B." lies behind the brown teapot on Luise's desk. The wind puffs up my coat like a parachute. I make myself light, lie into the current, spread my arms as if I wanted to swim, and I float. I see my feet break free of the ground in the show window of the shoe store. One meter, two meters, slowly at first. The wind carries me across the street to the Neptune Fountain. I circle around it halfway up then quickly ascend, once fast around the Marienkirche and I'm already flying in a straight line above Unter den Linden toward the Brandenburg Gate. The precious giant takes on a more human dimension from this height, only you can't see the people anymore. Watch out, a vent hole, too late, I'm falling. Most frightening thought about death: dying when I'm happy. Sharp crash, the roof; no, a countercurrent lifts me up gently out of danger. And now to the sun. Daedalus, ah, I know that already, that's not allowed. "Arise, ye wretched of the earth." We don't have any time to play. We have to hurry, keep on hurrying. To the butchers, to the bank, to the office, to the kindergarten, to the elevated train. We can be late everywhere. The money is sold out, the bank has driven off, the boss is closed, the child is crying.

I hear a rustling above me and bright sunlight shines through a parted cloud. I feel a hand on my shoulder. When I raise my head, I'm looking into dark blue eyes, blue as the night-time sky and deep as the earth below.

"Hello," the boy says.

"Hello."

"I'm taking a walk."

"I'm taking a walk, too."

The boy waves his arms twice with all his might and flies a bit ahead. He flies wonderfully.

"I haven't seen you here before," he says.

"Am I really flying? I thought it was a dream."

The boy laughs and makes a little loop. "You are beautiful. You are beautiful; your eyes are like a dove's. You are Josefa, I recognize you."

That's my boyfriend's voice, he comes and flies through the clouds and floats above the roofs.

"I see, I see and I don't believe it. I'm flying under an icy sky, and the winter sun is warming me."

My boyfriend answers and talks to me: "Stand up, my friend, my beauty, and come here. For behold, winter is gone, the rain is gone. The flowers are sprouting, spring has come, and the turtledoves let their voice sound throughout the land."

"Come, my friend, let's fly over the city until the day is cool and the shadows give way."

The boy takes my hand and we fly together, fall into mountains of cotton and fly on. I close my eyes and float through the darkness, which flickers through my eyelids like silver. Arise, north wind, and come, south wind, and blow through my garden. We take a rest on a cloud.

"And your name is Pawel."

"If you so desire, my name is Pawel."

"Tell me more of your beautiful sentences."

"But you know them yourself."

"I want to hear them from you."

The boy says: "Where has thy friend gone, thou fairest among women? Whence has thy friend turned? Thus will I seek him with thee."

"I seek him but do not find him; I call him but he answers me not. The guardians, who roam the city, found me; they smote me, the guardians on the Wall took away my veil."

The boy kisses me on the mouth.

"I must go now."

"Stay a while."

"Luise is waiting."

"Will you come again?"

"Perhaps."

"Come again, you will find me with the north wind." He waves.

I quickly fly back to the publishing house without glancing at the ground. I'd rather land on the fifteenth floor and walk to the sixteenth. Otherwise I'll shock Luise, and who knows if her window is open. I knock, open the door before Luise's "Yes" lets me in. She is sitting as always in the black imitation leather chair on the metal swivel. She looks me over, wrinkles her brow in disapproval and says sternly: "Look at you. Why don't you comb your hair?" I'd like to tell her about my flight and about my meeting with Pawel, but I know Luise wouldn't believe me. She would tap on her forehead with her index finger and say with distinct contempt: "You're nuts!" Well, then I'll tell her about the terrible storm instead where you could almost have thought you'd be blown away like a piece of paper. And then...I just can't let it go, hazard putting my foot forward encouraged by the hope of an unexpected reaction from Luise: "Just imagine that you could suddenly fly around the Neptune Fountain and then around the Marienkirche..."

"Stay on the ground if you don't mind," Luise says soberly and reaches for my manuscript, which is no longer next to the teapot but instead lies open in front of her. Nine pages. Nine times thirty lines at sixty spaces a line. Nothing sensational, no discovery, no idea that anyone else couldn't have had who had walked through

B. Nothing more than the timid attempt to describe conditions there as they are. All the same, reason enough to fly, important enough to sit in front of Luise well-behaved and well-groomed as before a civil magistrate. Only the roles are reversed. It's up to Luise to say "I do", or not.

The outside cold that I brought into the room has already been sucked up by the central heating, which makes me thirsty. Or the thirst comes from the excitement. I'm always thirsty when I get excited, dried-out mouth membranes that stick together and distort my mouth and voice when I speak. I've thought and played this conversation through at least ten times until I was sure I had anticipated every surprise and was ready for every eventuality. And now fear is creeping in. The fear of having to fight with Luise. This damned sentimental yearning for harmony. People, love one another! The inveterate remains of childhood: the search for security. Nothing corrupts us so thoroughly and painlessly as love or friendship. I don't want to fight with Luise.

Luise puts a piece of licorice in her mouth, carefully brushes a few crumbs from her skirt and finally looks at me. Wherever did she get that smile from one instant to the next? Not just a mouth screwed up out of embarrassment or well-meaning friendship; a deep, unmistakable smile, which isn't only meant for me, but for my report on B. as well.

"This is a report right after my own heart," Luise says. I've never heard a phrase from her with anything like this amount of bombast. She quotes a passage that she especially likes. I try desperately to suppress a broad grin so as not to look like a child under the Christmas tree. I'm so very sorry, Luise, that I had doubts about you. I should have known you're no coward. And Christian is right. We cross half of it out ourselves because we think we know that the others would cross it out. We see ghosts. We act like trained dogs at court who end up guarding nothing more than their own chains.

"Well, as far as I'm concerned, right away and immediately," Luise says, "but we have to show it to Rudi. There'll be problems for sure. I don't care about that if it's worth it. And this is worth it. But you know Rudi. And we can't just stick him with this thing."

"No?"

"No."

"Then nothing'll come of it." Our delegate doesn't have the guts, Hodriwitzka had said when he heard that the union would have to write an invitation to the Minister, and quickly forgot the dream of the large culture hall without the rostrum.

Luise looks at me as if she expected confirmation, verbal approval. I'd like to scream "Shit!" so that they hear me through the paper-thin walls, in the Editor-in-Chief's office.

"Listen, what did you expect? I have nothing against your writing all this, definitely not. But I am against it when someone writes something like this without knowing what they're getting in for. I can't listen to this constant moaning about the terrible times in which we're living and the horrible people we have to deal with. My nerves can't take it. You work at the paper. A paper is like that. If you can't take it, find another profession."

I remain silent. Luise stirs her cup with a teaspoon, carefully watching what she's doing. She swivels her chair in my direction, smiles with resignation. "That's the way it is," she says and puts down the spoon. The situations in which Luise reacts with indignation and irritation at the emotional outbursts of her colleagues are almost always the same. Outbursts of anger that Luise doesn't allow herself are forbidden to the others in her presence as well.

I was sitting nearby when she went to Günter Rassow in the open-plan office, hopping mad, to return a manuscript to him about a village that was sitting on top of a brown coal deposit and was going to be torn down, with the comment that she had just gone through an hour arguing with Strutzer. Without success. The article was killed because Strutzer insisted that the villagers had to give up their homes and gooseberry bushes with greater optimism than he found in the text. Luise said she was sick with rage and fell into a chair exhausted.

Günter Rassow looked at Luise as if he expected her to revoke this announcement the next minute, April fools or something. Then he understood, jumped up, banged with his ruler, which always lies on the desk at a right angle to the edge; and screamed wildly that he had finally had enough of this newspaper, that he wanted to resign, they'd see. Günter got a few decibels louder after each attempt to calm him down. "Then I'll become a construction worker or bake rolls," he screamed.

"Do that," Luise said sharply and left the room with a wounded smile on her collapsed face. Günter Rassow didn't resign, Luise didn't mention the incident anymore, but she was visibly reserved towards Günter for the next few weeks.

Since then I've tried to spare Luise similar situations even though this sort of self-control goes against my nature. I think a person has a right to his anger. And Luise's anger at Günter Rassow was actually no more than Günter's lack of consideration for Luise. Neither Günter or Luise had brought about the situation. They were carrying out a proxy argument that was nothing more than the expression of their defenselessness against Strutzer. Luise was offended nonetheless, though less by Günter's row than by the equivocal position he put her in. She was the boss, she had to return the manuscript for changes although this went against her own judgment. She expected understanding and sympathy from Günter. Instead of which he forced her into the role that Siegfried Strutzer had played five minutes earlier. That had offended her. And if I had really screamed shit a few moments ago, it would have offended her although she knew quite well that it wasn't meant for her.

But I don't want a fight with Luise, or a proxy fight. "Go to B. again," she said, "arrange it with the Party secretary or with your Alfred Thal or whatever his name is; he was quite reasonable. If they agree, Rudi is rid of half the responsibility, you know, and then I can talk with him."

Luise offers me the licorice bag, I take two, but nothing happens except for an astonished look at my fingertips, where two cat's heads are stuck. "Well, all right," she says, referring either to the licorice or my article.

I'm sitting stiffly in the black imitation leather chair, my jeans are pinching me in the stomach although I have nothing in it except two cups of coffee. My sweater itches. My boots are tight. I feel arms, hands, legs, rump, clumsy and heavy; everything is hanging on an empty bloated thing: my head.

No, that's not me. I know from this morning: I can fly. Spread out my arms as if I wanted to swim and I'm flying. An evil spell must come over me as soon as I enter the building; the concrete white ceilings, hallways, rooms; everything white with black imitation leather chairs on shiny swivels. I can fly so high that all the magnificent buildings of all periods shrink to the point of being bearable and you can't see them any longer.

"Sometimes I feel I'm being cheated out of my life," I say.

Luise looks up with a slightly defensive expression in her eyes. "Now don't exaggerate."

"I'm not exaggerating. I'm being cheated out of myself. I'm not even talking about the fact that I'll die in the age of space exploration without having taken a walk in Montmartre, without knowing what it smells like in the desert or what a fresh oyster tastes like. I can come to terms with that. Our forefathers didn't get very far in their mail coaches either, but they understood something about the world all the same. The greater deception: they are cheating me out of me, out of my qualities. I'm not allowed to be everything I am. They put a 'too' on every one of my attributes: you are too spontaneous, too naive, too honest, too quick to judge. They demand my understanding where I can't understand: to be sensible where I don't want to be sensible, my patience when I tremble with impatience. I'm not allowed to decide when I have to decide. I'm supposed to get out of the habit of being myself. Why can't they use me like I am?

Sometimes I think that maybe I would have been more useful in another age when order, discipline and loyalty weren't the highest precepts. Luise, if you drive a car for a hundred kilometers with the handbrake on, you ruin it. And do you think that a person stays in one piece? He gets broken, too. He doesn't stop, doesn't fall down, but he gets weaker all the time; he can't produce anything any more. His most important activity becomes checking himself: the denial of his mind, of his feelings. He wears himself out in the struggle against himself, clips his thoughts before he thinks them, discards words before he has spoken them, distrusts his own judgment, is ashamed of his own individuality, doesn't allow himself feelings. And if he doesn't prohibit them, he keeps them to himself. Worse still: he gradually begins to suffer from the artifical impoverishment of his personality and invents new qualities that bring him praise and recognition. He becomes reasonable, cautious, regular, well-organized, busy. At the beginning his abused character still twitches under the constraint, but the old thoughts and feelings slowly die: he dares to come out only in his dreams. But during the day our poor, restrained person wears a uniform character, a nice, moderate, sensible being, until one day he forgets his original nature, or screams out in pain, or dies.

Another forty or fifty years like this, Luise, and mankind will bore itself to death. Then the last rebels will have died out, and no one will encourage their children to play with the world any more. They will learn the hard truth of this life from the first days of their lives. Their desires will be destroyed through temperate regulation of eating, playing, learning. They learn reason without ever having been unreasonable. Wretched cretins will grow up, and the creative among them will feel a vague mourning and a longing for something alive. Woe be to them if they find it in themselves. They will become mocked outcasts. Crazy, madmen, incorrigible. You are too lively, they'll be told, as the worst possible reproach. But I think that our nature is stronger than every system bent on leveling it, no matter how perfect, and that it springs back when bent too far.''

Luise had listened to me the whole while in silence without her shocked blue child's eyes in her wrinkled face leaving me for an instant.

"Do you really mean everything you just said?"

"I don't know. Maybe. Today for sure.''

Luise is still looking at me as if she wanted to look inside me. She stares at a point above my eyes quietly and pensively, her head gently resting on her hand.

"I don't know whether you're right. In many things, surely. But I have to see it differently, you know. I lived through fascism. Your basic experiences are different, I know. You can't measure the advantages of socialism with a past you didn't live through. But when you talk about a perfect system of leveling, I have to say: I know one incomparably worse. For me what we have here is the best I've ever seen. But it may be that you simply have to see that as the starting point for something better. Perhaps you have to measure the present by the future as long as you don't have a past. And it isn't the sentimentality of old age to declare the present to be the goal because someone doesn't have much of a future left. All the same, Josefa, it pains me when you tell me that you are being cheated out of your life; you simply forget the immeasurably greater brutality with which all previous generations were cheated before you."

"Do you seriously want us to prove how much better off we are now than we were under the Nazis? When you began in '45, you had entirely different goals, didn't you? Didn't they receive you with open arms when all of a sudden, you, an anti-fascist and social democrat, wanted to help with a newspaper for the communists? They could use you the way you were. I know all that: you had too little to eat, you worked late into the night and you even broke stones on Sunday. And why do all your eyes light up in spite of that when you talk about this period? Why not when you talk about '55 or '65? Because at some point or other all the years began to resemble one another, from one election to the next, from one Party Congress to the next Party Congress; competitions, anniversaries, campaigns. But for the first three years, you know every day, every face you knew back then. Why then? Why not later?"

"Listen," Luise says, "we really don't have to argue about things we agree on." She has regained her sober tone. She gets up, walks slowly around her desk, opens the window. She fans the cold air to her face, probably to show the exertion that our conversation is causing her. Or she's thinking over what she wants to tell me now.

"I wouldn't think of trying to talk you out of your feelings. You have them and you've every right. But how do you expect to be a journalist with feelings like that? You'd be able to afford them in another profession. Be consistent, then. Use the freedom of choice you have. Go into a factory, learn a profession, get an engineering degree, too, as far as I'm concerned. You are intelligent enough. No one is forcing you to put on paper what you find so questionable every day.''

Bulls-eye, Luise, in my heart. Well, what answer do I have to that?

I've been travelling through steelworks, textile mills, chemical plants, engineering collective combines for six years without being able to get used to the violence of industrial labor, without losing the horror that gets hold of me when I see the maiming that labor still does to people. Flayed wind pipes, crushed legs, deaf ears, growths jutting out of bones. Not to mention the invisible deformation through constant and unvarying signals to the brain. Grip left with the left hand, push down with the right hand. Eight hours a day, senses deadened out of self-defense, gone insensitive through time and neglect, nothing more than shrivelled roots of dead yearnings; betrayed childhood dreams worth no more than a derisive smile: ''Oh God, I wanted to be a dancer; yeah, the crazy things you think up when you're a kid.'' And then she punches her 3000th or 4000th hole in a piece of leather that will become a handbag. When she wants to go to the toilet, she has to call the sub. When she goes to the dentist, she has to make up the half hour of work. Every backside in an office can sit two hours in a hairdresser's chair during working hours without having to make up the time. But half an hour on the line, punching twenty or thirty rivets a minute, six hundred in half an hour, or nine hundred, that needs making up. She gets up at 4:00 a.m, at 5:00 drops her child off at kindergarten, shift begins at 5:15. Grip left with the left hand, push down with the right hand, grip left with the left hand, push down with the right hand. And on top of that, the clockwork noise of the punch machine: tac, tac, tac, tac. Eight hours a day. I can't, Luise, I can't do that. It would be slow, very slow suicide for me. To forget who I am eight hours a day, to practise forgetting eight hours a day. Throw yearnings on the dunghill of impossibilities. Every thought cut to shreds by the tactactactac. Counting eyelets and punch holes. Forget that I can fly.

Luise's phone rings. She doesn't pick up the receiver.

''Well, why do you stay?'' she asks again.

The phone is still ringing.

''Why does the rabbit stay in the woods when the fox is chasing

59

it? He ought to become an aquatic animal instead. Some freedom of choice you're offering me! Please, Comrade, if you don't like it here with us, you are free to go where things are worse..."

"There you have it!" Luise points at me with her index finger as if it were a pistol. "You're not a rabbit who ought to be a frog, Josefa, fine as that sounds. My proposal isn't all that impossible. But you don't want to get up at 4:00, you don't want to be chained eight hours to a machine, you don't want to give up your thousand Marks a month. You want to keep your privileges, even if it's only one: work that you enjoy. Listen, Marx knew a long time ago why he bet on the proletariat and not on the intellectuals, for heaven's sake. You simply have more to lose than your chains. In that case you just put up with a small loss of freedom at least more willingly than a loss of privileges."

Luise is merciless. I have a headache and I feel dizzy. I don't want to argue with Luise. It'll be all right, Josie, my mother always used to say when I had worries, stroked my head and when things were really bad she cooked me apple snow. I liked the green ones best. I'd like to sleep. Eyes closed, face to the wall and sleep, fourteen hours or even longer.

I hear the door open behind my back. Someone asks whether Luise would have just five minutes time.

"Later," Luise says and smiles obligingly over my head.

"You're unfair," I say when the door is closed again, "you act as if I were the most cowardly and corrupt person in sight because I don't want to have my life punched to pieces on an assembly line. Do you really think people who are insensitive to their situation and don't even think about it are more honest?"

Luise screws up her mouth impatiently. "Now don't make such a fuss. Of course I don't think that. But you can't always play the desperate heroine if you're simply doing what you have to anyway. You want to write, alright then, you write. You want to write honestly; well, who's stopping you?"

Luise places her open hand on my manuscript as proof. "You don't want to go to the assembly line? Nobody's forcing you to. You want to take aim at things, be one of the critical minds? That's in your nature, too. Fine, no society can do without its critics.

But fight then and stop complaining. These are just the oft-quoted everyday toils, and no one has promised us that we wouldn't have them. If I wasn't profoundly convinced that the effort is worth it, even if it lasts longer than we had planned, I would have left long ago. Listen, I learned an honest profession as well, I can do tailoring. But I firmly believe in the victory of communism, I just have to tell you this plainly, even if you probably think it's nothing more than rhetoric."

I think of Werner Grellmann, who couldn't hear the word *believe* without raising his eyebrows.

"Faith," I ask, "what is faith?"

Luise pretends not to have heard the question, gets up, looks at herself briefly in the unframed mirror on the wall as she walks past it, redoes a few strands of hair.

"Do you expect people to embrace you with joy and cry: 'Just look, our dear Josefa is coming who always has such nice insults and criticism for us,' just because we have our wee bit of socialism?"

Luise has let her theatrical inclinations take over now. The last sentence was already reinforced with stage gestures: arm swung high, shrill voice. There's no doubt about it, she'd like to act out in detail her idea of how the martyr Josefa imagines the homage of the insulted masses.

Luise passed the entrance examination for the State Acting School when she was twenty-one, even though the whole thing had been a mistake. The first anniversary of the school was supposed to be featured in an article, and the official Party organ had given the task to its youngest female reporter. There are very few possibilities for a reporter to be anonymous, to experience genuine situations and atmospheres, ideally as someone touched by the events they are supposed to report. Here was such a possibility. Luise applied for entrance. She was svelte, pale, blonde, pretty, although she had an unusually pointed nose even then. She always wore a light trench coat and a black beret. Thus, by her appearance alone, a much sought-after presence for postwar German film. She hadn't prepared any role, which meant she had to take her stage test with an improvisation.

61

Just imagine, the fat, agile man with a moustache said, you are a young girl who is head over heels in love with a young man. Your parents do not approve of the relationship. The girl leaves her parents. The young man in question, however, leaves her soon afterwards. The young girl, played by Luise, now returns to her parents, full of remorse and shame after having been abandoned, lonely, without a roof over her head. She steals furtively into the familiar apartment and meets her father. And Luise is supposed to play this crucial moment for the warmly smiling critics.

Luise told us this story once after a planning meeting, as we sat exhausted and tormented from competition plans and problems, large and small. As she told the story she suddenly jumped up. "So you have to imagine they were down in front of me there, grinning at me like sick people." She demonstrated bared, grinning teeth, unnatural wrinkles around her eyes. "You have to pretend this is the stage." Luise pointed to the empty space in front of the door. "Well, I come in." She suggested opening and closing a door. She crept a few steps forward on tiptoe, her index finger in front of her mouth, her shoulders drawn in. Suddenly she froze, looked around on all sides with a jerk, put her empty hand to her ear and cried loudly: "Oh, horror, what noise is this!" Then she crept forward.

Günter Rassow slapped his thigh and laughed uproariously. Luise, undaunted, went on. She lifted an arm in front of her face for protection as though she were blinded. "Oh God, my father!" she yelled shrilly, then pointed upwards with her eyes: "What shall I do?" She looked around again wildly and helplessly, threw herself at the knees of the imaginary father and sobbed: "Father, forgive me!" sat down again at the table and savored the success of her performance.

The jury, according to Luise, was highly impressed with her presentation. The friendly gentleman with the moustache told her that she had comic talent, which deeply offended Luise, who had meant her acting to be serious. It's possible that Luise's reluctance to express her feelings except in a bottled-up or slightly ironic way was responsible for her success. Since then she has cultivated her comic abilities. And when Luise recounts conversations with disagreeable people, she usually acts them out so that the person she is talking about becomes a comic character who loses every chance from the outset. "You know how he talks," Luise says by way of introduction, then revels in every idiosyncrasy of stress, every sneer or lisp, until those listening are no longer interested in the arguments of her ridiculous opponent, admiring instead Luise's ability, clapping and crying: "Yes, that's just the way he talks!"

I have to give up if Luise decides to play the martyr Josefa before the devoted masses. You can't reach her anymore with objections. My role is set. All I can do is to keep myself from becoming a comic figure by refusing to play audience. Luise is just sketching the congratulatory speech by the First Secretary to his critic Josefa.

"Gotta go," I say, and leave.

V

The park is bare. No leaf, no snow, even the wilted foliage lies sparsely on the brown meadows; twisted branches stick out in the grey, damp air. In autumn, parks look like uninhabited, unheated rooms—unnatural and cold.

My son runs across the meadow to the slope where the ducks regularly await their visitors. He opens a plastic bag with bread crumbs and calls out like a market crier trying to beat his competitors. I sit down to one side on a tree stump—in winter the benches are cleared away— and stare at the white wall that separates the park from the palace it once belonged to. An elector built the palace for his electoress because he wanted to keep her as far away from court and off his back as possible.

They say he visited her now and then. I was told by a very old woman when I was still a child that he is said to have rowed a skiff along the greygreen, muddy creek that flows through the park and half of the city district. I must have looked in disbelief at the pitiful creek. A long time ago, the old woman said, when she was young, it used to be an exceedingly fine large river, and you could ride into the city on it. And the king travelled on it, she said, and

63

her eyes were moist with the debility of old age and the spring wind. The old woman's tale made a lasting impression on me although I was an exemplary and conscientious Youth Pioneer; for I can't look at that narrow, filthy stream without imagining a skiff with a red baldachin on it, the king standing in the middle in his white uniform and black three-cornered hat. He executes a broad, majestic, wide-arching gesture with his right arm and has his left foot poised slightly forward in the gracious manner of a monarch, with the point of his foot turned slightly outwards. The king is fat and resembles Siegfried Strutzer.

The palace was taken over by the government. The park is open to all, at their own risk when the ice is slippery.

I don't want to think about Siegfried Strutzer.

My son is wooing a beautiful, green-necked drake who is eagerly waddling around an old lady with a rainhat who apparently has something better to offer than stale bread—perhaps homemade cake.

"She doesn't want to come to me," my son says.

"She is a he."

"No, the brightly-colored ones are the girls."

"The bright ones are the boys."

"Political viciousness or political stupidity," Strutzer said.

"Girls, I know that for sure."

His infamous smile on his small mouth.

"And how?"

"Girls look prettier than boys, too."

"Why?" I should have said something.

"Because they have such cute braids and bright little skirts!"

"And if they cut off the braids and take off the skirts?"

He thinks. "Not then. But why are the boy ducks prettier?"

"I don't know. So that the mother is protected and no one bothers her when she's brooding."

"And what protects you?"

"Nobody wants to eat you," I reassure him.

Strutzer with his petty, infamous smile, his eyes hidden behind his glasses, which reflect the artificial light and lend to the upper half of his face an inscrutable rigidity. Thin, dark-toned glasses, perhaps merely intended to hide Strutzer's excitement behind two patches of reflected light. He tapped on the desk with his pencil, allowing long, regular pauses between the taps, increasing my tension.

"All right then, I'll put it another way," he said after I had been staring at him for half a minute without having gotten back my tongue. "Did you seriously think we would publish this as you've written it?"

I could have answered with a simple yes. He had asked before whether I had written it out of political viciousness or simply out of political stupidity. When he said "this", he tapped casually with his pencil on my manuscript. I wanted to light a cigarette just to gain time to think of a suitable answer. My hands were trembling. I put the pack back on the desk. My mouth was dry. Strutzer's eyeless face stared at me, although the infamous smile was hardly to be seen on his small mouth. The white walls blinded me. I looked at the floor. In the upper portion of my field of vision Siegfried Strutzer's foot was tapping in the same rhythm as his pencil. I got hot and began to hear a rumbling in my ears.

Strutzer leaned back, put both hands on the back of his chair, the tapping stopped. "Your arrogance isn't helping us at all. Neither are you. If you don't want to talk to me because of a personal aversion, then we'll just have to talk to each other in front of the Party leadership."

I couldn't think of anything to answer, nothing that would mitigate the situation. The white walls blurred into a soft mass that alternately oozed towards and away from me. The rumbling in my ears grew louder.

The pencil was tapping again. The foot in the cowhide shoe seemed to come closer with each tap. It was idiotic to remain silent. But it was too late to say something normal, casual, perhaps even something humorous. By now it had to be a statement of principle, something that could be quoted in front of the Party leadership or the Editor-in-Chief. He knew why the conversation had begun with his pronouncement of guilt. He had to put me on the defensive, to provoke me until I finally blurted out the unchecked idiocy that he was expecting. We laughed at him too often. Luise had gone over his trap too often with a hot iron, with her shrewd intelligence. Luise would never have let herself get into my tricky situation. She would probably have left the room after Strutzer's first question, though not without informing him that Comrade Strutzer would, of course, have to institute a Party proceeding against her after having brought such monstrous charges against her, which could no longer remain the topic of a private conference. Then Siegfried Strutzer would have had to make an effort to calm Luise down again.

My son is hanging on the highest rung of a jungle gym, screaming. "Hold on tight, I'm coming."

There was nothing left to salvage, all that was left to do was to avoid the mistake of saying anything at all.

"I see no other way except to inform the Party leadership about your opinions. Hopefully you'll have something to explain to the comrades." He wishes me a nice weekend. He's beating a march rhythm as I leave.

Luise had the day off. I called Rudi's secretary, heard that the Chief had gone home an hour ago, isn't coming back, either.

"Excuse me, could you please get off, we'd like to play seesaw," a girl says. I switch to an old tire. Strutzer called me shortly after lunch and told me he wanted to read the article about B.; I should bring it up right away. He reacted with unaccustomed sharpness when I told him that I had reservations and wanted to clear the text with the plant first. That's the whole point, he said with an ambiguous animation in his voice. Someone must have informed him about the form and content of the article, although no one knew about it except Luise, Günter Rassow and the secretary who had copied it. I took the manuscript to Rudi, asked him to read it himself before passing it on to Strutzer, and waited. Three hours later Strutzer called me in.

My son is standing in front of the seesaw, is following the up and down of the beam and the giggling of the girls with envy. "I want to ride too."

"Leave me alone. I want to get out of here."

"But I haven't done anything," he says, frightened.

"I'm cold, stop yelling."

"But I have to cry when you scream like that."

"Me too."

Maybe I shouldn't have had a child. Always the feeling that I'm keeping something from him that he has a right to. Don't burden the child, Ida says. I don't want to put on a show from morning to night, live with him like a stranger, only to be found out one day when he's grown up, as most mothers are found out to be liars—that I was a woman when he took me to be a good-natured neuter, a woman who slept with men, yelled, was despondent or happy. There are men who don't understand to their dying day how they ever came into the world, because they never dared to undress their mothers in their imaginations. And when they dare, all they find are wrinkled old women. Most see through their mothers' hypocrisy; as soon as they sleep with their wives, they imagine the spread legs and the sighs groaned into pillows so that the children won't hear. They understand what monstrous lies they have been told, how cunning grownups are when keeping their secrets is at stake, the talent they have for pretending. Mysterious scenes in the distant past are explained: terrified faces, hastily closed doors, Father's confused smile. They are warned for the future, enlightened about how to be expert in lying, a skill they still have to perfect. They watch grownups more closely at close range, especially mothers, since they are best at lying. They greedily register every inconsistent word with contempt, don't believe even the truth any more. My son has become a stranger to me, the mothers complain. But they have read something in a magazine article about the naturalness of this phase and aren't surprised...Until years later they come before them as men enlightened through their own lies, which they have mastered by then. They have forgiven their mothers for being women.

I don't want to keep anything from him that concerns me; I could only have kept him from me, had him removed in time. I yelled with joy when he was born and for weeks I couldn't fall asleep with the baby next to me until I was sure he wouldn't suddenly stop breathing.

"Are we going home?" he asks with fright when he notices that I've started on the path to the exit.

I dread having to spend the rest of the day talking to myself. Visit someone, barge in on a family idyll, drink coffee in company, conversations about children, newspaper gossip. To my mother's. The admonishing face: you really are inclined to see everything as grey-in-grey, long-winded descriptions of yesterday's TV programs. I miss Christian.

We haven't spoken to each other since my last visit to his place. First he makes outrageous suggestions and when someone is frivolous enough to follow them, he leaves them in the lurch. But perhaps he's waiting for me, hopes I'll come, just ring: I'm here, it was nothing, we are the way we were before, and I need you now.

"You're an idiot," Christian said.

"Why me? You said: write two versions."

"Well, did you write two?"

Silence.

"Am I supposed to give you some good advice now?"

What advice could he have given anyway? Talk to Luise, go to B., don't bitch. She knew that already. She warmed her hands on the burner of the kitchen stove and watched Christian slice onions. Cut them in half, then lengthwise. He had learned that from his grandmother, who was cook to a bishop. As if only grandmothers who had once cooked for a bishop could slice onions.

She had repeated sentence for sentence Strutzer's threats, and as she told them, felt herself how childish her panic was. Strutzer was an underhanded insect, everyone knew that. Perhaps he could prevent the article from being printed. But nothing more. Neither Hans Schütz nor Günter Rassow, who were both in the Party leadership, would allow Strutzer to construct a Nadler Affair.

"And why did you yell?"

"I don't know any more," she said. And suddenly in the silence: "Because I can't stand looking at the fat women and the hollow eggheads and the fat asses and the whole upright German nation."

It didn't occur to her that she had used exactly the same words as Fred Müller when he vomited his innermost self dead drunk at Hans Schütz's place. She minced the bacon as if she had someone or something under the knife that deserved her rage.

Christian sometimes considered her an adorable monster who possessed limited abilities to deal with personal conflict. More than once he had seen her in a state of deepest dejection, from which she always emerged marvellously fresh but never clean. She had been running blindly into disasters for fifteen years, all of which bore a fatal structural resemblance, different as they appeared on the surface. Admission to the Party, marriage, divorce, all according to the same scheme.

During her last year at university Josefa had been dismissed as secretary of the Free German Youth because of "sectarianism". The reason was this Mohnkopf or Mohnhaupt, one of the two comrades in the seminar, a foul intriguer and Josefa's special enemy. She used to tell him at regular intervals back then how she had brought Mohnhaupt low through supplementary questions or by pointing out to him that he had misused a foreign word. Christian had never shown much understanding for Josefa's little wars, although her childlike enthusiasm, which she considered a sort of class struggle, touched him. But one day Mohnhaupt or Mohnkopf had had a bellyful, charged her with wanting to damage the Party with her cunning attacks on him. Josefa had sworn heaven knows how many times that she couldn't stand Mohnhaupt. No good, she was replaced. A few days later she made an application to be accepted into the Party. This, she thought, would make them ashamed and convince them of the injustice done to her. What happened instead could be seen in advance by everyone except Josefa. She believed with naive stubborness that the comrades would have to disassociate themselves from Mohnhaupt's sly farce as if she were able to prove his assertions wrong. The comrades decided in an admission session, which according to Josefa was more like a formal proceeding, not to tolerate Youth member Nadler in their ranks any longer. He needed to make sure, Mohnhaupt had declared, that the person to his rear wouldn't shoot him in the back if he had to stand guard duty on the Wall sometime.

For days on end Josefa was crazed with rage and impotence. Christian tried to calm her down, but she trembled as soon as she thought of the affair, and she thought about it constantly. She sat in her chair as if it were a fortress, her eyes swollen from tears, throwing obscenities all around her, talked of killing Mohnhaupt or Mohnkopf and snapped at everyone who tried to console her. Then she disappeared. She was back after two days. "I was with your father in Halle," she explained. She seemed calm, almost contented. The next day she went to the university Party leadership, pointed to a Party statute underlined in red by Werner Grellmann that proved that her application had been dealt with incorrectly. Two months later she was reaccepted as a candidate, was solemnly presented with the red carnation and a book with a dedication saying that the comrades of the Party group were happy to have Josefa back in their ranks.

Christian sat at the kitchen table, smoked a cigarette and compared the Josefa doggedly slicing bacon with the one he had known ten years earlier.

"Did you know that all witches were good and beautiful when they were young?" he asked.

"And where did you find that out?"

"I knew one, the fair witch Yala-Niya, the daughter of heaven and the night. She loved a giant who lived across the mountains, but she didn't want to marry him until his heart was just as great as his strength. She sent him into the wide world where he was supposed to find out what he did not know. And he was supposed to return to her as soon as he had found it. She waited a hundred years and her nose grew longer and her chin pointy; she waited two hundred years and she got a bent back and a cackly voice. She waited three hundred years and two long fangs grew over her lip, and she hated all those who didn't wait. And if she's not dead, she is still waiting to this day."

"And the giant?" Josefa asked.

"Must have found out what he didn't know."

"I won't wait."

"But you'll grow evil."

She wondered whether she should contradict him or admit her fears. A few weeks ago she had found a picture that dated back to her school days when she was six or seven years old. Josefa with a broad, Slavic child's face in which you couldn't see the concave curvature between cheek and jaw bone. And although she had done her best to put on a serious and dignified graduate face for the photo, without a trace of a smile, the corner of her mouth was turned slightly upwards. She had compared her image in the mirror with the face in the photo: smooth hair down to her shoulders, the flat forehead free. It wasn't the thin lines caught in the light's harsh shadows that brought about the change in her face, which looked at her stiffly and seriously from the mirror. She drew the corners of her mouth and eyes slightly upwards with her fingertips, pulled her skin without being able to correct the changes. The little wrinkles weren't to blame. Aging begins inside; wrinkles only advertise it. Things had changed behind her eyes, extinguished hope, a bitter line between nose and mouth that had still to dig a groove, but let it be known how it would soon be running. The way the lips closed. The mouth in the photo wasn't open, incidentally. The mouth in the mirror was closed.

There were six or seven years between them. She remembered the unpaved street. A blazing hot summer day, the water shimmered above the embankment, it smelled like dust and melted tar. Sour beer fumes billowed out of the open door of a bar, repelling and inviting at the same time. Mulackstraße, Linienstraße, Große Hamburger, alternately soda on tap and peppermint liqueur: "A small green one, please." Old women in the windows of the uniformly grey apartments with their elbows leaning on sofa pillows. Cats sunned themselves in the flower boxes, all house and cellar doors open against dry rot. Half-naked children had spread out towels in their backyards and pretended to be at the seashore. Tadeus had put his arm around Josefa, the heat had melted her down into a quadruped, and when they kissed, a toothless old woman snapped, asking whether they didn't have a bed they could use.

"On the contrary," Tadeus said, "we have one, but unfortunately we don't have it along."

At that point she had to laugh at the old woman.

Later on she used to go there alone, without Tadeus, with others. But always in the summer on hot days when the odors of saucepans, roasting tins and musty cellars streamed through the doors and windows and hung over the streets like festoons.

71

She no longer knew the last time she had been there, or with whom. She remembered that in recent years there was bitter lemon from the drink collective combine instead of soda on tap, and the small street-level bar in Linienstraße was closed because the innkeeper's wife, who had always sat out in front of the door on a small wooden stool when the weather was fine, had died.

She had put the photo in a book, one she wouldn't read right away. After all, she was thirty, a working woman, living alone with a child (did she really think "living alone"?), and it was normal to grow older.

She stood up, washed the bacon fat from her hands, looked at herself in the mirror that hung over the washbasin, combed her hair so that she could continue to look at herself without embarrassment.

"Bull", she said, "my nose is no longer than it usually is."

She sat on the window sill and watched Christian toss the spaghetti into the boiling water. She was too tired and too tense to fight back. Perhaps she really was waiting for someone or something. She could not have said herself exactly where her restlessness came from, the gradually mounting tension that discharged itself in loud groaning and spurts of strength when it exceeded a certain level, without ever disappearing completely.

There were weeks during which she constantly suspected herself of doing the wrong thing. She slept with a man, then wondered whether it should have been another one; wrote a report and was sure she should have picked a different topic; visited people, only to find out half an hour later that it would have been better to stay at home alone; couldn't finish reading a book for fear that another was more important.

Restless states which often ended in extremes: in deluded infatuations that became her reason for living for a few weeks, or in crazy projects of cleaning and straightening up her apartment in order to create at least the illusion of order. The security of having to do this and nothing else was never realized. On the contrary: the fear of missing her real self grew to a panic when she lay down alone in bed at night and checked off another day of her life.

The real self she was looking for was the biography tailored to her uniquely and which fit no one else. She didn't know how many people she could assume were identical with their real selves. Grandfather Pawel belonged to them and grandmother Josefa; Werner Grellmann, too. Each of these biographies rested on an avowal of faith. Her grandfather avowed his Judaism (probably because he simply had no other choice). Her grandmother avowed her husband, Werner Grellmann avowed science. These were active avowals, effective, fatal for her grandparents. Or put it another way: the biography doesn't rest on the avowal, rather the avowal was a necessary result of the biography, was loyalty to one's self. The meaning of life adopted as the concrete content of this concretely unique life.

Luise's life was also determined by an avowal. Nevertheless, the plan of her biography and its realization in action were no longer one. Luise was a communist and her ideal avowal was meant for all those oppressed and exploited. But the result of her work appeared week after week in a newspaper that she didn't like and wasn't intended for those who read it, where what Luise wanted to talk about was kept out, where there was nothing about ash chambers, defoliated trees or forgotten towns. The long road that Luise's plans had to travel before they became deeds led past innumerable small compromises, disciplinary considerations, inner and outer checkpoints, at the end of which was action that was not the flesh of her plans but a cretinous offshoot.

Thirty years ago Luise had different experiences. Back then she wanted to rebuild the country, and she broke stones on Sundays. She wanted to expropriate Junker property and wrote impassioned reports on land reform. Back then Luise's deeds were the firm flesh of her ideas. Josefa had never experienced anything like that. She learned who her ancestors were: from Spartacus to Saint-Just, from Marx to the anti-Nazis, all fighters in the history of the world were her ancestors. The roots of her designs were there. But she let Strutzer decide the extent of her deeds, one who condemned Josefa's avowal to remain a loose, shrivelled shell.

She looked at Christian as he carefully watched the spaghetti and stirred the sauce. She wanted to grab him, just like that, touch his neck or arms, his sweater, which was sure to be warm from his skin.

She had noticed a change in her body in the last few years that couldn't be explained any longer by loss or gain of weight or the results of pregnancy. The skin on her forearms pushed up into innumerable wrinkles when she pressed against it with her thumb, the first disgusting pockets of fat swelled up inside her upper thigh. Decay. The approach of old age. Death. And always the fear of throwing away one's only life. She had written a composition in the tenth grade about the meaning of life. She remembered the last sentence: A person cannot live without giving his life a meaning. Everyone believed in the meaning of life as they believed in the Lord God, a Great Idea that shines before them and would show them the right path. The inside of her upper thigh had begun to decay, and she still didn't know what she was to do with her life. She had brought a child into the world, and she wrote articles for a weekly. When she was seven years old, she didn't think any life was worth living where she wasn't famous. She didn't even consider becoming someone whose name wouldn't get into schoolbooks.

"What should I wait for," she asked exhausted. "Get married maybe? Are you racked by migraine? Get married. Do you suffer from overweight? Get married. Is your nose too long? Well, what can you tell the people who are married already?"

"Divorce. Besides, I wasn't talking about marriage," Christian said.

"Then don't tell me any stories. Say: Josefa dear, you ought to fuck more often, or else your nose will grow too long. Then I could answer: Christian dear, I fuck often enough, but that won't keep my nose from getting longer. When I become a witch, the men won't be to blame. As long as they're not my bosses."

Josefa sat on the window sill. Christian could only see her outline against the white sun, which had come through the clouds. She sat quietly, more loose than relaxed. Her sudden transformation irritated him. She could just as easily jump up in the next instant and fall back into her aggressive alertness for reasons even she didn't understand.

"The worst thing about it is," she said, "that they told us so

74

much about revolution that a life without revolution seems meaningless. And then they pretend there are none left, as if all the revolutions in German history had already taken place. Theirs was the last one. They allow us to sweep the dust that it stirred up to one side. Your revolution is to defend the achievements, they say, and make us into museum attendants. You save yourself in history: now you play Marat or Robespierre, certainly Robespierre, and can pump yourself full of the revolutionary storm until you fly. But I should purge the revolution of 180 tons of flue ash; I ought to clean and polish it with polish from a spray can, and I am supposed to praise it in newsprint as a super horsepower vehicle to the future. After that I'll go to the hairdressers and have my hair dyed blonde because I'm crazy for change.''

Josefa's spontaneity, which had always yearned for action, was foreign to Christian. He planned for the long run. He was disconcerted by hectic activity, large groups of people, and he avoided them whenever he could. He viewed the country and century he had been born into as an accident, which he accepted as a barrier of fact and not as a barrier to thought.

''You wrote about B. the way you wanted to. Now just wait for the time being. Your Strutzer is no doubt sitting peacefully at his coffee table right now and isn't wasting his thoughts on you, while you are pulling thorns out of your scalp that aren't even there. A kind of hypochondria, as well.''

After dinner they took her son to his grandmother and drove to Karl Brommel, a friend of Christian's whom Josefa had seen three or four times. ''I can't take being alone with you today,'' Christian said. Karl Brommel was an Alsatian, a compact man whose broad cat's head rested on a streamlined body with no apparent help from his neck. Slit-like eyes, a narrow slit-like mouth. He had stayed in Berlin fifteen years ago because he had met a girl on an excursion in the GDR for French journalists. She was in her early twenties at the time; he was over thirty. She didn't live long; she died at twenty-eight of a kidney disease. Her name was Brunnhilde, they called her Bunni, and she was the sister of that successful musician Hartmut whom Josefa cried over at her graduation party.

In addition to his city apartment in a new complex, Brommel owned a country house, which looked rustic, but offered every convenience. It even had a sauna which, as he liked to tell, was used extensively by the locals from the village. In exchange Brommel received homemade sausages in the spring, every kind of fruit and vegetable that grew there in the summer and in the autumn, fine yellow boletus and a genuine, individually force-fed goose for Christmas. Brommel needed his house to work in. On weekends he often went to the city, visited friends, went to the theater, took care of official business. During the week he worked like an ox on the yoke, but with joy, he said. He was correspondent for a French newspaper. But most of all Brommel wrote books. Books about other countries he had been to and what he had experienced and seen there. Books like that were always in demand; and since Brommel was a Frenchman, he had already written about France, as well as Africa and India—no fewer than three about France.

Brommel was happy they had come. He seldom had visitors during this kind of weather. He put on water for tea and steaks on the grill. Brommel always had a supply of steaks. He sat down at the table and squinted his eyes together to slits and asked Christian, "How are you?" When he spoke, his mouth formed a small round opening, and it was remarkable that Brommel could articulate at all. This time Brommel smoked a pipe. Josefa remembered when he had been a cigarette smoker, a cigar smoker and a non-smoker. Brommel smoked with conviction. No matter what kind of smoker he was at the moment, he left no doubt that he considered the present way the only one possible.

Josefa's presence did not seem to interest Brommel, either to amuse or to irritate him. He ignored her. Josefa leaned back, stared into space, smelled the raw wood the furniture was made of. Tables and chairs of unfinished wood. The Braun electric heaters hummed softly. She drank some of the tea Brummel poured for her. Earl Grey, she registered; it was her favorite tea. Brommel praised Christian for his latest essay in a philosophy journal. Josefa didn't know what essay; she stopped listening.

Warm current rippled through her scalp; her jaw had the urge to open. She placed her head in her hands because she couldn't hold her face in any other way. A candle flickered between Brommel and her, through which Brommel looked like a fat faun blowing on an invisible flute. Josefa watched him through the flicker. Brommel bathed pleasantly in the benevolence he poured over Christian. He belongs to those people, Josefa thought, who confer their praise like a medal. Later on, Brommel said he wanted to walk a bit along the village street. Josefa would have preferred to stay in the warm house, but she was outvoted.

It was dead quiet. Not even a watchdog was barking. There were no sounds except the steps of three people who walked silently along the village street. The houses left and right stooped beneath the darkness.

Josefa took a deep breath and the frosty air ran across her nose and neck with a bite. The sky seemed higher, the stars closer, the cold more pleasant. Brommel coughed. The cough echoed across the village like thunder. It then became still again. We are the last humans on earth, Christian, me and Brommel. The others are dead, gone like Bunni. We too will soon be dead. Then it will be quiet on earth. Nothing will move between heaven and the paving stones under our feet except small creatures: lizards and beetles. No one will be able to bury the last of us, the stench of his decaying body won't disturb anyone.

The paving stones shone in the greywhite light that fell from the windows onto the street like the skullcaps of a subterranean army. Stone heads. We are walking over the dead, over the billions who have lived before us. They lie under us meter deep. No doubt Brommel is thinking of Bunni now. She died eight years ago and since then Brommel hasn't been able to last more than three months with a woman. Or no woman has been able to put up with him. Josefa visited him once in his city apartment. Five or six large photos hung on the walls and stood on the shelves: Bunni was in all of them with her narrow head and her overly large, fleshy nose and those eyes that you couldn't imagine as being anything but grey. The eyes reminded her of her brother, who had said as early as fifteen years before that his sister would die before she was thirty. The eyes in the photo looked as though they belonged to someone who knew she would die soon. Or it seemed that way to Josefa because Bunni had died.

"Let's turn around," Brommel said.

The paving stones broke off, the street ran into a rutty sand-path, which disappeared in the darkness ten meters further on. They walked back the way they had come.

Lower right in the paper a medium large announcement framed in black. In large letters: JOSEFA NADLER. In small print above: Tragically and inexplicably for us all, torn from life too early. Below: She was a talented journalist always ready for duty. Then one more sentence, which mentions "memory in honor". They would almost certainly replace talented with faithful or dependable. But they would say talented in the funeral oration and talk about the many unwritten articles they would have to do without. Her critical mind...Josefa imagined a gentleman in black tails who floated over the wreaths and flowers. The man looked like Siegfried Strutzer. "The unwritten articles with critical reason...," she heard.

She didn't even have to wait to die to hear this phrase.

They'll still use the subjunctive in the beginning: "She could have been a brilliant journalist." They'll become bolder in forget-ting. "She would have been a brilliant journalist." Until they've gotten used to the fact that my claim to the future is extinguished and they strike me from the list of the living once and for all: "She was a brilliant journalist," they'll say and it will bother no one. They'll need one or two years perhaps to mold and make me perfect. They'll make me more beautiful, more clever, better than I was and bathe me in metamorphosis. A few decades and they'll have to look at the birth records in order to find out that I ever existed. Despite it all, one runs over the earth like an ant, learns the multiplication tables, gathers up a bit of literature, a little economics, a little pile of knowledge as a viaticum for life; one boxes with Siegfried Strutzer, runs after the newest fashion as if it were a matter of life and death. Why don't we sit down under the stars, plant vegetables, milk the cow, shear the sheep and on dark evenings weave the material for our jeans?

Brommel held his grog glass in his hands as if he wanted to warm his fingers. He more lay in his chair than sat in it. Christian leafed through a Western magazine. Brommel viewed Josefa through his slit eyes. "You've changed since the last time we saw each other," he said.

"I think so," Josefa said. "Why?"

"You look as if you had been infected by the bacillus doubt." Brommel's pretense of being able to look into people's souls was something that Josefa could never stand about him. Surely he felt indebted to his father, who was a psychoanalyst.

"Christian has predicted a future for me as a witch. Well, what do you have to offer?"

Brommel laughed and his eyes disappeared completely behind the slits. "That depends on what you have to offer."

"My inner life has already been the topic of discussion today. I don't feel like bringing it up again."

"Your inner life must have a club foot then."

Josefa looked at Christian. He was reading.

"Maybe," she said, took a cigarette, then looked at the floor with effort. Brommel had bent forward. He was watching her with open curiosity. "You seemed much surer of yourself earlier," he said.

"But I haven't even said anything yet today."

"It's just that that puzzles me," Brommel said. "Do you remember our discussion about carrying out sentence and the death penalty?"

Josefa turned red: "That's a good seven years ago," she said.

"Six," Brommel said, "exactly six. It was the second anniversary of Bunni's death. And I remember that you talked about other people's lives the way someone who rents boats talks about canoes. If memory serves me correctly, you even quoted Lenin and the French Revolution." Brommel savored his good memory.

"Our conversation was very important for me then," Josefa said. She stopped looking at the floor and turned to Brommel. Brommel leaned back in his chair.

"But still more important was a girl, Heidi Arndt."

"That's interesting," Brommel said, who liked hearing stories, "tell me about her."

"A colleague was investigating a story in a Berlin clothing factory

79

and met a young woman who had been serving out work rehabilitation for two years. She had since gotten married; the work requirement she had been sentenced to had just run out as well. No doubt her story would soon have been forgotten by the others. In spite of that the young woman said that she was prepared to have someone write about herself and her life. You have to keep that in mind—in a magazine with photos. My colleague got sick or had a vacation; I got the assignment. I visited Heidi Arndt at her home. She lived near the Warsaw Bridge. A dark apartment in an old building: full-length wardrobe, living-room suite, linoleum on the floor, polyester curtains.

"Heidi Arndt was twenty-three years old. She was small and dainty. She had soft bags under her eyes like a child. When she opened her mouth she looked ten years older. That was due to her gnawed teeth. Since then I've often noticed that people who have been in jail have bad teeth or too few teeth for their age. Heidi Arndt told me her story objectively, it seemed to me, and without shame, without anything added. She was the youngest of three children. Her father was a locksmith; her mother helped in a factory kitchen. The children had a strict upbringing. The two elder children didn't resist. Heidi, the most intelligent and the liveliest of the three, had to submit, too. She had a boyfriend at sixteen and was secretly engaged. She had to be back home every evening at 8:00 p.m. and from the balcony could see her fiancé ride by on his motorcycle, first alone, later with other girls. The engagement fell apart. Half a year later she fell in love again. She had a baby; her parents threw her out. She found a room with an old woman around the corner. Her new boyfriend was a loafer who drank too much and did little work. Heidi gave up her apprenticeship because she was too tired in the morning after nights spent drinking and screwing. Her boyfriend always had money; she didn't know where he got it and didn't care either. She moved into her boyfriend's apartment. A year later the police were standing at the door and Heidi was sentenced to one to two years work-training for criminal endangerment, which meant that after one year they had to decide whether to release her or not. The baby went to her parents. Heidi was put in a cell with twenty other women: prostitutes, unsuccessful

80

emigrants, alcoholics. She tried for a year to do good work. She filled her quota during the day but not on the night shift. She had to fight off sleep at 3:00 a.m., sometimes she did fall asleep. She had just turned eighteen. She was shunned by the other prisoners because of her good behavior. Most of the women in the cells were lesbians. Heidi didn't want to. Although it was strictly forbidden, most of the women had themselves tattooed. Not Heidi. She was told after a year by the institution that she could not be released yet because she had not filled her quota. They were considering whether to put her child up for adoption. Her parents didn't write to her. Heidi didn't know where her child was. Shortly after that she was told that her child had just been adopted. The same day she had herself tattooed. She began an affair with a woman who was, according to Heidi, very smart and loving. The second year was easier. She became friends with most of the women. Only, the food was bad, sometimes even rotten. She never had to go to solitary confinement, but the others always talked about it. Prison within prison; she was afraid of that. Heidi was released before her girlfriend. They promised each other to live together when she got out. They talked a lot about the outside. All the same Heidi would rather have remained inside with her girlfriend. She was afraid of the outside. She found her daughter at her parents. That was the only thing that gave her courage, she said. She found work in the clothing factory and was allowed to move into the room in the old woman's apartment. The old woman had a grandson whom Heidi had liked for a long time. He had only gotten past the sixth grade and was a coal heaver. He hadn't had the courage before to talk to Heidi. He wanted to help her now. But Heidi waited for her girlfriend. When her girlfriend got out of jail she had another woman. Heidi married the coal heaver. They understood each other...but she couldn't sleep with him. She desired a woman. Women are more tender, she said. She took it upon herself to see a psychiatrist to correct her sexual preference. When they went to the beach in the summer they had to find a hidden place or Heidi had to wear a sweater with a collar despite the heat. She went to the doctor once a week to have the tattoos rubbed out of her skin. The doctor did it without anaesthetic and it left behind scars that looked like cigarette burns. She had to wait a year until she was accepted as a patient; many had to wait longer, she said. Although the people in the factory were friendly, Heidi wanted to quit on the day her work obligation ran out. She wanted to spend a year without working. "I can do that now," she said, "now that I'm married." I asked her why she wanted to allow her story to be published or even wanted to tell it after all that had happened. "I want everyone to know how awful it is. And before they lock someone up, they ought to think over the fact that no one gets better in there. And it is never over."

Brommel waited to see if Josefa wanted to add something, laid his hand on the backrest of his chair, stared intensely for a few seconds at a point in the ceiling, brought himself out of this position with a jerk, and said: "Yes, you can learn something from stories like that. Was the case ever printed?"

"I never wrote it," Josefa said. "None of the competent authorities agreed to publish it."

"Well, it's no wonder," Brommel said and pulled his fat cat's head even deeper into his shoulders. "But why don't you write it down anyway?"

"Maybe I should do that."

"You definitely should," Brommel said. "They can regulate which stories get printed. The writing itself is immune to any regulation. Think of yourself as a chronicler, as one, excuse me, who collects documents. And don't let yourself be bothered as you do it by the thought of when they'll be read."

Christian looked up from his magazine. "Leave her alone, Karl, there's no point. She wants what she writes to get printed. All or nothing, she won't do it for any less. Ask Josefa what tactics are, and she'll tell you: put your head through the wall next to the open door."

"When there's 'no admittance' written on the door," Josefa said.

"Yes, isn't it more advisable, then, to sneak through the door at the right moment?" Brommel asked.

"Maybe," Josefa said, "but I can't lead two lives: one legal and one illegal. I don't want to give up the claim to be able to live with others as I am. I don't want to break off the dialogue with them or emigrate later on. I'm the black sheep now, but I belong to the flock."

"Perhaps you don't even belong to it now, and you just don't want to admit it," Brommel said with the self-satisfied benevolence in his voice that he had already used with Christian. "Don't get me wrong, I don't want to keep you from your, as I hear, admirable and straight path through the wall; but experience simply teaches that heads are softened in the process, not walls."

"We'll see," Josefa said and smiled at Brommel's curious cat's face.

"Lots of luck," Brommel said and raised his glass.

Josefa was happy that she had escaped his questions. She got chills down her back with his slit-hidden eyes and with his mania to creep into other people's souls.

They sat until night fell at Brommel's bare wooden table, and although the conversation didn't turn to Josefa any more, Brommel fixed her every so often with an expression as if he found it difficult to suppress a question or a comment. He threw a sentence abruptly into a pause in the discussion: "Beware of too much self-pity." Before Josefa could answer, he continued talking about a book he had just read. When they wanted to leave he offered them a guest room for the night.

A small room with a large bed. Christian closed the door, leaned against her with his arms folded and with a brash smile: "Well, now what?"

The whole day long Josefa had felt the desire to touch him, to feel with hands and feet the closeness that she sensed. When Brommel had asked her then: whom do you belong to? she had thought of Christian for an instant. The prospect of a split personality seemed less threatening to her as long as she could stay the way she was with Christian. She was grateful for Brommel's offer to spend the night in his guest room. She took it to be an oracle, which, if it didn't spare them the decision, at least made it easier. They'd now have to spend the night playing cards on the edge of the bed, or she would have Christian between her thighs until morning, 'til he had pumped the fear out of her that the day had pumped in.

Christian was still standing in front of the door. He wasn't smiling any longer. "Take off your clothes," he said quietly.

He stayed at the door as if he had to guard her. Josefa sat on the bed. Christian hung his sweater on the back of the chair, he then picked Josefa's clothes up off the floor. Even now, Josefa thought. Christian pulled the covers from Josefa although it was cold in the room, looked at her for a long while. Josefa was shivering. She pulled Christian over her like the covers. They lay a moment without touching each other. Then Josefa felt the warmth that spread from her womb over her breasts and neck. She abandoned herself to the waves her body was floating in. Closed her eyes. Dark. A squid is holding me in his arms and drifting with me on the ocean. From one wave to the next. He's holding tight so I won't drown. He's keeping my mouth closed so I won't swallow water. Hold on, he says, and dives with me through a huge wave. He presses the air out of me with his arms. Float, he says, and lets me go. I'm holding on to only one of his arms and don't go under. The squid's head has sprouted wings. We're flying now, he whispers and lifts himself into the air. He musn't let me fall. Higher, faster, faster. We're falling, the squid cries. We race to earth in a nose dive. Now I sprout wings, large wings of maple leaves. We're flying just above the water, and the waves are splashing against our stomachs. My arms are white soft hoses with suckers on the inside. I have many arms. I am a squid.

VI

A red sock with a blue strip around the ankle glowed between Siegfried Strutzer's hitched-up pantleg and his grey cowhide shoes. The foot inside the red nylon and grey cowhide rocked back and forth. Luise sat down on the edge of her chair with her elbow on the edge of the table and scribbled something in a notepad. Josefa sat between Luise and Strutzer. He hoped that she had had a nice weekend, Strutzer said. She hoped that she had had a nice weekend, Luise said. Josefa remained silent.

"Luise must know what it's all about," Strutzer began.

No, Luise said, she didn't know anything about it.

Josefa looked out the window. Except for the blue-white sky she didn't see anything. She would have had to stand up to see the bright lines of cars that crept across the Alexanderplatz mornings in mysterious order. She tried not to hear what Siegfried Strutzer was talking about. "Keep out of it as long as you can," Luise had said, "or else you'll spoil everything with that buzzing in your ears, and you might throw paper clips around the room again."

Strutzer placed both his arms on the back of the chair, put his legs one next to the other, the left foot turned slightly outwards, opened his mouth hardly at all when he spoke, as if he had to avoid every exertion. The king on the skiff with the red baldachin. Strutzer had a son who looked like Strutzer. Already pasty-faced, small red mouth, tired eyes turned down at the far corners. Strutzer had a wife whom Josefa estimated must weigh two hundredweights. In addition, Strutzer had a four-room apartment and a car. Josefa didn't know anything about a *dacha*, but had to assume that there was one.

"Josefa shouldn't have even given you the manuscript before clearing it with the plant," Luise said.

Strutzer raised his hands in defense. "Wait a minute, wait a minute," he said softly and formed an offended smile. Rudi Goldammer had charged him with taking up the matter.

Don't listen, Josefa thought, think of something else. She tried to imagine how Strutzer spent a Sunday with his fat wife and his pasty-faced son, who looked like Strutzer. He gets up at 9:00 at the latest, showers, puts on an old but clean pair of pants and a sweater which had been thrown in the clothes bin to use for painting. There is coffee, an egg, jam for breakfast. No—no jam. Ham. Mrs. Strutzer is on good terms with the butcher. Strutzer reads the newspaper out loud to his family, gets mad about the lapses of style on the local page, then opens to national politics. Strutzer is in charge of the national politics section at the *Illustrated Weekly*. He pushes his cup over to his wife to call her attention to the fact that it is empty. She pours.

"Well, fancy that," Strutzer says, "he was there after all." He informs his son and wife, who aren't as initiated as he is, about the background involved. The Minister had spoken at the Writers' Congress after all, although, as Strutzer had heard, it was generally agreed that these crybabies had gotten more than enough attention.

"What is Josefa's position?" Siegfried Strutzer asked.

Josefa didn't have any other position on that point than her own, Luise said emphatically and looked reassuringly at Josefa. Josefa nodded in case they debated the matter.

She was dissatisfied with her picture of Strutzer's Sunday. Perhaps Strutzer gets up on Sunday at 6:30 as always, is happy that he can fall asleep again because he doesn't have to compete in the struggle for the *Illustrated Weekly*. He moves closer to his fat wife, who is still asleep, puts his head between her two large breasts, thinks for an instant about the fine day he'll have with his docile wife, and with his son, who is turning out just like him.

After breakfast, while his son is cleaning the aquarium, Strutzer tells his wife that Rudi Goldammer is sick again and that the entire responsibility for the *Illustrated Weekly* rests once again on his, Strutzer's, shoulders. All this for the salary of a deputy editor-in-chief, which in all fairness should go to Goldammer instead of Strutzer. Strutzer's wife looks at her husband's shiny brown eyes. "You're just too good," she says, "anyone else in your place would have tripped up Goldammer long ago. You're too soft."

Strutzer sighs; stands up. As long as he could prevent the grossest political errors by his efforts he could find some kind of sense in this injustice, he said. And the absolute necessity of always defending the Party line has been proven right by the report by this Nadler, which would be grist to the mill of the class enemy if it were up to her. Strutzer tapped on the back of his chair with a pencil. "Well, I can't be responsible for the article as it stands," he said, "and there's no telling when Rudi will be back."

Give up, Luise, you can't handle it. Maybe he really believes in his mission and suffers at our hands the way we suffer at his. Strutzer between his wife's fat breasts relaxing after his guerrilla war against deviant colleagues. Does Strutzer sleep with his wife? Josefa took a cigarette. Fat white fingers on Strutzer's fat wife. Josefa saw Strutzer wallowing, rubbing himself into her until he came and then fell from her. Strutzer was wearing pyjamas, his wife had on a coarse nightgown, which Strutzer had just pulled up as far as necessary.

"Josefa," Luise said, "do you agree?" Luise was leading the hearing; Luise nodded to Josefa.

"Yes," Josefa said.

She looked Strutzer over, who was jotting down everything. Strutzer wrote down everything, he always had everything in writing. Every telephone call was noted in his files. Strutzer's Sunday stayed lifeless, doughy, hidden behind tinted glasses, like Strutzer's eyes. Once again Josefa put Strutzer with his son and wife behind the full-length wardrobe, television and couch and watched Strutzer for the third time. King Siegfried is reading the Party paper, smells of good shaving lotion and is smoking a cigarillo. Mrs. Strutzer is clearing away the breakfast dishes. Son Strutzer is standing clumsily in the room and asks his father with real interest about recent political developments in the Middle East. Strutzer puts down the paper, rubs the corners of his eyes thoughtfully with his thumb and forefinger. Strutzer doesn't wear glasses at home, not even when he reads.

"Please sit down," Strutzer says to his son. "Yes, that looks very problematic just now," he says, offers his son a cigarillo and elucidates the most recent political events in the Middle East to him. His wife brings in a tray from the kitchen with a few glasses on it. She polishes the glasses while listening to her husband's exposition. She is glad that she has a clever husband and a son who is turning out just like his father.

"Bring us a beer, why don't you," Strutzer says to his wife. His wife gets the beer, polishes the glasses. Strutzer and his son sit like this until noon. His wife is cooking.

What Josefa saw in her head resembled scenes she had often seen on TV about everyday life in the GDR: clichés, interchangeable and boring.

She didn't know much about Strutzer. She had only once been able to gain accidental access to his true self when he was under the influence and talked about his school days. Strutzer came from a small village in Thuringia. He went to a boarding school when

87

he was fourteen, one that was a hundred kilometers from his village and had been a Nazi prison until the year before. The pupils still felt themselves bound to the traditions of the house when Strutzer moved in. Strutzer told about the punishments that the older boys imposed on the younger ones when they refused to obey orders. Strutzer had had to drink his own urine. When he took an interest in a girl whom an older student claimed as his own, Strutzer's genitals were smeared with black shoe polish one night. It was a disgusting business washing the stuff off, Strutzer said.

Josefa had asked why he didn't run away to his village. After all, fascism was over. He thought back then that it was all right, Strutzer had answered. His sense of justice hadn't been offended. Later on, when he belonged to the older group, he too blackened others' genitals.

"So I'm taking down a note," Strutzer said, "manuscript by Nadler to be voted on Thursday by the Council. Settled."

Luise got up. Strutzer pushed his chair up to the table, a bit crooked, with the open corner towards the room. Like his left foot, Josefa thought. She looked for the fourteen-year-old Strutzer behind the tinted glasses. Thin, blonde, crooked mouth he had to drink his own piss with. His mouth hadn't forgotten that, doesn't want to either. Nor does the other: blacken or be blackened. Strutzer went to the university. Strutzer had attended the Party school. Strutzer was never again interested in a girl someone older had his eyes on. He could surely distinguish between someone of importance and the unimportant. Strutzer belonged to the important ones on the *Illustrated Weekly*.

They walked down the corridor, one behind the other, in silence. They were quiet, too, when Luise opened the door to her room. After Luise had closed the door behind her, Josefa took a deep breath. "The fat jellyfish." Luise laughed. Then she indicated the white wall with her head. "Talk a little softer." Luise took a cellophane bag out of her handbag and put a little black licorice cat into her mouth and put the bag back in her pocket without offering any to Josefa. "You'd have to know whether Rudi has read it or not. If he hasn't we still have a chance. If he's read it, then we know why he isn't here today." She reached for the telephone.

"Get us some coffee," she said as she dialled Rudi's number. Presumably Luise's scheme went beyond even her own limitations if she didn't want an audience. Luise waited to dial the last digit until Josefa had left the room.

Poor Rudi, now she's going to catch you. Josefa walked through the white hallway. The hallway was long. When she walked slowly it seemed even longer. Josefa had gotten used to greeting everyone she met in the hallway ever since a secretary had accused her of arrogance in an offended tone. Josefa hadn't said hello to the secretary because she was sure that she had seen her there an hour ago. That wasn't an hour ago, that was yesterday, her colleague said, who remained convinced of Josefa's arrogance.

Every day was the same in the hallway. The white endless monotony, smell of coffee, doors opening and closing. Nothing that would have made one day different from any other. The open-plan office provided memory aids with its empty or occupied desks: Günter wasn't here on that day, then it's Thursday. The weather helped too: the day of the storm. Josefa didn't believe that Rudi was sick. She was sure that he had read her article on Friday. His trained sense for impending confrontation had warned him, and Rudi had gone into seclusion.

He was sitting at home in his mouse hole now, translating children's books. Rudi spoke English like an Englishman and translated English children's books in his spare time or when he was sick, although, as Rudi said, English humor was untranslatable, least of all into German. When Rudi discovered a phrase during his work that he found particularly funny, he would often use it for days on end at the slightest excuse with a childlike joy. Rudi had never offered any of his translations to a publisher. Most of the books had already been translated, in general badly, he said.

Rudi will have put on a Mozart violin concerto. There's a pot of tea standing next to him, not too strong. And when Rudi looks for a word that is supposed to sound as funny as the English word he has to translate, he looks out his window onto his garden with its tall pines and bare poplars. Now and then thoughts will force themselves to his attention, about Luise, about Strutzer and the 180 tons of flue ash that he's hiding from. And Rudi has to make an effort to get these thoughts out of his mind. He cooks soup for himself at noon, cream of asparagus or cream of mushroom for his delicate stomach. When Rudi Goldammer isn't sick he gets driven every day at 1:00 p.m. to the Ganymed Restaurant to eat soup there. There's no soup in Berlin as good as the ones at Ganymed, Rudi says. When he doesn't have the time to drive there himself, he has his driver get it for him. Rudi's eccentric habits were often the subject of secret criticism among the personnel of the *Ilustrated Weekly*, who accused Rudi of putting on airs and abuse of his office. Many laughed at him. Josefa understood Rudi's mania for soups. Rudi had eaten dogs, although he liked dogs. He had caught them, skinned them, boiled or roasted them and with them had fed his comrades, who would otherwise have starved to death. He sometimes ate dog meat himself. He laughed when he told the story, consoled us and himself by saying that they were Nazi dogs, after all, which belonged to the wives of the officers of the concentration camp. But Rudi didn't like meat any more. He liked the delicate white soups from the Ganymed.

The lunchroom was full. The lunchroom was always full. There were five lunchrooms in the building, and all of them were always full. The lunchrooms were located in the middle of the hallway, nine tables at each, thirty-six chairs, a buffet. The walls on the corridor side were made of glass. The bosses and the busy editors could identify people out of the corner of their eye as they busily ran up and down the hallways. You could also make out what they were doing there by a march past the glass front: whether it was necessary nourishment or idle coffee drinking... or if they went so far as to booze it up against the lunchroom regulations. Anyone who drank cola was suspicious. Anyone who had bitter lemon was also suspicious. There could be vodka in the bitter lemon. Sometimes there was bockwurst in natural casing. Then the lines in front of the counter were even longer; some even ate two sausages immediately. Women saved four or five cold sausages for their suppers at home.

Josefa filled two thick earthenware cups under the automat, poured cream into Luise's coffee, took two cubes of sugar. The way to the stairs led past two heavy glass and aluminium doors, which could scarcely be opened with both hands, much less with elbows and feet. Josefa waited for someone to open the doors. Then she walked slowly in order not to spill any coffee and to give Luise some time on the floor below in the *Illustrated Weekly*. She could already hear screaming from Luise's room. She could hear Luise's sharp voice: "I've had it with this play-acting," Josefa heard. Poor Rudi, she thought. She stood in the hallway, a cup in each hand. Ulrike Kuwiak flitted past. "Did you get thrown out?" she asked and flitted on into the main office. Josefa tried to make up her mind whether to walk down the left side of the hallway or the right. The open-plan office was on the right. "If the responsibility is too much for you, why don't you have yourself replaced?" Luise screamed. Josefa walked on the left side. Perhaps Hans Schütz was there. She knocked on the door with her foot, opened it when she heard no answer. The room was empty, it had the odor of cold tobacco smoke, there was a pile of English and French periodicals on the table. It was quiet, the window was at the rear of the building and the street in which the publishing building was located was the border between the new monumental center and the filthy old quarter where Reni's bar was located. This is where Josefa had walked with Tadeus on hot summer days through the narrow, pleasant streets—and later on with other men.

Josefa leafed through the magazines, drank coffee and enjoyed being alone and unobserved. It was difficult to avoid the view of others in this building unless you were a group director like Luise or Hans Schütz. The only refuge for people who wanted to rage in peace or who simply wanted to be alone for five minutes was the toilet. But here too you had to wait for the right moment because one or two of the five stalls were usually occupied. But even if you were lucky enough and could put your cried-out, contorted face back in order undisturbed or clean up your runny makeup, you couldn't stand to be in the green-tiled room for more than five or ten minutes. Then the asylum changed back into the toilet that it was.

Josefa pulled up her sweater and scratched her stomach. The phone rang; she didn't pick up the receiver. The argument between Luise and Rudi Goldammer was calming down. She began to feel pangs of guilt. She was a troublemaker. It was her decision that Rudi didn't want to take responsibility for. She had often asked herself what Rudi was afraid of. As a victim of Nazi oppression he could have retired two years ago, to translate English children's books from morning to night, cook white soups and listen to Mozart. Perhaps he was afraid of his quiet marriage. Or of Strutzer, who would then become boss of the *Illustrated Weekly*. Or of the discussions that would precede his life as a pensioner. Rudi was afraid of decisions. The need to make weighty decisions terrified him. As *kapo* in the concentration camp Rudi had had the power of life and death. The lists of the death transports went through his hands; he was responsible for putting together the transports and he substituted the names of irreplaceable comrades with those of criminals or weak old people he knew wouldn't survive. Rudi switched the names on Party orders. He still dreams about some of them to this day. He is tortured by the thought that he submitted the wrong names. As though he had given right ones as well. And now Luise was yelling at him because he had run away from the choice between Strutzer and Josefa.

Josefa dialled Luise's number. It was still busy. Josefa remembered her first meeting with Rudi Goldammer six years ago. All she needed to complete her language degree was her exam in Middle High German. She had had it up to here with her studies. The reading lists, attendance lists, but most of all the exams, when she sat trembling with pale hands, bloody nail cuticles on her fingers. The examiners seated across from her were permitted to ask her anything that happened to cross their minds, which was then graded between one and five according to the approval or disapproval she had aroused. She considered her studies an undignified form of intellectual exercise in which every thought was subject to being judged by strangers before it could sprout even the tiniest of wings with which to fly to another thought in order to procreate a generation of new thoughts. They were laid out in the morgue of student brains strangled or in a state of suspended animation, waiting for the resurrection. Only Euler was excluded from her curses: Euler with his special seminar on contemporary literature. After the war Euler had become a teacher, then a taxidriver. There were rumors about an affair with a student. He later studied at the university and remained at the Institute as an assistant. Euler had a pedagogic character. He thought logically, was patient, and enjoyed the intellectual achievements of others. It seemed to make him happy when he could take even the smallest amount of credit in the intellectual activities of others. Euler wasn't a brilliant teacher. Brilliant teachers shine by their irony, create witty anecdotes that their students still remember when they grow old. The color grey fit Euler, who even preferred it. It was said that Euler had written an excellent dissertation but that he hadn't submitted it because he always thought it was in need of improvement. Euler's sole ambition seemed to consist in having two or three students finish their studies each year whom he regarded as his own. Although Euler devoted equal attention to all during class time, he favored a few students every school year, to whom he offered his free time and weekends as soon as they asked for help. His choice seemed arbitrary; only rarely were the students whom Euler reared painstakingly for five years those with the best grades.

Josefa's friendship with Euler began shortly before the end of her first year at school, when she stormed into the teaching assistants' lounge to quit school after she had learned of the new cultural-political line from the daily papers. The room was empty. It was only as Josefa was getting ready to close the door again that she noticed Euler, who was sitting inconspicuously on the sofa, as befitted his grey self, opening a packet of three honey tarts. Josefa wasn't sure whether to tell Euler about her decision. He wasn't in the Party, wasn't consulted by the Institute on matters of political importance either. So why should she spill her guts to Euler of all people?

"Whom are you looking for?" Euler asked.

"I really just wanted to let someone know that I'm dropping out of school," Josefa said. If Euler didn't have any authority, then he might know after all how she felt about banning films and books, what she thought about the tirades being directed against actors and directors.

Euler asked her to close the door, offered her a chair and a honey

93

tart.

"Why?" he asked.

"I wanted to work in a publishing house after I graduate," she said, "as a proofreader; I might even have written something myself. I wanted to publish books, not to keep them from being published. I don't want to have a profession where you end up doing the opposite thing overnight. In that case I'd rather be a baker or a doctor, for Christ's sake, anything but something that has to do with the arts."

Josefa remembered the last sentence of the long lecture that Euler had given her that day.

"Read the classics," Euler had said, "especially Engels. Reflect on the dark age in which they lived and be sure to note the serenity with which they were able to write about it."

She went with Tadeus to the Baltic Sea for the vacations. They rented a tent and a kerosene burner. It was their first vacation together. They knew they wouldn't be seeing much of each other afterwards. Two years in Moscow for the physics student Tadeus T: "This is a great honor, my young friend." There was no time for the classics.

The first day of the new school year she met Euler in the hallway in front of the seminar room. He was happy to see her again, even if she didn't seem exactly cheerful, he said with a touch of irony. Since then Euler felt responsible for Josefa as if it had been his decision not to become a baker or doctor. Perhaps that's even how it was. Perhaps she wouldn't have been able to stand the next four years if Euler hadn't constantly sermonized about intellectual independence outside the curriculum. He gave her many books to read that weren't on the reading list, directed her term paper although she had picked a ridiculous topic. It was only when Mohnhaupt declared war on Josefa that Euler was helpless.

"And why do you have to join the Party at all costs?"

"If you were in it you could help me now. Maybe that's the reason," Josefa said.

"I'm afraid that's an illusion," Euler said sadly, "but go ahead and try."

After five years at the university she didn't find it difficult to say goodbye to Euler. She was happy that he had been there. But he belonged to a period she finally wanted to put behind her; one she didn't want to feel nostalgic about in the bargain. She was sceptical of all the stories of easy-going college days and the wistful prediction: "Some day you'll wish you could go back."

Back then the editorial department of the *Illustrated Weekly* was housed in a narrow grey-black building in the old Berlin newspaper district. Josefa had a cup of coffee in an espresso bar at Unter den Linden and walked slowly, because she still had half an hour's time, along Friedrichstraße in the direction of the Wall. She tried to picture in her mind the person who might fit the name Rudi Goldammer. When she shook the hand of the real Rudi Goldammer half an hour later, she was astonished at how closely he resembled the figure in her imagination: short, soft facial features, careworn lines around his mouth, childlike, friendly eyes.

"So you are Josefa. You're a Party member aren't you? Well then, we'll use first names, otherwise it's so complicated. Do you want a cognac?" He drank nothing himself. "My stomach, you know."

"Are you talented?" he asked.

"Yes," Josefa said.

Rudi giggled. "That's good," he said, "I'm glad you said that. If you don't believe in your own talent, no one else will either." Rudi sat down, folded his hands on his lap, placed his right ankle on his left knee and took a long look at Josefa with undisguised satisfaction.

"You are young," he said, "that's good. There are too many old people here. I'm too old, too." He chuckled like a child who has secretly said something naughty and is happy that his parents haven't heard him.

"You're pretty, too," Rudi said, "that's good, you'll have an easy time of it with our male colleagues. And don't let everybody talk your ear off. The stupid ones talk the most. But you know that: I've read your confidential report". Rudi giggled again. "They really did a number on you, but that doesn't matter. I like controversial colleagues."

From their first meeting, Josefa got the idea that Rudi Goldammer ought to be sitting in a large Viennese café, drinking a cup of mocca and eating whipped cream, reading newspapers and poems, listening to stories told by acquaintances and interrupting now and again: "I'm delighted, Franzl," or "That's nice of you, Josef." She also liked Rudi because he liked her. She found his childlike openness touching. But she no longer understood why she had never asked herself how Rudi could edit a newspaper given his naïveté—a newspaper that was better only for having headlines with a purer style.

What could Luise possibly change by yelling at Rudi with his stomach complaints and his toothaches? Then Rudi might cry. Josefa often suspected that Rudi secretly cried at home. Old people look ugly when they cry. Josefa dialled Luise's number again. The line was free now.

Luise had the windows in her room wide open. "Where were you so long?", she asked crossly. Luckily she had forgotten about the coffee. Josefa meanwhile had drunk both cups.

"He read it," Luise said.

"And what does he say?"

Luise got red spots on her neck when she got mad. Her neck was scarlet red. "I told him that I'll send him the manuscript. But the poor man feels so bad that he can't even read. He's got gastric ulcers coming out of his ears."

Josefa was tired. She didn't feel good. Lie down in bed. Someone fixes camomile tea and green apple snow for her. She isn't responsible for anything: not for B., not for her child. Only people like Strutzer could manage without being sick.

"You look like Saint Joan at the stake again," Luise said. "Go get us some coffee."

The lunchroom was full. The lunchroom was always full. There were five lunchrooms in the building and all of them were always full.

Today of all days the sun was shining in B. Evidence against the truth. The sun never shines in B. It can happen that dull yellow light struggles its way through the fog as through frosted glass.

But today the sun was shining. The small white ball stood visibly in the sky. The wind almost always blew in the opposite direction, and the town lay downwind from the power plant.

Alfred Thal sat bent over at his desk, more inconspicuous than usual, reading Josefa's article. He read slowly. Josefa saw his sad eyes scan the paper back and forth until they found a sentence or paragraph that he wanted to read twice. The sun reflected on the desk top. Josefa drank orange juice that the secretary had gotten from the General Director's refrigerator when she had asked for a glass of water. There was nothing in Thal's face to indicate approval or disapproval. In the next room the secretary imposed silence on the General Director by turning off the dictating machine. Alfred Thal turned the page.

"Hodriwitzka is dead," he said.

Josefa felt that her mouth had twisted into a nervous smile. She had to grin like this every time she heard of a person's death.

"Excuse me," she said.

Alfred Thal nodded. "An accident," he said.

"This fucking power plant," Josefa said.

"Not in the power plant; here on the street. He was run over. It happened a week after you were here. The burial was on the day before yesterday. Wanted to turn left with his bike and didn't signal. Run right over by the bus and died instantly."

Hodriwitzka with his square skull and his square hands was dead. When Josefa was telling Luise the story about Hodriwitzka, he was lying on a bier or in a box protected from decay until it was his turn to be carried to the grave, until the formalities were taken care of, the speaker arranged for and the music. Lay dead in a box with clean hands and was at fault. Had lived in a town where the people have five times more bronchitis than elsewhere, in which cherry blossoms shrivel overnight on the branches because the poisoned air has blown through them, had worked in a power plant where the word *safety* is not allowed and had died at fault under a bus.

Where could Thal have found out that Hodriwitzka was at fault? How did he know that he had wanted to turn left if he hadn't signalled? Maybe Hodriwitzka had simply lost his balance because a few grains of the 180 tons of flue ash had blown into his eyes. Or he didn't have the strength to steer the bike with one hand after he had been pushing cinders through the gratings of the furnaces with a five-meter-long poker. There were more than enough opportunities for Hodriwitzka to die in this town. He didn't need a bus for that; the bus was a coincidence. It could just as easily have been a leaky valve or carbon monoxide or the steep old iron stairs. Thal was happy that it was a bus. Not in the power plant. On the street. At fault.

For sixteen years Hodriwitzka had lifted his left arm at this corner when he had ridden home, like an electronically guided signal. It was only on this day that Hodriwitzka's brain hadn't given the signal or the arm had refused to carry it out. Why this of all days, a week after Josefa had been in B.?

Who would have been at fault if Hodriwitzka had been mentally writing a letter to the Minister on the way home, unsure of how to address him: "Dear Comrade Minister..." Hodriwitzka wasn't in the Party. "Dear Mr. Minister"... that sounded too polite. "Dear Colleague Minister..." Hodriwitzka wouldn't have been sure whether the Minister would have found that much friendliness to be tactless or presumptuous. Hodriwitzka would have wondered why a worker didn't know how to address his minister in a workers' and peasants' state. Or ought to, or had to. Then the curve. He had almost missed it: turn left without signalling. At fault. Hodriwitzka? The Minister? Josefa? But what reason would Hodriwitzka have had to drive under a bus because of a ridiculous form of address to a minister? It was more likely that Hodriwitzka had long since forgotten the letter by then. Josefa had never thought for an instant that he could write the letter either. She had been afraid of seeing Hodriwitzka again, his confused smile at the ten minutes they had understood each other, which had long since become blurred in coal dust and water vapor while she had brought into being that vaguely perceived agreement, pinned it down on writing paper, robbed it of its indecision until it was consent worthy of mention. They wouldn't have mentioned the letter any more. Not Hodriwitzka because he would have thought it over in the meantime and would have known why he couldn't write it. Not

Josefa because she knew that she was a tangent that drew away from the circle as soon as she touched it. This tangent existence was the worst thing about her profession. Everything was touched at the periphery, and the moment she touched it she was already moving away from the point of contact.

Away, constantly away from everyone. Hodriwitzka died beneath a bus. She came on a visit, rubbed the dirt from her eyes once or twice and rushed on to the next circle. A health inspector had the right to fight cockroaches after a visit; a medical commission was permitted to give out a few extra beds in the hospital; the safety inspector ordered handkerchiefs to be tied over long hair; the fire inspector ordered trash to be cleared away from an emergency exit. She was the democracy inspector. What was she permitted to order, fight, prescribe? A letter to the Minister.

Thal straightened up the pages of the manuscript without looking up. A suppressed smile trembled on his mouth.

"It's good," he said.

"What of it?" Josefa asked.

"Nothing. If that's what the people told you, then that's what you have to write," Thal said quietly, still with a smile.

"But the thing about safety…"

"It's right, isn't it?" Thal asked.

Of course it was right. Only: all of her experiences with press and public relations officials failed her with this little Alfred Thal. Press officials were usually loud, considered themselves answerable only to the General Director, made hypocritical references to their journalistic past with the local press, asked in passing about this or that prominent colleague whom they had studied with or had had a wild time with back then, which no doubt Josefa must have read about. "You are surprised," Alfred Thal said, "but look, the General Director gets his share of filth, Hodriwitzka got his share and I get mine, too. The stuff from the smoke stacks has no respect, and doesn't ask who the flowers belong to that it falls on." Alfred Thal laughed. He held his hand in front of his mouth to hide his brown tooth stumps from Josefa. "Our General Director has had a press blackout clapped on him by the Minister," he said. "Every interview has to be cleared; more often than not they're refused. Now he's happy when he finds someone to bring the dilemma of the power plant before the public. He recently carried on like a madman because there was an army of TV people here and they didn't film anything except the new indoor pool!'' Thal suddenly fell silent. He looked sadly at his nicotine-stained fingers, split a match and cleaned his fingernails with the thin splinter.

"It's like being under a spell," he said. "We live here in a haunted forest that no one dares to enter. And if someone stumbles his way to us, he closes his eyes as if he could escape the black magic by not looking at it. One of our chemists wrote a fairy tale for his little daughter. The dragon in it is the power plant with seven heads; each smoke stack is a head. The dragon had bewitched the town. Everyone had forgotten how to laugh. And it is dark in the town because the sun only shines where there is laughter. A very sad story until the dragon-slayer comes and strikes off the dragon's head and frees the town from the spell. We even printed the fairy tale in the house paper. Then there was a big stink with the district administration.'' Thal laughed again with his hand in front of his mouth. "Go ahead and write the way you want; as long as you don't give away any production secrets, nothing can happen to us that hasn't happened already."

The sun was shining. The General Director had a press blackout, Rudi Goldammer had stomach pains. Siegfried Strutzer had killed the article. Hodriwitzka was dead. The Minister couldn't find out that the stoker Hodriwitzka had lived in B., or that he had wanted to invite the Minister to the culture auditorium without a rostrum in order to discuss the future of B. with him.

Because Hodriwitzka would have written the letter. Josefa decided to believe that he would have written it. What could have happened to him that hadn't happened already? At fault beneath a bus. Josefa drank the General Director's orange juice. The chemist wrote a fairy tale. Thal was ashamed of his bad teeth and didn't go to a dentist. Josefa's good Samaritan look in Thal's resigned smile. I'm superfluous here, Josefa thought, I won't change anything.

Thal suggested that they go to eat. Food was still the best thing for a depressed stomach.

The lunchroom was grimy: dark green oil paint on the walls, peeled and faded wax cloth, a smell of old food, men and women in blue and grey smocks or overalls were standing in a twenty-meter-long line in front of the food counter. Their faces looked as if they were powdered white and grey, each according to the substance they processed. A redheaded man with a pockmarked face stood in front of Josefa. Grey-black dust had settled into his scar pits. "Graphite," Thal said, "he has that for life, it eats into his skin." The redhead turned around, smiled, shrugged his shoulders and turned around again. Two servings of meatballs with Bavarian cabbage. Thal got a soft drink. They found a table with two chairs right next to the toilet door. Thal squashed his potatoes and cabbage together into squares with a nimble motion before he pierced them with his fork. He chewed slowly with his tooth stumps. Josefa hardly touched her food.

"My oldest starts here in the fall," Thal said, "as an engineer. The middle one is already in the plant: apprentice in the PVC factory. My twins will be here in two years. All four are staying in B."

Josefa got the impression Thal was happy at the prospect.

"I couldn't stand it here alone with my wife," he said.

Josefa didn't know Thal's wife. Thal told how his wife had yelled at the twins in the morning because they had spilled the milk. "She's cantankerous," he said and looked at Josefa as if she would confirm the fact that his wife was cantankerous. "She has such a shrill voice," Thal said. "That doesn't bother me any more, but she shouldn't yell like that at the boys. I went bike riding with the boys on Sunday. A beautiful day. She can't ride a bike."

Josefa wasn't one of those people who get embarrassed when strangers tell them about their marriages. She was curious how others stood their quadruped existence, and in a certain way she found it a comfort that some limped along on four feet. Aunt Ida's tear-filled light blue eyes and the threats of a lonely old age palled before Alfred Thal's satisfaction at his stolen Sunday.

"Why don't you get a divorce?," she asked.

"In two years," Thal answered. "In two years," he repeated firmly, "when the twins get out of school."

He pedantically scraped the last bits of food on his plate together with his knife and his sad owl's eyes shone dreamily behind his thick glasses. Suddenly an unusually loud, malicious laugh in which he freely bared his deformed teeth. "Divorce instead of a silver anniversary," he said. He then crouched down again and shovelled the last carefully squashed bits of potato into his mouth. He really ought to go to a dentist, Josefa thought.

All around them people were standing in line, eating, clearing dirty dishes. Dish in the right hand, apple in the left when they looked for a place to sit. Then knife on the right, fork on the left; nothing peculiar except for a few left-handed people. Dirty dishes on the right, knives and forks on the left, the grey-blue smocks, the faces covered with dust. Oppressive monotony. The redhead stood out in the group of grey faces, laughing loudly. Large-scale enterprises reminded Josefa of reservations. Of course no one herded the people here by force or compelled them to stay on the terrain they had been allotted, but weren't the accident of their birth, their average grades in school and unrecognized talent violent forces that drove them behind the walls, among poisonous gases and the thudding monsters? And if it wasn't them it would be others. Insecticides, fabric softeners, fertilizers. Couldn't they at least do without the fabric softeners?

Thal offered her a cigarette. Even the no smoking campaign didn't make it to B. No indication in the lunchroom that smoking was prohibited. It would have been ridiculous as well to combat that little bit of nicotine, given all the visible poisons in B. The redhead got up from the group of grey faces, took his plate to the dish stand, rinsed his knife and fork in the tin bucket, then walked slowly to their table. He reached for an empty chair from the next table. Instead of sitting down he propped a knee on the seat. "You're from the newspaper, aren't you?", he asked Josefa.

"Yes."

"Well then, why don't you write about electrolysis? Here, this little bit of dust on the skin doesn't do any harm. Doesn't even hurt. But those guys there get a wrist like that." The redhead pointed at a growth on a wrist bone the size of a tomato.

"That's called fluorosis. From the fluorine floating around here. You can write about that. Don't even want to recognize it as an occupational disease. My brother-in-law was 49, died. Twenty years of electrolysis. Go right ahead and take a look."

The redhead hadn't spoken loudly, but his aggressive tone brought the conversations at the surrounding tables to a halt. The men and women with the dusty faces watched the scene cautiously; many kept on eating with their eyes to the table as if nothing had happened.

"Why don't you sit down," Josefa said to the redhead.

"Thanks," the redhead said and remained standing.

Thal tugged gently on his forearm. "Don't act like an idiot, Hermann, sit down. She can't help it either."

The redhead waved him off but sat down even if it was only on the edge of the chair. Although Josefa was a little scared by the redhead's belligerence, his appearance was somehow a relief to her. The resigned silence with which Hodriwitzka had waited for the decision about the power plant and Thal's dreamy longing for a life without a cantankerous wife depressed her and spread a paralyzing despair.

"Taking a turn in the indoor pool, eh?" the redhead asked contemptuously.

Josefa pulled the manuscript out of her bag and gave it to the redhead. He took the sheaf of paper with ostentatious indifference. After a while he shook his head: "Well, look at this: she had the guts to go into the power plant. I used to be there. But that was a while back."

Power plant, redheaded, freckles: Hodriwitzka's anarchist, Josefa thought. "Were you the delegate at the power plant?" she asked. The redhead looked up warily and took a drag on his cigarette like Belmondo when he's thinking something over. "Where d'ya find that out?"

Thal stood up. "I'll get three coffees," he said and looked inquisitively at the redhead Hermann as he said it. Hermann didn't answer.

"From the Works Union Management, huh?"

"From Hodriwitzka," Josefa said, hanging on the reaction that the name Hodriwitzka would produce in the redhead.

The redhead blew the air through his nose with a short, sad

sound. "A fine human being he was; little too kind, too weak, but he never beat around the bush. We was like a team. Him the master, me the delegate. We got results. When we met with the WUMers he just rolled his eyes. 'Cos he knew somethin' was gonna come. Oh well, that's over."

Hermann sighed and wiped a few bits of tobacco from the table. He remained silent. All of a sudden the redhead looked Josefa over with growing suspicion. "Was you here already four weeks back?" he asked.

"While Hodriwitzka was still alive," Josefa said.

The redhead must have been expecting this answer; he nodded, satisfied. "Then you must 'a been the one who put the idea in Hodriwitzka's head to write a letter to the Minister, right?"

The redhead's condescending rudeness aroused Josefa's disgust. His ugly face disfigured with scars filled her more with disgust than pity, as it had before when he stood in front of her in line. She looked around for Thal; he was third in the coffee line.

So Hodriwitzka hadn't forgotten. "Did he write the letter?" Josefa asked.

"You're even proud of it, eh? Ran around like a little idiot writing his girl for the first time. 'Man', I said to him, 'you're nuts. You'll get to see the Minister in the paper and then you'll have the guys from State Security on yer neck.' We once collected signatures years ago 'cos our yearly bonus was supposed to be cut. Six months long we had one breakdown after another—our equipment belonged on the junk heap and they didn't buy any new stuff. The quota wasn't met and we was supposed to pay the difference. Eighty people signed: a hundred percent. We got the bonus, but don't ask how much they run around the place after that lookin' for somethin' else. And then a letter to the Minister...Either you're as dumb as they make 'em..."

"OK, let's drop it..."

Thal put a light green plastic tray with three cups of coffee on the table. "Such a pretty girl, Hermann, and all you do is fight," he said.

Hermann smiled. "Nothin' else she'd do with me anyhow. Or ya got an itch for redheads?"

Hermann had dimples when he laughed. He didn't look all that brutal after all, Josefa thought, trying to give the redhead a smile.

"No," she said.

"There, ya see," the redhead said to Thal, who was holding a sugar cube in his coffee, waiting until it was all soaked up. "Nothin'. Ya'd put up with a redhead doctor or actor. But a redhead worker, that's the limit. Ever make it with a worker?" he asked mockingly.

Josefa looked around to see if anyone except her and Thal had understood the redhead's question.

"Hermann, you're going too far," Thal said softly.

The redhead laughed raucously. "Just asking. He wouldn't have to have red hair. But for sure a lady's a lady." He stubbed out his cigarette in the saucer and lit another. Josefa had recovered from the embarrassment his question had caused her. "Go right ahead," she said, "I haven't yet. Just one who used to be a worker, but he's gotten his qualification since then." She looked defiantly at the redhead. "Ever make it with a college girl?"

"Now she's shootin' back," Hermann said and slapped himself on the knee amused. "Didn't mean it like that, really." He offered Josefa a cigarette: "Here—peace pipe."

Thal laughed with relief.

"Now lemme see this stuff," the redhead said, grabbing the manuscript, which still lay in front of him.

The redhead's question stuck with Josefa. Fine, she had never slept with a geologist, a sculptor, a biologist or a mathematician. But the redhead hadn't asked whether he was a locksmith, a lathe operator or a mechanic. The fact itself bothered her even less. It could have been an accident that there were no workers among the men she knew well. But it wasn't an accident. When she had seen the broad-shouldered, muscular men in the factories she had been touring for the past six years, the cocky sureness with which they carried the huge metal parts, their forearms crisscrossed with veins, she had sometimes thought to herself that it would be nice to lie under a body like that, what someone like that would say to her as he caressed her, just what he would be like: tender, rough, imaginative or unimaginative. It would never have occurred to her just to go ahead and do it. She was afraid of leaving her accustomed level of communication, of putting herself at the mercy of a value system foreign to her, of having to listen to patriarchal or petty bourgeois moral phrases foreign to her, without daring to argue against them as she did with Christian. Perhaps it was nothing more than an unacknowledged socially-veiled class arrogance, if not a class barrier?

Had there ever been a ruling class that didn't rule in bed as well?

Josefa briefly ran through the epochs of history from slavery to capitalism: slaves, mistresses, virgins who had to spend their wedding nights in the beds of princes: noblewomen who steered their fat capitalists to a knighthood; servant girls gotten pregnant by masters' sons. The result was staggeringly clear. A topic for sociologists: "An analysis of the political and economic power relationships on the basis of the sexual relations between the classes." Josefa had no doubt as to the outcome of the analysis. The rulers in bed would turn out to be actors, pop singers, doctors and craftsmen. This association of professional groups, however, fit into no class definition, and it would thereby be proven that the conditions of sexual life in socialist society were no longer determined by class relationships because there were no classes except the class of workers and peasants. But the class of peasants and workers had associate groups, to which actors, pop singers, doctors and craftsmen belong. If this calculation is correct, then it would mean that the ruling class of workers and peasants is ruled by its allied groups in sexual intercourse. That couldn't be right. There must be a mistake somewhere in Josefa's thought.

The redhead shoved the manuscript back across the table. "Alright," he said, "I take back what I said before. And that's gonna be printed?" he asked in disbelief.

"God willing," Josefa said.

"Who's your god? Editor-in-Chief, or higher up?"

"God only knows," Josefa said, happy that she had changed the redhead's opinion.

The redhead laughed. "Well then, good luck. Gotta go. Back to the salt mines." As he left he rapped his knuckles in approval on the table.

Alfred Thal asked whether he would come along with them for a beer after his shift.

"Maybe," the redhead said. When he had taken a few steps he turned around again. "By the way, my wife's a teacher," he said.

PART TWO

I

The dreams grew more frequent, coming to Josefa whenever she could find an escape route from the remarks made all around her and which she made herself, even though she was angry afterwards at having said things she had said ten times before. Up to a year ago she had to close her eyes in order to summon figures from the blackness, those figures she didn't know but who brazenly paraded behind her closed eyes. It was enough for her now to get the chance to close her ears to all this noise, to let the veil fall that was unseen by others, but which protected her from the glances of those outside. Then the devils came, afflicting her with their serious grimaces and going to it. Josefa was aghast at these horrible things that existed, which had to exist because they were inside her, pieced together from reality, which needed more room than her head but had settled down in her—so she believed—and had taken possession. She merely had to stare into the reflecting surface of a table or into a grey cloud until the curtain became taut in front of her eyes, then she could conjure up her creatures, who said little but revealed their identity unhesitatingly. They were always different, as if, once having assumed a shape and played a scene, they had to die. They looked like no one Josefa knew. They showed only parts of faces: mouth and nose or only chin. Josefa often didn't want to wake up in the morning, even though sleep was a thin cloth torn to shreds by the sounds of cars speeding past and rumbling street cars or by her son's fingers, which carefully lifted her eyelids to see whether she was still asleep. She wanted to know how the story turned out that her creatures had played for her or with her, evil and base though they were. They had never spared Josefa when they accepted her into their world. She had never been allowed to play a devil with them before, not even one of the weaker one. They had given her the role of victim and if she didn't want to play, she had to content herself with the role of spectator. But even as victim she didn't want to wake up too early; she'd rather wait and see what would happen to her:

whether she would be able to defend herself against her malicious attackers whom she didn't hate even when they tortured and mocked her. All she had to do to escape was to open her eyes; she could lock them up in the crate until she felt a longing for them and once more allowed them to play their games.

She pulled the covers over her shoulder as there was a cool draft coming from the windowframe, and her bed stood directly underneath. She briefly opened her eyes: a light blue sky decorated with irregular patterns of still-bare branches that belonged to the linden tree in front of her building. She registered the image behind her eyelids, where the sky was transformed into a river set against a black background. The river was the Spree. The Spree was as wide as the Danube. You could get to three bridges via a huge staircase. From there the bridges led across the river: one straight, the others leading left and right in sloping arches. On the other side each bridge ended in a building as if it were a tunnel. Each of the buildings was three hundred meters from the next. They were theaters. Josefa crossed the straight bridge; it was already dark when she entered the auditorium. Her friends called to her softly that they had kept a seat for her. The play had already begun. There were two women on stage. They were lilac. The light that fell on them from above, the wallpaper, the curtains, the silk bedspread were all lilac, too. Both women were very old; one was older. The older one was tall and gaunt, the younger one wore braids that fell across her flabby breasts. Skin, hair, teeth were lilac. The women didn't move and their whispering sounded like scratchy hissing. The audience was impatient. The women began to move slowly, as if they had awakened from a frozen state. The younger one tied lilac ribbons on her braids and smiled. She had long teeth. The older stood stiffly and looked with scorn at the younger. She said something and the younger one cried. The old one smiled; her teeth were even longer. The eyes of the old one sat in sockets fissured like craters; they shone feverishly. The younger one was still crying. The old one took a stick and hit the younger one on the head. The younger one stopped crying and adjusted her wig, which had slipped under the blows. The old one laughed so hard that she held her stomach. Then she took a liquor bottle out of a cabinet that stood behind a curtain, poured two full glasses and gave a glass to the younger one. The liquor was lilac. They drank it in a single draught. The younger one sat on the old one's lap, stroked her wrinkled cheeks and said in a whiny child's voice:"I still can't write, Mommy." The old one fixed the ribbon on the younger one's braid.

"You still have time," she said. "You aren't even eighty yet."

"I'd so much like to be able to read," the younger one said, "it's so boring."

"You have your picture books."

"I don't want to be in this room all the time, Mommy. It's so lilac."

Now the younger one spoke with the brittle voice of an old woman. She knelt down in front of the old one and folded her mole-blemished, wrinkled hands. "Please, please, Mommy."

You could see sparks flying out of the craters in the old one's face. She grabbed for a lilac glass bowl and smashed it over the head of the younger one. "Why are you lying?" she screamed.

The younger one threw herself to the ground so that her old bones made a cracking sound, and she clasped the old one's feet. "I didn't lie," she moaned, "I really didn't."

The old one sat down and caressed the younger one, who was still lying on the floor. "Then why did you say: the room is lilac?"

"It looks so lilac, Mommy."

The old one took a piece of glass from the floor and cut the younger one's hand with it. "Look here," she said and pointed to the blood, which ran through the wrinkles in the younger one's hand like a thin red thread. "This is lilac."

The younger one licked the blood from her hand.

"Say the word ten times as punishment," the old one said.

The younger one said the word ten times quickly and monotonously. She crept toward the bed on her hands and knees, lay down on the lilac bedside rug and loudly blew her nose on the silk spread that lay on the bed.

"That's a good girl," the old woman said, took a newspaper from under the table and read. The paper was lilac. The younger one slid towards the old one on her stomach without her noticing.

When the younger one was close enough, she shot up like a rabid wolf and tore her blouse to shreds. The old one had no breasts. The younger one shrieked with joy, hopped around the old woman on her skinny legs and pointed with her finger at her thin, bony torso.

The old woman bared her long teeth like an animal. She tore the cloth from the table and draped it around her shoulders. A woman in a nurse's uniform stepped through the door, which hadn't been visible until then. The uniform was white. "He's coming," she said.

The younger one stopped screaming, slid the wig off her forehead, pulled her skirt up to her bony knees and placed herself next to the door. The old woman stood in front of her.

He came. He wore a top hat and tails. Both were black. He walked past the women to the middle of the room. The two old women at the door stood as stiffly as they had at the beginning. The black man also stood stiffly. They whispered something that Josefa couldn't understand.

Someone behind her was crying. She turned around but she couldn't see anyone. There was no one in the theater except her. The theater was lilac.

Josefa woke up because her son was crying. He was hungry. She got up slowly because if she got up quickly a painful emptiness would fill her head, blinding her for a few seconds. She comforted her son, brought him milk and bread and began the day, which hung mild and sunny over the streets. Josefa remained standing at the window, looked numbly at the street below her as if at something unreal that she had never seen before. Small, upright creatures that maneuvered nimbly between fast-moving metal boxes in order to reach the other side of the street where they disappeared into the same building entrance, which they later left with bags and bottles.

The alarm clock showed 9:00 and Josefa wondered why it hadn't rung at 7:00 as it did every morning. She slowly realized what day it was and that she was standing calmly at the window in her nightgown at 9:00 instead of having long since dropped her son

114

off at kindergarten and having settled into her chair in the open-plan office at the *Illustated Weekly*. This realization caused an ever stronger and more sickly feeling in her stomach. She brushed her teeth, quickly washed up, put on the first thing she found, left the bedclothes where they were and took her child to kindergarten. She bought cigarettes on the way and a bottle of red wine as a precaution in case she couldn't get back to sleep. Waiting for Luise's call became unbearable.

She wondered whether she should turn on the heat, as the night time temperatures still fell to freezing and the apartment beneath the attic cooled down rapidly. But she would first have had to go to the basement and get coal, and since she had made up her mind to stay in bed as it was, she did without the luxury of a little additional warmth. She put on water for coffee, got undressed again, put a cup, the sugar bowl, the wine and a glass on the small stool next to the bed, picked up bits of clothing that were lying around and put them in the clothes closet and waited for the kettle to whistle. It was 9:40. The meeting was supposed to begin in three hours and twenty minutes. Perhaps they would wait ten minutes before they told someone to telephone her to find out where she was. Luise was the only one who knew that she wouldn't be coming and Luise wouldn't tell. She will tell them that she's prepared to telephone Josefa once the others begin to feel uneasy, to find out whether she is ill or on her way to the editorial office. She will then go back to the conference room, where they are assembled in order to discuss Comrade Nadler's irresponsible behaviour, and will inform those present what they already decided yesterday: Comrade Nadler considers it pointless to take part in this meeting. She requests that they deliberate without her.

What possible concern could it be to her if they sat around the horseshoe-shaped conference table with facial expressions befitting the seriousness of the situation, as if they were bearing someone to the grave who had meant a great deal to them. They had prepared their funeral orations, practised their sorrowing faces in front of the mirror. They had reserved the bar where they would later drink a toast to the soul of the dearly departed. But the corpse wouldn't show up. The burial would have to take place without her.

Josefa poured herself a cup of coffee and got back into bed. She felt a secret satisfaction in doing the most forbidden and brazen thing anyone could do in her position. She had too often had to explain to others and to herself during the last six weeks what had actually happened: what had caused her to be excluded from the community, why she was a corpse and why the others had to mourn.

She had told them about Hodriwitzka, about the town he lived in, this miserable filthy hole on which 180 tons of flue ash fell every day. She was tired now. But they couldn't hear enough explanations, they wanted someone to tell them over and over: No, I won't change the manuscript; yes, I've written a letter to the Supreme Council; I'm right, I'm right, I'm right, as though Josefa could make amends to them for the sentences she herself had never uttered.

Josefa got up to get a book from the shelf, although she knew that she wouldn't read much of it. She combed her hair in front of the oval mirror, was surprised by her face, which looked no different than it had six weeks before; a bit thinner, perhaps. So this was the one everything happened to: broad cheek bones and jaw bones, grey eyes, said to be slanty, although Josefa could never see why, a large mouth that she suspected of being too narrow, a slightly arched nose with a flattened point, smooth hair falling to her shoulders. The noise of approaching motors filtered through the open window behind her forehead; she was shivering, closed the window, went back to bed, said to herself that she was here because she wanted to be. It didn't concern her anymore. Later she was surprised at how long they had been able to do this to her, to pacify and enlighten her month after month when she handed in her articles, which she knew weren't false but weren't true either. And who knows how long it would have kept going on if Luise hadn't sent her to B., if she hadn't met Hodriwitzka and the redheaded anarchist and the others with their grey and white faces?

In the beginning it had seemed as if events had befallen her by accident. Suddenly, without warning, something was gone that she had considered secure. She had thought that there wasn't much

116

certainty in her life since the certainties of childhood had gradually lost their worth; Tadeus, much less her marriage; in its place the child: her child and her profession. Now and then she was horrified at the thought of the thirty years that she would have to take the tram day after day to the subway, board the subway downtown, walk along the windy tunnel that went under Alexanderplatz, through the heavy glass door at the publishing house, which she could open only by throwing her entire body weight against it, ride the overcrowded elevator to the sixteenth floor. Thirty years of that, until she retired or, if she died before that, until death. The idea that a Monday morning in the year 2000 could resemble any given Monday this year was uncanny. The hallways still white, the small honeycomb-shaped rooms, the open-plan office, other faces behind the green plants, no more Luise, no more Rudi Goldammer, though there wouldn't be any Siegfried Strutzer either. To the same extent it had soothed her to belong to this earthquake-proof colossus, to read her name every so often in bold-face type in an edition of a million copies. Proof of the existence of a certain Josefa Nadler: thirty years old, divorced, mother of a child. That was all over. In six or seven hours at the most, the telephone would ring and Luise would give her a report of the meeting about whose outcome Josefa had no doubt.

It was only in the last few days, during which she had been on leave, that she slowly began to grasp the logical consistency of events that for weeks she felt had been random, which she had been fighting like a madwoman without understanding that they were unfolding with the regularity of physical processes. It seemed to her after the fact as if none of the persons involved in the drama could have acted any differently than they did. Each step was prescribed, therefore predictable. She knew that Strutzer would soon be declaiming his last monologue on this affair. They all lay in front of her like dissected fish. Luise, Strutzer, Rudi Goldammer, Ulrike, Hans Schütz, herself—all of them lay intricately divided into heads, bones, fillets and skins on the horseshoe-shaped conference table of light-colored wood.

The evening she returned from B. she took a taxi from the train station to Christian's apartment. She had the taxi driver wait five minutes in front of the building in order not to have to walk through the night alone in case she didn't find Christian. She didn't catch the train until 8 p.m. though she had been standing at track 2 of the station in B. at 5:30 on the dot, accompanied by Alfred Thal and the redhead. As the train arrived, the redhead had asked whether she would like another beer instead, one fresh as the dew—eat, drink and be merry, he said, for tomorrow...and she knew what he meant. Thal was pleased at the redhead's suggestion. The twins had a disco dancing course and he'd otherwise have to spend the evening alone with his wife. They drank beer and schnapps in the waiting room, which was overcrowded with men, tobacco smoke and noise. They no longer talked about Hodriwitzka and the power plant. They told stories about their children, exchanged their favorite dishes: the redhead liked eating rice pudding with sugar and cinnamon best, Alfred Thal preferred sauerbraten with dumplings. Josefa was the only one who couldn't decide on a favorite dish. The redhead said that he absolutely had to get to Ireland once in his life, on account of the Irish, who were all redheaded and anarchists. He would definitely find out in Ireland what the connection was between red hair and a person's character. Alfred Thal wanted his one imaginary visa to be for Greece. The civilization, he said, the Acropolis, he wanted to see that before he died. The redhead sang another song on the train platform, a sailor's song that his uncle, who had gone to sea as a young man, had taught him.

Since the visit to Brommel, Christian and Josefa were only apart during the hours he had to spend at the university and she in the editorial office. He would ask in the morning almost indifferently if she would be home in the evening; he came in the evening and stayed. They behaved freely with each other as they had been doing for fifteen years. Only in the evening, when they lay down in Josefa's wide bed, did they become transformed into speechless creatures, into flying squid with maple-leaf wings, revealing what they had kept secret from each other until then. The excessive longing to be dissolved into this feeling that dulls every other sensation; to be simply this one piece of body, to forget who they were, to keep silent so as not to remember that there was an ocean beneath them. Their life together was strictly divided into day and night, into friendship and ecstasy. Christian seemed to want to catch up on what he had missed since the morning of the milk truck, and Josefa was astonished at his lust mixed with gentleness. She couldn't recall any man with whom she had felt nearly so free. It was difficult in the morning to connect her nocturnal loss of consciousness with Christian, who leafed through the paper and pointed to Josefa's tired eyes with gentle mockery as they ate breakfast.

The night she had spent with Christian after she had returned from B. was the only one Josefa could clearly remember and could still identify with a particular day. For one night she was a being in a life that had nothing to do with the *Illustrated Weekly*, or power relationships and ideologies, or the arbitrariness of the age she was born to. All those weren't life. They were images of life, not life itself. Living was breathing, loving, producing children and giving, earning a living, and nothing more. She had felt all kinds of longings before, but she had always held something back to escape into the shadows of her being, to leave the twentieth century in front of her or behind her and simply to be. She had always been held back by the knowledge of the impossibility of such a life or by the suspicion that it was an undignified form of existence and that real life consisted in forever struggling to change things. This night suddenly drew a straight line from her birth to her death, separated the natural from the absurd; and almost everything about Josefa's profession was found to be on the absurd side, seemed to her perverse, contriving to impose on her and the others a meaning that lay outside their natural lives. A desperate desire to love overcame her, the mania to experience pain and to inflict pain, and she loved Christain because he followed her into those animalistic depths where she sped as if she might find her salvation there.

She tried to find the line of thought of that night again, to reduce herself to a living, feeling being. But it already failed with the very word *reduce*. Why didn't she think of elevating herself to a living, feeling being? Josefa lay in bed with her eyes closed, held the book that she had not yet looked at open in her left hand. With the other hand she sought the paths along her body that Christian had found that night, she tried to convince herself that this was Christian caressing her, was startled, sat up, lit a cigarette. She couldn't find the image again that accompanied this idea of life. A small girl with a long braid on a green meadow saw her, but if she thought of this image now it looked like a postcard, flat and mawkish. That night it had been vivid and Josefa had seen it in perspective: the girl and the cow were very small but still clearly recognizable. She knew that it would make little sense to search for the clarity of those hours or even of those minutes.

She had already lost it the day she had taken the elevator to the white hallway on the sixteenth floor where Siegfried Strutzer stood in a new burgundy shirt he had bought in an exclusive shop along with the matching dark red tie. He didn't say anything except good morning, but that was enough to fix his place in Josefa's life. He smelled of disgusting shaving lotion. It might have been a good aftershave, too, but that was all the same to Josefa as soon as Strutzer smelled of it. Josefa remembered that when she opened the paper that morning, she had felt a boundless anger against men, not against any particular man, not even against Strutzer. She wouldn't have liked him any better had he been a woman, and there were already enough women like that. "Greetings to our wives and girls" went the bright thick red headline on page one. So that's why Strutzer was smiling. One day in the year was reserved for women; Strutzer acted correctly. There were nine men in the photo, which took up a third of the page. They were standing in a row smiling at a woman who had a tight black skirt covering her round derrière. One of the men was shaking the woman's hand, apparently after having carefully pinned a medal on her, for there was a shiny badge on the woman's white blouse just above her left breast. The woman's legs were bent at the knees as if she had just made a curtsy. The woman looked happy, and the men, who were as alike as peas in a pod, seemed to be satisfied with themselves.

Josefa wanted for once to belong to those who got medals pinned on their left breast. Then she could tell them words of thanks thought out long ago. She would make a speech about the joy of being a woman.

Josefa rolled over to her left side so that the light that was shining through the window wouldn't bother her while she dreamt. She crept under the covers away from the noise from the street and the droning of the vacuum cleaner, which the Rickert woman ran through her apartment every day at eleven on the dot, and closed her eyes. Josefa walked slowly from her seat in the first row, where the people sat who were being given awards, in a long white gown which fell over her shoulders in heavy pleats and whose waist was tied with a hemp cord, walked up the low stairs onto the stage, looked out slowly across the heads in the hall, walked onto the podium, and when she stood behind it, she pulled it close. Her hair was cut short. Josefa watched with satisfaction as the crop-haired Josefa began to speak in front of the assembled women who were supposed to be honored and in front of the men present who had decided to honor them.

"Women and men," Josefa said in a soft voice that she didn't recognize as her own. "Women and men," she repeated louder still, "we have come together; we women to let ourselves be honored, you men to do us honor. The time has come, women, when we have to thank men for the honor they have bestowed upon us. For there are still those among us who do not appreciate the tremendous changes men have brought about in us. I once heard a woman complain about the small salary she received in comparison with the men in her family. But the men were strong, they could carry furniture and drive trucks. Each according to his abilities, women. Women are the ornaments of our husbands, as delicate as the fine wires we solder in dust-free rooms. Where does a woman get the right to argue about the price of strength if strength is, after all, a man's business?

Or the other one who stops thinking about her work the moment her child gets sick, thinks only about the child, although the men in the union have set up a sick room in which that child could have his fever in peace and quiet, so she could still operate the crane that otherwise stands idle. Instead she talks about motherly love, even about her longing for her sick child who she says will need more time to recover if it doesn't see its mother. The same woman,

121

however, incredible as it may seem, complains loudly that she doesn't get a penny for her work as a nurse. Freed from the compulsions of animal instinct, the woman persists, blind to the progress of her own sex, of her nature as she calls it, and grumbles when she is taken to task, that she thought socialism was going to be different. Under socialism, she thought, anyone who wanted to be a mother could be one. Simplicity, women, is reactionary. Does this woman seriously believe that the struggle millions have died for had the sole, simple goal of letting women kiss their babies all day long instead of proving that they are as useful as their husbands?

Now, women, on to the third topic, which I have to admit is a delicate one. Men have recently been talking a great deal about the freedom of our bodies and about the discovery of female sexuality. I see that you are smiling, and I smile too when they have their enlightened brothers in the magazines draw the thing in cross-section and in longitudinal section with an arrow going to every little part they look for with such enthusiasm, instead of asking us who have known that since we were three or four. Still, their touching concern for us, their childishly eager smile when they wait for confirmation of what they have read, yes, even the annoyance on their faces when we become stiff with so much diligence and they classify us as frigid, just as they are taught— this isn't a reason to smile, women. A few brief hours from here by jet they cut it off their women so they won't get the urge to go after other men. Our men don't do that. On the contrary, they allow us and themselves pleasure. We should thank them for their willingness and not laugh at them arrogantly. For if they decided tomorrow in the Supreme Council to cut ours off, then it would be our turn as well. The one woman on the Council can't help us either. For that reason alone, women, we should be reasonable and recognize what has been accomplished. Men often lack a sense for the little things; where could they have gotten it the way their bodies are put together? We should recognize, however, the extent of their merit and not close our eyes to the epochal change, for the clitoral age is upon us. Thanks to our men.

There is something further that causes me concern. One often hears a question among women which, to be sure, was originally justifiable, though if you are perceptive, women, you will notice by yourselves that the question was dictated by an unjust attitude. You ask why you always have to be young and beautiful, be ashamed of every grey hair, while men wear grey at their temples as a mark of dignity. You demand equal standards for fat and wrinkles, and, just though these demands sound, they are unjust all the same. I'll show you why. What beauty is for us, a man's strength is to him. It fades away with the years as does our firm, smooth skin. The man follows with dread every failure that occurs after drinking alcohol or when he is sick. From youth onwards he is terrified by visions of becoming impotent, of how one day he will have to look at a woman without a stirring in his loins, instead of fucking her. What then could be more just than to compensate for this injustice in a way that also offers to put a stop to women's desires, who are still able to when they are old, but aren't allowed to because their beauty has vanished like men's strength. And the fears are distributed evenly as well, for what else should we fear, women, if not the withered flesh on our stomachs and thighs and the wrinkles under our eyes? We even have advantages, as we can dye our hair and wear corsets. If that doesn't help, then the surgeon can, by sewing folds in our skin like clothes which are too wide. It could not be more just. Stop your wailing. What you bring on with your racket is much worse. There are already men who go out of their way, impressed by the criticism of women, to have flat stomachs and hairless breasts. They run to cosmetics, dye their beards, put on flower-patterned shirts as if they were women. Worse still: the weak ones among them, with a weakly developed male awareness, already regard women almost as men. They look at what women can do and only then do they look at their legs. This can't be what you wanted, women, that one pressure leads to the next. If you continue marching forward for equal rights, they will put us in the government one day. We would become prisoners, would have to play according to men's rules. I ask you, do you want that?'' The crop-haired Josefa fell silent. The women in the hall began to applaud; just a few at first, then more and more: a drugged rhythm from the

123

front rows was slowly picked up by the others.

"Why are you applauding?" Josefa asked.

The women applauded again, not very long.

"Don't you understand anything?" Josefa yelled and hit the podium with her fist. The women applauded.

The phone rang. Instead of saying her name or hello, Luise said: "Listen, Josefa." She had thought everything over again in detail, had also spoken about it with her husband and they had come to the same conclusion, that it would be better for Josefa to show up at the meeting. It wouldn't change the outcome, of course, she knew that. But why should Josefa want to provoke people even more? She didn't have to say much; her presence alone would be enough to keep the matter from getting worse than it already was. Otherwise Luise would, of course, stick by her promise and carry out what they agreed on yesterday. "But just think it through a little further, won't you," Luise said, "after all, you have to work somewhere or other. Up till now everything can still be straightened out. But if you defy them again today..."

"Luise," Josefa interrupted, "you said I should go to a factory, get trained. Do you think that they're all that choosy about who they take on a conveyor belt? It doesn't concern me anymore. I'm not coming."

Luise stopped talking, then she asked in a tone that had none of the motherly urgency of her earlier admonitions: "Do you really want to work in a factory?"

"Yes," Josefa said.

"We'll talk about this later," Luise said, "I'll call you back after the meeting."

Josefa sat on the edge of the bed, poured wine into her half-empty glass, took a sip, put on a record of Greek music Christian had given her for her birthday, reached into the tin that stood on the shelf and bit into a cookie. It was stale. She threw it back into the tin, sat up again on the bed, lay down, rolled herself into the blankets. Yes, she said, yes, I'm going to work in a factory. She had thought over this possibility often during the last weeks, but had rejected it again and again because she was convinced that something would happen to save her. She hadn't known who or what was waiting for her; just an accident that would clarify her situation. In the beginning she had hoped Strutzer would break a leg or get a swollen appendix. That might have been a solution six weeks ago. If Strutzer had drunk two more glasses of wine at the women's testimonial, he might have slipped on the waxed floor of the white hallway and broken his ankle, couldn't have visited the Comrade-in-charge at the Supreme Council in order to submit the article on B. for a decision. Then the Comrade-in-charge could not have made a decision in accordance with Strutzer's wishes, nor could he have been told how unreasonable Comrade Nadler had shown herself to be and how little support Strutzer had gotten from the other comrades in the matter. But Strutzer didn't drink any more than he was offered, and he informed Josefa three days later that she was summoned to an exchange of views with the Comrade-in-charge tomorrow morning at ten.

Josefa entered the building through a small door on the broad frontage. She stood in a brightly lit room: chairs, table, an ashtray. On the left a window in a wooden wall: registration. Josefa stood in front of the counter, which was constructed in such a way that the only possible communication between porter and visitor and visitor and porter was between the lower edge of a frosted-glass disc and the wooden shoulder and through a sicvc that allowed sound through in the middle of the disc.

Who do you want to see? Your ID please, the official said, and looked through the slit between the disc and the shoulder through which Josefa was supposed to hand him her ID. She could just make out his profile when he bent forward to check her ID, but his face was covered as soon as he stood up straight and turned towards her. He dialled a telephone number. The visitor for the Comrade-in-charge, he announced. It was part of Josefa's profession to report, to be checked, to be allowed to pass or be sent away. In general, she followed the course of such procedures with indifference, but not this time, not toward this official with the disc in front of his face. She had thought of all sorts of accusations that the Comrade-in-charge could think up; she had arranged all the arguments she could offer in her defense, even to go on the offensive if necessary. She had practised a number of versions of her conversation with the Comrade-in-charge. Twice Christian, as the Comrade-in-charge, had decided to end the conversation and showed Josefa out of the room because she had made statements that were almost treasonous in the eyes of an intransigent Comrade-in-charge. Christian interrupted the third conversation because even he found Josefa's pretentious naiveté ridiculous. You talk like a decorated Youth Pioneer, he said. Christian praised the fourth attempt, but Josefa hadn't understood why. The drill had only made her more unsure. The Comrade-in-charge had arrived at his decision: he had communicated his precise and irrevocable *No* through Strutzer. Even Luise had given up; it's the end now, she said, and too bad. Josefa didn't know what there was left to talk about between her and the Comrade-in-charge.

The official pushed a paper through the slit underneath the glass disc which entitled Josefa to pass through the main entrance around the corner. The main portal was located on the broad side of the building at a height of six or seven meters and was surmounted by a stairway about twenty meters wide. In the high entrance hall, decorated with small tapestries and portraits, a soldier carefully compared Josefa with the ID and the ID with the pass, leafing carefully through each page. The soldier gave the ID and pass back to Josefa, put his right hand to the visor of his cap, said nothing. In the right rear corner of the foyer Josefa found the paternoster elevator.

Josefa didn't know how to use a paternoster elevator. Every time she had tried to use one, she got in too early and off too early, and when she tried to wait for the right moment, she missed it and had to wait for the next cabin or ride a floor in the other direction, which put her up against the same difficulties again. The cabin rose slowly from the shaft. Josefa waited. Not yet. Only when the platform of the cabin had risen to the level of the floor under her feet did she have to jump. Now, this instant. She put one foot forward, took a step into the void, found her footing. In two, at most three, minutes she would locate the room of the Comrade-in-charge, would know what he looked like, the person whose name Strutzer mentioned every chance he got. Josefa rose through the second floor. A man watched her ascent with indifference. Josefa was wearing a skirt and stepped to the rear of the cage. "And, for heaven's sake, don't wear jeans when you go there," Luise had counselled. Luise didn't know the Comrade-in-charge. He had replaced the former Comrade-in-charge, a rude man from Saxony who wore trousers that were too short, and except for Rudi Goldammer and Siegfried Strutzer, none of the contributors to the *Illustrated Weekly* had ever seen him.

Where had she read: "The most important thing before a battle is to be the first one who feels fear, so that you have fear far behind you when everyone else experiences it?" But why should she be afraid? In half an hour she would be floating earthward again in the paternoster elevator, would leave the building and far enough away that the portal guard couldn't see her, would place herself in the spring wind, which blew today from the northeast; and she would fly towards Alexanderplatz in endless knots and loops to where the earthquake-proof publishing house stood. An electrically lit three moved into Josefa's line of vision. Josefa positioned herself right up against the front edge of the cabin. She lifted her right foot so that she could set it on terra firma at the right moment. Another twenty centimeters, ten centimeters, away—getting off was easier.

Three corridors led from the foyer in front of the paternoster elevator to the center of the building. Josefa was unsure which one of the three ways she should choose. She compared the room number written on her card with the numbers on the first three doors of the three corridors, but all three numbers were almost equally far away from the one she was looking for. There was no man or woman to be seen to ask the way. Artificial light streamed out of a door the upper third of which consisted of a glass pane— frosted glass like the window at reception. Josefa knocked. It remained quiet. She knocked again, this time even softer because the sound her first attempt had produced still rang all too loudly in her ears. She pushed down on the door handle carefully, so as not to startle anyone in case there was someone in the room, also because she had the feeling of doing something forbidden. The door didn't give way; it was locked. Without any good reason

Josefa set off down the middle corridor. When she had gone a few meters she heard rapid steps coming from another direction getting closer to the foyer. Josefa turned to ask directions from whoever was the cause of those steps. A man was standing in front of the paternoster elevator in an anthracite black suit. His fingers were thin and powerful. He held himself like an athlete, and Josefa thought that here was someone with an exerciser in his apartment—and a sun lamp. He could have been fifty years old or even a bit younger. He wore the oval decoration with clasped hands on the left lapel of his suit, the emblem of good people since her childhood. When she had gotten lost or wanted to know what time it was, she had waited for someone who wore the badge. These were her friends, her mother had explained to her. Later on, too, when Josefa had long since met others who wore the badge and weren't her friends, she still felt a spontaneous surge of trust as soon as a comrade stood across from her, a feeling she quickly suppressed because it blocked her judgment and because it forced her time and again into a childlike credulity that matched neither her age nor her views.

The man who stood in front of the paternoster elevator took a few steps towards Josefa. "Are you Comrade Nadler from the *Illustrated Weekly*?" He introduced himself as the Comrade-in-charge, said that it was difficult for visitors to find their way in this monstrous, frightening building. This is why he meets his visitors at the elevator, then only the building was frightening, not those inside it. He laughed. Josefa laughed. The man led her through corridors full of corners and Josefa tried to note where they turned left or right.

The Comrade-in-charge opened the door and let Josefa enter the room in front of him in which his secretary was sitting, who then looked up from her work and said hello to Josefa in a friendly tone of voice. The Comrade-in-charge asked his secretary to be so kind as to bring some coffee from the snack bar, two or three cups, whatever she saw fit. He then led Josefa through a communicating door into a second room, offered her a seat on the sofa, lowered the blinds so that the sun was no longer glaring. He was suffering from conjunctivitis, he said, as he placed a Bohemian glass ashtray

128

on the table. Normally he loved it when light fell on the people and things he dealt with. He gave Josefa an ambiguous look as he said this. He asked whether it bothered Josefa for him to use formal address with her; he found it difficult to use familiar forms with people he didn't know better. With women especially he had a feeling of exaggerated intimacy, especially when a beautiful woman was involved. He grew serious. "And you cause our Comrade Strutzer so much grief?" he asked.

Josefa thought that she detected a hint of irony in the smile of the Comrade-in-charge, though she wasn't sure whether it was intended for Strutzer or for her, or whether this facial expression was peculiar to the Comrade. "I don't think I give Comrade Strutzer any more grief than he gives me," Josefa said. She too smiled, in case the Comrade found her answer presumptuous, in order to have an out with a jest. But he seemed to enjoy Josefa's disrespectful statement. He laughed and asked whether she might like a cognac to drink along with her coffee. He got a liquor bottle out of the case behind a curtain, poured two glasses full and gave a glass to Josefa. "All kidding aside," he said, "I read your article. I want you to understand our decision." He said that he liked the report, he had clearly felt the passion and commitment. Nor had he noticed any errors of fact. All this, he just had to say so, won him over very much to Josefa and her work.

The secretary brought the coffee. Josefa drank alternately a sip of cognac and a sip of coffee, and drew on her cigarette. The strips of sun that ran across the furniture and the floor, the melodious voice of the Comrade—he must have been from the north and Josefa liked the sound of the northern accent with its rolled r's—these things confused her. She sat relaxed in the chair as if she had never felt the unpleasantness of the building, the security checks and her own insecurity. She was lightly flushing under the Comrade's words of praise and had the relieved feeling of belonging in spite of it all, just as she had felt in childhood when she had asked these strangers like him for the correct time or the correct road. But her mistrust was reawakened. After all, this comrade had communicated a plain *No*, and through Strutzer at that.

He wished, he now said, that all journalists could be as honest

129

and combative in supporting the cause. "Our cause," he stated. In that case, Josefa said, he must prefer the unprinted page to those now appearing in the newspapers.

The Comrade nodded, satisfied. With this remark, he said, Josefa had revealed a fundamental error. "You are too absolute," he said. At every point in the class struggle there is a tactical and a strategic goal. Now the strategic goal most certainly included the elimination of a town like B. And, of course, Josefa knew as much herself, that there were proposals made years ago to give B. up as a residential town, to move the inhabitants to a healthier place from which they could ride to work in buses. But then the apartments wouldn't have been enough and the plan was abandoned. How and when the elimination of B. was to take place was a tactical matter. The misunderstanding between himself and Josefa—for he didn't want to consider it as anything more than a misunderstanding—was purely a question of tactics. Without moving a muscle the Comrade altered his facial expression by a sudden perceptible severity in his eyes, which he fixed sternly on Josefa. There was also another tactical consideration which, although not concerned with the class enemy, was still of considerable importance, he said with a monotone voice that overwhelmed Josefa; and it was regrettable that it was precisely the most valuable comrades who could find so little understanding for certain impossibilities that he would change immediately if he could. The Comrade had stressed every word distinctly as if a different one could have fitted in its place— words which were infused with the sternness of his gaze as he waited silently for an answer.

Josefa tried to grasp what the Comrade had just told her. He was a different type from the one she and Christian had imagined in their rehearsals. The expected admonitions didn't materialize. There was instead an urgent effort to enlist her understanding, which he could have done without but didn't want to. What need did he have for that here behind his Venetian blinds?

"I can't think that way," she said, "I don't understand."

"You are too impatient," the Comrade said. "Perhaps we will need the same article urgently in a year. Not now. Think of Brecht: Galileo. Sometimes it's wiser to keep quiet when one has much to say.''

He fell silent.

"Comrade Nadler, why did I ask you to come to me? Why am I talking myself silly so that you will understand?'' The Comrade waited an instant before he went ahead with his answer. "Because we can't do without comrades like you, nor do we want to. I am going to tell you something now that must stay between us: people like Comrade Strutzer are necessary for the smooth operation of an editor's office or an institute. But we can't build socialism with only people like him. For that we need people with imagination, courage, yes, even people who are awkward for us. That, Comrade Nadler, is what I am struggling for, and now I really have to become informal to enlist your understanding.''

She had understood the anarchist and Thal, but most of all she had understood Hodriwitzka. Too much understanding is bad. One understanding cancels out the other. She couldn't bear that much understanding.

Hodriwitzka is dead, she said, he can no longer write a letter. Someone has to write it.

She told him about her talk with Hodriwitzka; the Comrade-in-charge had to know that if he wanted to understand. And she told him how the anarchist had abused her, and how she had wished that Strutzer would break his leg. And what Luise thought about Strutzer and why Rudi Goldammer was ill and would die one day because of Strutzer. Josefa sensed how the room was becoming filled with her sentences and with her voice, and she thought that she must stop talking but she kept on.

The man seemed to understand, to nod encouragement.

Strutzer is a fat jellyfish, she said, and he, the Comrade-in-charge, wanted to back him up. She was afraid of Strutzer, fear that became a rumbling in her ears. And she was angry, she didn't want to understand anything about Strutzer. She had already understood enough, she had even felt pity because he had had to drink his own piss. But now that Hodriwitzka was dead, she had finally had enough and she refused to understand this tactical idiocy.

The Comrade-in-charge was distressed. "Not only don't you understand Comrade Strutzer,'' he said, "you don't understand me either. Don't you think it unfair that although you don't understand anyone, I have to understand you and Comrade Strutzer and Comrade Goldammer and the comrade who is in charge of me? I understand you, Comrade Nadler, I even think I understand you very well, your revolutionary impatience, your wish to make things better than they are. I have a daughter a few years younger than you: a pretty, intelligent girl. She reminds me of you. How many times do I say: girl, I say, when you lose your patience who is supposed to keep it for you? You have to learn to live with defeat.''

The Comrade filled Josefa's glass with cognac a second time. His own glass was still half full. ''Hold on, girl, and observe moderation. Don't try to break a butterfly on the wheel.''

''Strutzer is an odd butterfly,'' Josefa said, ''an immortal butterfly. Nothing fazes him except cannon fire.''

''Is it the power plant that's at stake or Comrade Strutzer?'' the Comrade-in-charge asked.

''It's the power plant,'' Josefa said, ''and it's Strutzer.'' She was tired, from one minute to the next she was dead tired. The rehearsals with Christian, the fear before she had entered the building and again when she was looking for the right door, the cognac, the voice with the rolled r's. Josefa held the snifter, swirled the brown liquid. It was darker where her fingers held the glass. She stared into the watery mirror in which two fingers were floating. A colorful little bottle genie submerged the other figure and set it on its back. The bottle genie swung an invisible whip. The other figure, resembling a fish, from whose sides arms grew instead of fins, tried to throw the little devil off by hitting him hard with its tail fin and swimming wildly with its arms. The little devil swung the whip and sang: Arise, ye wretched of the earth!

''...More things in heaven and earth,'' the comrade concluded. Josefa hadn't been listening. Exhaustion walked on spider's feet from the soles of her feet to the skin under her scalp. What more did the man want from her? It was decided. Hang on, bear with him.

''Yes,'' she said.

''Why yes?'' the Comrade asked.

''Yes, why?'' Josefa said. Now I won't be able to fly to

Alexanderplatz, she thought, I'll have to walk. Why was she so tired, all of a sudden, for no reason? The man looked at the watch on his wrist.

"Excuse me, could you please tell me what time it is?" Josefa asked with a thin child's voice.

The man told her. He excused himself: an urgent meeting had already begun in the office of the Comrade-in-charge of him. Did she feel ill or could he help her? he asked. He accompanied her to the next turn in the corridor and told her the way to the paternoster elevator.

II

In the weeks that followed, Josefa was unable to think of the Comrade-in-charge without feeling a pang of diffuse fear in the pit of her stomach. As soon as she had left the building she was once again surrounded by rushed and sauntering pedestrians who blinked contentedly at the March sun or looked around for park benches, which the authorities couldn't get set up quickly enough. As soon as Josefa leaned over the bridge railing and looked into the foamy waters of the city's most important river, she felt a fright go through her slowly; it tasted salty. What would keep the Comrade-in-charge from telling Strutzer about her attack on him, or reporting to the comrade responsible for him that a certain Josefa Nadler had incited workers against the authorities and encouraged them to write letters? Or he could ask Rudi Goldammer to hand over his difficult job in light of his serious illness. Josefa stared at a point in the water that swelled the longer she looked at it, coming towards her. Yet the wet markings on the walled river bank proved that the water level was unchanged.

A meeting took place two weeks later in which the Comrade-in-charge was supposed to give a talk to the comrades of the *Illustrated Weekly* on the reporting of socialist competition. The Comrade-in-charge had already taken a seat next to Strutzer at the chair when Josefa entered the conference room. Strutzer spoke softly and confidentially with him, tapping the dossiers in front of him now and then with his pencil. The Comrade held his head slightly inclined

133

to Strutzer, looked absentmindedly among those assembled, and Josefa again noticed the expression between his mouth and nose that suggested irony. His eyes, which had been moving aimlessly around the room until then, remained fixed on Josefa—a fleeting nod across the table, noncommittal gestures while Strutzer continued talking. Josefa thought she saw traces of triumph in Strutzer's behavior: a victorious royal smile, unmistakable satisfaction in the tired eyes behind the tinted glasses. She expected him to stand up, tap for order with his pencil and say, not without an offended tone: "Comrades, there is a female comrade among us who has called another comrade a fat jellyfish and a queer butterfly and other species of beast. I would ask the comrade in question to make a statement on that." Luise, Günter Rassow and Hans Schütz would bury their heads in their hands and barely be able to suppress their laughter; the others would wait indignantly or spitefully to see how Josefa tried to get out of the snare.

At this point Josefa had already written her letter to the Supreme Council. When she looked back on it, the act seemed crazy to her, and her fear of the consequences spoiled getting up in the morning and coming home and looking in the mail box. A week had already gone by since she had put the envelope with the long typed address into the yellow box, and she hoped afterwards that the letter had gotten lost along the delivery route or had accidentally landed in the wastepaper basket at the Supreme Council's mail room. Such hope caused her not to mention the letter to anyone. She was still under the impression of an experience she had had on her usual evening trip home when she wrote it. She had left the editorial office an hour earlier than usual to order a hot water heater at the housing office. She hadn't noticed anything yet as she slowly went down the subway stairs into the stream of people returning from their offices. The only thing she noticed out of the ordinary was the mass of people at the tram stops, which was greater than on other days. She concluded that one or more trains weren't running. Josefa only had to take three stops or to walk twenty minutes, and since she wasn't in a hurry and the weather was tolerably mild, she decided to walk. After she had pushed her way through the stubbornly waiting crowd and had walked to the other side of the street, where the stores broke up the monotony of the way, fifty or a hundred meters further on Josefa noticed a strange quality in the air. At first she thought it was the light. A distinct twilight split the streets and objects into two layers that were shifted a few centimeters on top of each other. Josefa closed her eyes and the strangeness didn't go away; it became audible, although Josefa couldn't make out the type and character of the sound. A quiet rustling in the air: the rustling of leaves or wings. Josefa looked through the bare branches of the tree tops but couldn't find a cause for the rustling. A black bird sat on a branch, opened its yellow beak as if it wanted to sing, flapped its wings as if it were going to fly and fell silently to the ground. The air began to stir, and when Josefa turned around she saw a black limousine surrounded by a swarm of men in uniform on motorcycles floating above the roadway at the same speed. The noise of the motors swallowed up the stillness; all that reached Josefa was a muted hiss; waves of displaced air hit her face. The limousine disappeared behind the next turn. A shrill whistle tore the air like paper. Two policemen jumped out from the cover of the building onto the roadway and raised their arms covered by white oversleeves.

The blocked traffic flowed out of all the side streets with a loud screech into the main thoroughfare, moved sporadically along like thick blood in a dead vein or shot through it hectically, then grew gradually calmer and more rhythmic and the noise travelled across the rooftops. It was dead silent, Josefa thought. She pushed the silence away from her wherever she went. It must have made them deaf, Josefa thought. They can't know anything about B. They have no way of knowing. She put off buying the hot water heater until another day and rode home to write the letter. In it she told them that she, a journalist, thirty years of age, had to inform the government about conditions of which they presumably had no knowledge and that the stoker Hodriwitzka from B. had wanted to write this letter weeks ago, but had been run over by a bus as he tried to turn left without signalling. Since the comrades charged with this matter would not allow a public consideration of the problem in the press, she saw herself compelled to inform the government through this channel about omissions in the building of socialism.

There followed a brief and exact description of the occurrences in the power plant in B. Josefa looked for a clean envelope with straight corners, addressed it after she had found the complete address in the telephone book, bought stamps at a newsstand and put the letter into the yellow box. The next morning she tried to intercept the man who emptied the mail boxes in the area to get the letter back. But she came too late and was left with no alternative but to hope that the mail delivery would be undependable, which it wasn't.

For the first time since she had been waiting for an answer to her letter, Josefa felt no fear. She was still sceptical, waiting for the throbbing and spasms to return, which had until recently followed the very thought of rebellion. She lay on her barricade of quilted down, saw through closed eyes how bright red blood was pumped through her heart and flowed into delicate channels all the way to her fingertips. She was a functioning organism. She experienced for seconds at a time the clairvoyance she so clearly remembered from that night with Christian and which she had pursued in vain ever since. She saw herself in the middle of the road between birth and death, walked without stopping and without turning around; and the world was divided into her pain and that of others, into her own desperation and the desperation of others, into her own joy and joy belonging to others. It was only the things that were concentrated in her, that concerned her, that came out of her which were ultimately her life.

Josefa thought about her future. Think about your future, why don't you, child—one of Ida's favorite sayings. Right now Ida considered her only niece's future secure, and her light blue eyes would surely fill up with tears when she heard how frivolously Josefa had abandoned it.

An alarm clock that rings at 4:30, and next year her son will be going to school. She has to leave the building by 5:30; her son has to get up by 6:30, has to leave by 7:30, eating breakfast alone before that. She'll ask the others how you manage it. She'll come back in the afternoon at 3:00, that's a plus, but she'll be dead tired in the evening and if she doesn't get to bed by eight or nine, she'll scream in the morning from the exertion of getting up. At first they'll smile at her in the factory: a weirdo who was at the university; but they'll get over it sooner or later. They'll find out she's a tough customer, that they can't put anything over on her, and someone in the union will put her up for office, maybe cultural chairwoman, so she can get tickets for them at the operetta. If things turn out worse than that, they'll send her to a training course and make her a delegate. But she'll fight against it. That will be the penalty: beginning today they'll have to do without her. She'll get trained, but nothing more. She'll write a letter now and then to the Supreme Council, calling to their attention omissions in the development of socialism, and no one will be able to call her to account. Dear Gentlemen, she'll write, my work is very monotonous and allows me a great deal of time to think. This is how I've come to think over why my work, as can be deduced from the sum I am paid every month, is considered so insignificant in comparison with the work of others. I assure you...Josefa got up, took a piece of stationery out of a drawer, looked for a pen, didn't find one, got the typewriter instead, sat up on her bed and placed the typewriter on her upper thigh. She rolled the paper into it without a carbon—she always typed without carbon paper, much to Luise's aggravation—and wrote: I assure you that sitting for years on end staring at parts only millimeters in size, which have to be soldered with a steady hand, is a destructive kind of work against one's own nature. I am not in physical condition to do more than that. Ditto for my co-workers. There is no doctor and no artist forced to deny his nature as we are. But the work doesn't show up favorably in the books. The same goes for other professions: cleaning lady, garbage man, street cleaner, messenger, fish seller. No job is more difficult to replace than the toilet attendant at Alexanderplatz. That stench all day long and you still talk about light work. I, untrained solderer Josefa Nadler, propose: equal pay for every type of work. The only difference is between good and bad work. There is low pay for bad work and more pay for good work, regardless of whether it's man or woman, minister or mailman. Whoever has children receives that much more. For shift workers, miners and other professions that eat up people, more

137

vacations and shorter working hours because otherwise no one will do the tasks. Dear Gentlemen, she continued, I expect the result of this to be that whoever likes to work with wood will become a carpenter and not a poet writing songs for children or first grade primers, because there would be no advantage from giving up his joy. Then he wouldn't look angrily at the poet's new house, who now lives better from his bad verses than the other does from good carpentry. And the fellow will charge a pretty penny for his enjoyment. The carpenter will build us tables that we can only dream of now. And in exchange he'll be permitted to go free of charge to visit furniture makers in Sweden to exchange ideas. The work left over will be like mine: jobs that overwhelm, have the same effect as a steam roller, crushing and deforming people. All that is spared is what is necessary to work: patience, stupidity, nimble fingers, soft cushioned flesh in the rear, which the rest of the person can sit on. Dear Gentlemen, I am aware of the technological bonds of our age, the money needed for investments and the necessity of such tasks. Therefore I propose: every citizen of his country, I stress, every, should have to put up with these conditions. One year of his life or two will be taken up with work like this for four hours a day; in the time left he can learn languages or a musical instrument in order to retain his sanity and make use of the time. I await your reply with interest. You will hear from me again as soon as I can submit new proposals. (Signed) Josefa Nadler, untrained solderer.

Josefa read the letter out loud, imagined the surprised face of the addressee and decided to send it as soon as she had been a worker for three months. Starting then, she would send a letter every month. She'd become a corresponding member of the Supreme Council. And one day she would stand up in the market place among the most frequented vegetable carts and inform the crowd about her correspondence with the Supreme Council.

Everything in Josefa's life would probably have remained the way it was if she had gotten up earlier on the morning in question and hadn't missed the mail collector: she would have gotten back her letter to the Supreme Council, assuming that the collector would have handed it back to her. Postal regulations didn't expressly allow that. Josefa assumed that the man would have been sensitive to her diabolical situation and would have handed back the envelope. The *Illustrated Weekly* would then have quickly forgotten the day-to-day controversy over her story. There was scarcely anyone who still talked about it, only Luise now and again, said it was a shame, a real shame. Rudi Goldammer's gastric ulcer was better and Strutzer had to carry a mountain of periodicals and papers back to his own room with a grim smile. Josefa wrote in a letter to Alfred Thal: "Please say hello to the anarchist for me and tell him that I can't change things." She sat as always behind her desk in the chair of black imitation leather, surrounded by the noise of the open-plan office, looked at Günter Rassow's weak back, phoned the library, phoned the factory where she wanted to do her next report, arranged photo appointments, deciphered letters to the editor, answered them. And waited. Waited every day and every hour for the answer to her letter. Every telephone call frightened her and every envelope addressed to her. When Erna, Rudi Goldammer's secretary, who had a curt and arrogant way with everyone on the editorial staff, called and informed her that the Chief wanted to talk to her, Josefa's knees trembled. On the way to Rudi's office she drank a glass of cold water in the tea kitchen because her mouth was dry as cotton and bitter to the point of choking. Rudi greeted her with a hug. He was sorry, he said, that he had only now gotten around to reading the article. Too bad that it had gone so stupidly. This Strutzer, well, he just couldn't be changed. His gastric ulcers always but always came at the wrong time. She would simply have to believe him. The matter would have turned out differently if he hadn't been sick. Rudi suffered from the mission that he had taken upon himself and Josefa suffered with him. "I know," she said. "I know if you had been there then..." Rudi walked up and down the room with small steps looking at the toes of his shoes, then remained standing in front of Josefa and looked into her eyes probably to check how seriously she took his protestations. There were red carnations on the table. "Lovely flowers," Josefa said. "Yes," Rudi said, "from Erna. Erna always brought me flowers when I was sick."

139

Rudi went to the door and Josefa got up. Rudi said: "The next time…" and patted Josefa gently on the shoulder. Josefa nodded. On the way back to the open-plan office she drank another glass of water against the bitterness in her mouth. She should have been relieved but had to fight back tears.

There was no way Josefa could have known that a few minutes after she had left Rudi's office Siegfried Strutzer received a call concerning her: "I am connecting you with the Director of the Office for Citizens' Complaints of the Supreme Council," Strutzer heard and quietly cursed Rudi Goldammer, who was certain not to be in his office again, who once again hung the task of scapegoat around his neck. Some compulsive letter writer had complained about the *Illustrated Weekly* to the Supreme Council, and who had to face the music?—him of course, Strutzer. Strutzer's mental curses were interrupted by a male voice who wanted to be sure that he was speaking with Comrade Strutzer, Party Secretary of the *Illustrated Weekly*. "Yes, fine, Director of the Office of Citizens' Complaints of the Supreme Council here," the voice said "Comrade, we have a file to handle here that has to do with you as well."

Well, now we're in for it, Strutzer thought, rankling at his life as deputy, which brought him more aggravation than recognition. Just a little while ago he had found a large, elegant envelope in the letter box on the front door, which he went through every morning while Erna brewed tea for Rudi. This, according to Strutzer's experience, would be an invitation and from an important office as well. Strutzer found Goldammer's falseness at its most revolting when he pretended that he despised this sort of invitation because he couldn't enjoy either the food or drink due to his sick stomach. But it never occurred to him, Strutzer thought with bitterness, to pass along the invitation to me.

"We are turning to you, Comrade Strutzer," the voice said into Strutzer's ear, "and not to the State Director, Comrade Goldammer, because we believe that the Party Group has to be informed, and we further believe that the Party Group must urgently deal with the views of Comrade Nadler on certain matters."

It became very quiet around Strutzer. He listened to the voice

140

as if he were under a spell, to the voice that wanted him to do something other than what he had expected. It was meant for him, Strutzer. The Comrade on the other end wasn't talking to him because he couldn't get hold of Goldammer, but because he had wanted to talk to him from the very beginning.

The dossier will be sent in the next few days, Strutzer heard, also the dubious letter by Comrade Nadler. They merely wanted to let Strutzer know in advance so that he knew why they were turning to him in the matter. The office sent a confirmation of the receipt of the letter of complaint today to its sender. She will also be sent, as the law requires, an exhaustive answer to her questions. They simply thought the Comrade's confused ideas were in need of a more thorough treatment than the Office could indulge in.

Strutzer broke in with a ''hm'', which he drew out with serious concern between the Comrade's sentences. Comrade Nadler's behavior had seemed problematic to him for quite a while, and it didn't surprise him that things had become this serious. Strutzer thanked the Comrade for his confidential information. He promised that the Party Group would consider how they could help their comrade.

He carefully put the receiver back on the hook, pulled a smooth white folder out of the top drawer of his desk, smoothed it with his hand although there were no wrinkles in it, and wrote the date on the upper right-hand corner. Strutzer wrote on the upper left-hand corner: REGARDING : J. Nadler, Info of the Dir of Off of Cit Comp of the SC. He was full of good cheer. He wouldn't talk with anyone about it before he had the letter in his hands and could thoroughly calculate every step. He didn't want to make any mistakes. This was a case where neither Goldammer nor Luise should have the opportunity to get involved before it was dealt with by the Party meeting. Strutzer noted every word that the Director of the Office of Citizens' Complaints had told him. He wanted to be able to quote him at the proper time. He pulled a blue document file out of a pile of files, checked the heading—''B. File'' written on the inside of the cardboard cover in small letters—and he laid the white folder on which he had just been writing alongside the one that had already been filed. It was only then that Strutzer felt the burning pressure in his stomach, looked at the wall clock—it was four minutes to twelve—and went to eat.

The next day Jauer came back to the editor's office for the first time. Monday morning he sat at Luise's small conference table surrounded by Günter Rassow, Luise, Hans Schütz and Eva Sommer, who looked at him with open curiosity. Eva Sommer ran her fingers through Jauer's hair and said with her smoky voice: "You look good, boy, really." Jauer told how in order to get better he had to fish a ring out of a pot filled with flour with his teeth, while the other members of his group sat around him and laughed because, of course, he looked very funny. But the others, of course, looked funny too when they rummaged in the flour pot with their teeth. This way everyone had a laugh at everyone else, not nasty laughter, but a liberating laughter. Josefa felt uncomfortable at the thought of the patients full of flour. Why didn't they simply have you play blindman's buff, she asked. She hated the game, the blind anguish when you stumbled and were pushed, without knowing where you were going or coming from, the shame when the others who didn't have any scarf tied around their eyes, those standing around in the circle, laughed when she fell down.

"And that helped you?" she asked.

"As you can see," Jauer said. His voice seemed defensive. But that was only a tiny part of the therapy; there were group discussions and individual discussions, but most of all complete seclusion from everything that surrounded you. No contact with the office, the doctor said. As he said it Jauer looked with reproachful pride from one to the next until his glance came to rest on Luise.

"Well all right," Luise said, "nice that you're back again." She popped a piece of licorice into her mouth. Hans Schütz had put his black leather pipe case on the table and proceeded to clean one pipe after the other. He pushed the wire wound with pile threads through the opening in the mouthpiece, screwed the mouthpiece back into the bowl, blew into it again to get rid of the last bits of impurity, had a long look at the noble bend for the hundredth or thousandth time and put them back into the case with

142

cultic tranquility.

"So tell me: and you can really sleep again?" he asked Jauer with distinct scepticism.

Jauer smiled: "Yeah, sure."

There were some really amazing stories, Günter Rassow said. A boyhood friend of his had suddenly begun to limp after puberty for no reason at all. They diagnosed it as muscular dystrophy: incurable. To make a long story short—it was, until the boy went to a psychiatrist who discovered an Oedipus complex. Rassow's friend's mother often complained about the boy's lazy gait and his bad posture during the time in question. As a result the boy, who according to Rassow had an extraordinarily sensitive personality, became highly introverted, and that was the decisive impulse for his illness: he was unconsciously looking for an objective reason for his gait in order to elude his mother's admonitions. The doctor advised the boy to stop resisting his mother's love and concern.

"And did it help?" Eva Sommer asked.

He actually stopped limping, Rassow said. Of course, peculiar changes took place in his body at the same time. Rassow found it unpleasant to describe the process in detail, his voice grated under the effort it cost him to find a harmless way to put it. "You could observe a certain regression in him, not visible, but fraught with grave consequences all the same. Even his voice temporarily sounded clear and childlike again." Rassow cleared his throat and ended his account with a deep "Yes."

Eva Sommer laughed. "Better than limping."

"Who knows," Hans Schütz said.

Josefa looked into the others' faces in order to see if everyone was thinking what she was, that is, that Rassow himself could have been that extraordinarily sensitive boyhood friend. Hans Schütz concentrated on the enjoyment of his pipe, which he had finally cleaned and held filled between his teeth. Luise, who didn't know anything about psychiatry and similar psychic mumbo jumbo to begin with, chewed her licorice. Only Eva Sommer followed Rassow's story spellbound.

"Jauer definitely got his Oedipus complex from Luise," Josefa said.

Jauer blushed. "You really ought to take it more seriously," he said, and his voice trembled. In any case he felt as good now as he had ever felt in his life. He didn't want to ruin that with silly gossip and he didn't see any cause for jokes, which were simply proof of ignorance.

Josefa was dumbfounded. She had directed the remark more at Luise than at Jauer. She had missed him often during the last weeks and it was only the strict prohibition by his doctor that had kept her from visiting him. She muttered an apology and Jauer, who must also have felt that his violent temper was excessive, blurted out something like "all right". Hans Schütz was the first one to break the uneasy silence. "You've gotten fatter," he said after taking a good look at Jauer. Josefa had also noticed that Jauer's face was changed. The concave arches had filled out, which gave his face a uniformly oval appearance. The yellowish skin tone and the pale pink spots from his illness were gone. His skin was clearer; his cheeks were evenly flushed. But most noticeable of all was the different expression in his eyes, which Josefa couldn't quite describe, though she could no longer find the chronic casualty, the person hurt for life in him.

When Jauer brushed the hair from his forehead, she noticed a pale red line running obliquely across his brow and ending left and right in his hair line. Josefa couldn't remember the red line on Jauer's forehead. She didn't know whether she simply hadn't noticed it before or whether he hadn't had it. A fine red groove like the imprint of the edge of a coin or like a scratch or a scar, an unusually intricate scar. Perhaps a wound from childhood, Josefa thought, a fall off a scooter or down the basement stairs. The red line must have always run across Jauer's forehead, and she just hadn't noticed it before.

"I don't smoke anymore," Jauer said.

It suddenly seemed to Josefa that Jauer's voice had changed, as though the vocal cords had finally become his own. Generally speaking, Josefa noted, Jauer no longer gave the impression of being incomplete. She explained Jauer's changes to herself by the illness he had just gotten over and the isolation he had been in for three months. Three days later, he replaced his old yellow leather jacket with the sweat band on the collar, which his mother had given him ten or more years ago, with a doeskin jacket, underneath which he wore a bright shirt with a colorful matching tie. Even then, Josefa didn't imagine how deep Jauer's metamorphosis had gone. She would find that out only later when the letter from the Supreme Council to Strutzer had long since been delivered by a messenger and when "this outrageous arrogance on Comrade Nadler's part," as Strutzer called the affair, was the only item on the agenda at the Party meeting.

Josefa took the receiver off the hook after it had rung the third time, although she had placed the telephone right next to her bed. No one was supposed to think that she was sitting next to the phone waiting for someone to miss her.

"Why aren't you at the office?" Christian asked. "Are you sick?"

"No."

"What else?"

"Nothing."

"I think your hearing is today."

"Yes."

"Good heavens, go on and say something, won't you. Something happened?"

"Nothing's happened. I'm not going."

Silence.

"Josefa, look, something must have happened…"

"No."

Silence.

"Should I come to see you?"

"No."

Silence.

Josefa pushed down the white plastic parts into the black telephone housing with two fingers; only then did she put down the receiver. Drank a sip of red wine to swallow the choking pressure in her throat. Pulled the pillow over her face as if there were someone nearby to hear how loud and uncontrollably she was crying.

She had been awaiting this call for a week. Since the painful Wednesday when she had seen Christian for the last time. She had wanted to call him herself every day or simply to go to him, ring the doorbell as she had done two months or 1977 years ago. She wanted to make up for the mistakes of the last weeks every day since the Wednesday he had gone, when she had kept silent for two hours. And now it was too late. Or it was already too late on Wednesday, when it seemed to her that they were sitting in a train speeding irresistibly to where the tracks end. The end as only goal. The train ran on and on. They wouldn't be able to get off until it was up to its head in sand. To wait for the catastrophe, and every attempt to apply the emergency brake speeded up the tempo. She had been pondering for a week what had happened to make them sit across from each other, mute.

She had remembered having watched scenes day in and day out that she had taken part in and she was now their bewildered audience. Why hadn't she understood anything? She heard sentences that she had spoken, understood them in hindsight, heard Christian's sentences, which she had not heard and yet had been spoken. She had heard, heard and not noticed, hadn't translated them into experience. She found the same consistency in what had happened to them and in what had ended in the two hours of silence on Wednesday that had determined everything and everyone during the last weeks.

Christian suffered from Josefa's fits of depression, for which he couldn't find any adequate explanation. Even though he understood her agitation at the setbacks that were inevitably waiting for her, he nonetheless was bothered by the fear, almost panic, with which she faced events. Her letter to the Supreme Council was simply ridiculous. Josefa's naiveté, often bordering on infantile unpredictability, used to amuse or aggravate him, depending on the degree of ignorance he saw in it. Fine, you didn't need to be particularly sensitive to be shaken by a town like B.—Josefa was sensitive. And he had understood her when she had told him horror stories, screaming between spoonfuls of goulash soup, as if she had just taken a tour of hell. But this letter was childish. "Simply say you're sorry," he advised her, when Josefa showed him the invitation to the Party meeting and told him about the letter for the first time. "Say you know the letter is idiotic, say you were drunk or had a fever. And everything will be all right."

Josefa had moved her chair to the stove, warmed her back and hands on the hot tile stove and shivered. "Why is the letter idiotic? It's all true, though." She tore off bits of skin from her lower lip with her teeth.

Christian groaned: "But you can't just let a whole government know in writing that you think they are stupid."

Josefa looked at him in despair. "But I simply wrote about what I saw and what they may not have seen. Why won't you understand me?"

"Josefa," Christian scanned the syllables of her name like a starting command, "there are certain conventions, norms in human social life, which a grownup considers normal. You can like them, you can also not like them, but you do have to recognize them if you want to accomplish anything at all. Do you seriously think that anyone needs your letter to find out what B. looks like? You can really smell it quite a long way off..."

Josefa bitterly pursed her mouth. "Spare me the speech," she said, "I don't understand it anyway."

"Why don't you understand? When you want to catch a fish you use a fishing road, not a blowgun. It's the means, that's all."

"You act as if I'd thrown a bomb." She wiped the back of her hand across her bitten lower lip. She was bleeding. Christian was silent. He felt sorry for her. She really did not understand. She didn't grasp the fact that there were rules of the game. Just as she had ignored all terminology since they had known each other. She thought up her own according to her mood and was indignant as soon as he corrected her. If he was able to correct her, she said, he had obviously understood her correctly. As a result, his translation into precise technical language was superfluous.

"OK," he said, "then you have to do what you think is right. Then you have to bombard people with crazy letters. But then don't tremble with fear after the fact. If you yourself consider that a reasonable kind of discussion, you'll be able to explain that to them as well."

147

Josefa cringed and pulled in her head. "Cut it out with this logic of yours," she pleaded, "I just don't understand it. I wrote a letter. So what. You can throw a letter away if you don't like it. Nothing happened. But even you get worked up about it. I think that I'm afraid simply because I can't get anything right. And this Strutzer is always around. I talk with the Comrade-in-charge, I write a letter to the Supreme Council, and I always end up with Strutzer sitting at one end of the table and me at the other."

Christian sat down next to her against the stove. Josefa felt his shoulders and his arms, imagined that they could exchange feelings like current this way. She would direct some of her fear into Christian, draw a few amperes of composure in exchange.

"Do you want to quit?" Christian asked.

"No."

"Then straighten things out with the letter. At least listen to their censure without contradicting; say at the end that you understand," he said, and quoted one of his favorite sayings: "It isn't important to be right, but to remain right."

She had felt powerless against this saying as long as she had known him. She couldn't calculate answers, reactions, phone calls like the ingredients for a soup. She didn't know in advance what Strutzer would do next, and what she would have to do after that. "I'll try," she said. And then she thought again as she had that evening at Brommel's country house, that her divided self was easier to bear as long as she could remain who she was with Christian. The mere thought that they might part again one day threatened her existence.

The meeting of the Party leadership was set for Monday. All the collaborators of the *Illustrated Weekly* had already been informed of Josefa's strange behavior Monday morning, although the members of the leadership, whom Strutzer had informed at a brief gathering, were pledged to strictest silence. When Josefa opened the door to Luise's room, Luise sat up in her imitation leather chair, put the teapot back on the table, said: "Would you look at her," shook her head, pursed her lips and said: "Shut the door." Picked up the teapot again, said: "You could hardly have thought of anything stupider.''

"No," Josefa said, remained standing, thought about whether she should say something, remained silent.

Luise took a deep breath. "So you know..." she began, stopped talking, struck her forehead three times with the flat of her hand. She took great pleasure in this gesture, which apparently expressed everything she wanted to say. She leafed through the newspaper and read. Or she didn't read, to guess from the nervous movement of her eyelids. Josefa quietly left the room, met Ulrike Kuwiak in the white hallway, who greeted her rather sternly. Günter Rassow was standing at Josefa's desk and waved excitedly to her with the receiver of her phone. "The chief," he whispered and smiled sympathetically.

"Why'd you run away? Come on back," Luise said and hung up.

Luise did not belong to the leadership. During the last election Strutzer had told those assembled that she had asked not to run for office again due to her poor health. He regretted deeply, he assured them, and he went on to thank her, and he would miss her... He presented Luise with twenty red carnations Erna had bought and reached for Luise's limp hand with his fat white fingers. The truth was that Luise had put drops for her circulation in her teacup after every leadership meeting because she had argued herself into exhaustion with Strutzer or had gotten mad at him.

"Listen, you can't expect much good to come out of it," Luise said. She counted the seven members of the leadership committee on her fingers: the likely no votes on the right hand, the likely yes votes on her left. The five fingers of her right hand weren't enough; on the left you could only see her index finger. Hans Schütz. But only if you get lucky. If you have bad luck he'll just chew around on his pipe and won't say a thing."

"And Günter?" Josefa asked.

Luise shook her head. "I've talked to him," she said, "unless he gets a choleric fit and cuts loose without rhyme or reason, he'll raise his hand like a good boy. Besides which your letter goes against his sense of order. So he even has a defense."

Josefa watched how Luise's pointy nose chopped holes in the air. For the first time she wasn't grateful to Luise for her accounting

149

talents, for her practical business sense by which she weighed relative strengths like green herring, computed answers like prices carefully calculated according to the principles of supply and demand. It also seemed to her for the first time that these methods were utterly inadequate in her case. The last weeks had reduced her plans and goals to a minimum: she wanted to be understood properly. What good were Luise's tare, gross and net computations in all this? Sentence in this package is light, sentence in that package is heavy, same sentence in a letter envelope weighs the most. She wanted to be properly understood, nothing more. This intention alone forbade her every strategy. Even the attempt to limit herself to half truths would mean abandoning her goal, giving up success from the very start.

Luise was still calculating, although she had already anticipated the result. She said the very least would be not to contradict, to listen to the reproaches and show at least a trace of regret. Josefa had already promised that to Christian.

A few hours later, in the afternoon dusk of early spring, surrounded by three members of the leadership committee on either side of the table, sat Strutzer, who had shown Josefa the unoccupied seat at the other end of the table, and who then had sat down at the forward side opposite. Josefa was certain that she had already heard every word that was spoken and that she knew in detail how the hearing would continue.

Strutzer read the letter out loud. He indicated sentences he considered especially troublesome with an ironic voice and ensuing pauses, while he looked knowingly at the members of the committee and encouraged them to react with an assenting smile. "...now and then it seems to me that the silence surrounding you, the motorcycles riding in front of you, the busy preparations for your visits, the false reports, prevent you from seeing things as they are," Strutzer read. With every syllable a tap of his pencil. Ulrike Kuwiak hissed that it was really impertinent, Elli Meseke looked reproachfully at Josefa and said: "But, girl, how could you ever say such a thing?" Strutzer continued reading. It must be two letters, Josefa thought. She had written a letter, had typed the address on the envelope, had placed it in the yellow box, but a different letter had reached the addressee. Mail boxes, mailbags, sortings, receipt boxes, bureaucrats' eyes and bureaucrats' brains had transformed her letter into a cynical insult. Puzzling metamorphosis of language along the way from her apartment to the Ministry, through the Ministry into Strutzer's white fingers, into Strutzer's mouth, into Josefa's ears, no longer recognizable as her words: cynical, vain. She hadn't written that, not that way.

"May I read the letter myself?" she asked.

"Please do," Strutzer's red mouth smiled. He handed the letter to Elli Meseke, who passed it to Ulrike Kuwiak with a reluctant glance at the paper as if it were a disgusting animal the sight of which she feared but which she wanted to look at all the same. Ulrike Kuwiak pushed the letter over to Josefa. No doubt: this was her letter. The paper, the dislocated small-case *s*, which always struck a millimeter too high on her typewriter. The paper trembled slightly in her hands, she put it on the table, repeated the sentence where she had interrupted Strutzer: "...now and then it seems to me that the silence surrounding you, the motorcycles riding in front of you, the busy preparations for your visits, the false reports, prevent you from seeing things as they are." She read quietly, breathlessly, without emphasizing one word more than another, scarcely paying attention to periods and commas. This way her sentences sounded familiar again, she recognized the thought that had gone into them. She threw a quick glance at the faces of the others. On the right, Hans Schütz smiled with the corner of his mouth turned towards Josefa. Günter Rassow held his head bowed, his face covered with his hands, which he held at his temples like blinders. The faces of the rest were unchanged between sympathy and demonstrative imcomprehension. "Since I find it impossible," Josefa went on reading, "to fulfil my professional duty and to inform the public about urgently needed changes, I had to choose this way to inform you about conditions in B. I ask you to reexamine operations and to change your decision." And although she recognized the language as the one she used every day, it was reflected back to her as a foreign tongue by the chalky walls and the perplexed faces. She heard the words with the others' ears, went through their thoughts and felt like a blow the presumption hidden in the letter that surfaced as soon as it struck obedient souls. Now that she was finally sender and addressee in one person, she comprehended the second life of her letter. The improper, arrogant, indeed dangerous and intolerable presumption of the writer confronted her and drove out her better knowledge of her own intentions.

"Shall we listen to what Comrade Nadler has to say to us herself about her letter," Strutzer said.

The sighs of relief by the others were more visible than audible; the tension disappeared from their backs and shoulders; hands and pens relaxed. Josefa was hot. And if they were all right, well what if a letter like this was really subversive? Had she perhaps given herself a role she had no right to? Hadn't she declared that she knew more about B. than all the institutions and all the comrades-in-charge? She stared at the letter lying in front of her. "Dear Comrades," the letters ran into each other, "Dearades" was what trembled in front of her eyes: tears, don't lift up your head. Swallow.

"Please, Josefa, you have the floor," Strutzer said.

Josefa tried to open her mouth. Her lips stuck firmly together, wouldn't let go of each other. At least say that she hadn't meant it that way. Stick her tongue between her lips until they opened. Her tongue was swollen and dry. Her mouth was paralyzed. Speechless. "I have to conclude from Comrade Nadler's silence that she has nothing to tell us," Strutzer said, regretfully. "Then I would now like to ask for the comrades to ask to speak."

She knew this. It had already been like this once before. Also between chalk-white walls. But there had been another color then. Green. Green cloths that they had covered her with like flags over the coffin at a state funeral. And a voice full of practised compassion: "Don't be afraid, nothing serious, even our doorman performs this nowadays." Not serious. All the same leather bonds on her wrists, the black rubber mask over mouth and nose: "Take a deep breath, this is oxygen." Injection in the left arm. Last thought: I'm not going to wake up again. Soon, soon the great pain. She tries to groan. Exerts herself. No sound. Her eyes open. Only a millimeter. Only one eye. No good. Nothing works. No fingers. Pain coming soon. And me a living corpse. Speechless. Motionless. Dissected fully conscious. Turned off like a washing machine. Knows what's going to happen to her. Knows what she'd have to do to save herself. Can only know. Dead. But not dead. Condemned to endure. She belongs to them. To them with the knives. Then a male voice: "She's still wide awake, let's give her another 150 cc's." Then nothing more. They explained to her later that her muscles were paralyzed during the operation. Her muscles had still reacted, they had observed that: "You've too active, you still feel."

Elli Meseke raised her hand, forearm up with her index finger pointed straight. She had only one question for Josefa: why didn't she come to them with her problems, to her comrades?

The others sighed in relief. Josefa had the floor. Why didn't she come? Why not? But she did want to talk to them. She had written everything down about B. for them. Strutzer had read it. Rudi, the Comrade-in-charge. But they knew that. Why did the fat woman ask that?

A twitch ran across Günter Rassow's thin back, ran into his arm, which he slowly raised; odd that it doesn't creak, moving stubbornly like a rusty hinge. But it doesn't creak. His arm doesn't either. He is concerned with another question. What, another question? Why don't they notice that she just can't think of any answers? A question, Günter said, that seems more serious to him. "How could it happen that a comrade we see every day, who works with us, nursed cares and problems that finally drove her to this act of despair, without us ever knowing about it? And I ask you, how is it possible that Josefa could be this far gone? What have we neglected?"

Thank heavens he hadn't asked her that. But he was crazy. Act of despair. As if she had actually thrown a bomb. Or committed a murder. Günter winked at her. Josefa didn't understand. Or did he think that he had just helped her? He hadn't asked her a question, nothing more. She would have to say something. No act of despair, civil rights, right of appeal and all that. But her mouth was stuck together. Her tongue was stuck fast to her palate. That's why people in movies always drink water when they get excited.

But there was no water here and she couldn't ask for it. They'd think she was putting on an act. Strutzer had now brought a wavering Günter over to his position. Picked up his pencil, took a deep breath. As much as he valued Comrade Rassow's self-critical attitude, there was, however, no reason for him to reproach himself in this matter. He himself had had long and intensive discussions with Comrade Nadler. Even the Comrade-in-charge had tried. But the Comrade had shown that she wouldn't listen to reason. And in addition, the Comrade-in-charge had also noted her distasteful arrogance.

So that, too. She had almost forgotten about that. Her blind confidence in the Comrade-in-charge. So he had passed on her complaints against Strutzer after all. Or Strutzer was lying. Josefa looked for the offense on Strutzer's face. Only the royal smile playing around his curved mouth. The eyes hidden behind tinted glasses. She had said fat jellyfish. Josefa didn't believe that the Comrade-in-charge had repeated words like these. But he could have informed Strutzer about his general impression of her. Arrogant then, well all right.

Strutzer remained silent. Waited and looked around the table, avoiding the direction of Hans Schütz. Schütz wouldn't have suited him as next speaker. Josefa looked out the wide window front at the sky, at white and grey mountains of clouds, which then just as unhurriedly dissolved again. A cold sky unwarmed by any earthly bonds, no branches, no rooftops climbed to these heights that Josefa's eyes reached. Flowed endlessly past her, like the ones before, like the next ones. Was simply there. Simply there. The thought spread through her, warm and unexpected, suddenly, as if she hadn't known it all along. Or had to know it all the same. The indivisible sky, no, it was divisible, sovereign territory, the word existed but the clouds flew against air traffic regulations obeying only the wind. That remained. It seemed to her that no one sitting at the long angular table except her knew that the clouds went by or where they had to go. It was as though the sky was coming through the window for her alone at this moment. What could interest Strutzer about the sky, although Strutzer called himself a nature lover. He raised tulips in a small flowerbed in

154

front of his building. Flaming tulips, violet tulips brought back from a business trip; Dutch bulbs that he had shown to some connoisseurs at the *Illustrated Weekly*. During tulip blossom time, Strutzer put an especially beautiful specimen of his breeding every so often on his desk and told everyone who saw it that he was the one who had brought it about. But Strutzer's tulip season had been destroyed last year. Wild rabbits had discovered his tulips and every morning when he came to look at them, he found a few stems without flowers. Strutzer lay in wait with a shotgun. But the rabbits, hardened city rabbits, always got there after Strutzer, tired and full of hope that his tulips would be spared that night, had gone to bed. For days on end Strutzer went careworn and irascible through the editorial office. One weekend he decided to stand watch the whole night. The rabbits came in the early dawn. Strutzer shot. In spite of his military training he wasn't a good shot. But most of all, Strutzer said later on, the visibility that morning was poor due to the dampness and haze. Strutzer hit the rabbit but didn't kill it. After it was hit it fled into the bushes where it died slowly. The rabbit cried. Strutzer, satisfied with his just retribution, went to sleep. The other tenants were waked up early this Sunday by the animal's cries. No one in the apartment building except Strutzer owned a weapon with which they could have finished off the rabbit, and Strutzer was asleep. The following Monday he complained to Luise, to whom he had given three of his tulips and who he knew planted herbs in her garden, about his neighbors who refused to say hello after that.

Strutzer wasn't interested in clouds.

Josefa couldn't stop looking through the wavy glass, and she wished that all the black clouds in the world would come together inside this rectangular room and explode into a rainstorm for five or six minutes. That was all she needed. Thunder, pouring rain, lightning bolts, all in one, so that the window panes groaned, the earthquake-proof walls shook, that words and screams were swallowed up by the terrible thunderclaps. Everyone looks up at the sky and the streets; nothing to be seen. All they can do is have presentiments like people gripped by panic, whipped by the rain in the entrances to buildings, standing like abandoned cars on a flooded roadway, in the raging storm teeming with sirens. They are thinking—oh, dear God, help, and words like *heavenly hosts* and *Flood*. Strutzer secretly folds his hands; Ulrike Kuwiak screams, Josefa isn't afraid, she knows that the clouds are merely protesting against a lack of respect by man, against his forgetfulness and his pettiness. And then: calm. The clouds draw away quietly laughing to the eight directions they've come from and behind them the sun is waiting. Everyone looks up again at the sky, stunned and pensive. They've forgotten Josefa and her letter.

Strutzer's clipped shout tore Josefa from her vision. "Not only don't you have anything to say to us, but you don't listen either. All of us here have better things to do than to deal with you." Strutzer's mouth tensed up into sharp wrinkles as he spoke. He propped himself up on the table with his hands as if he had to hold on, his pencil lay obliquely on his writing paper. Josefa started, opened her mouth, closed it again without saying anything. Slowly blood began to rush into her head, quietly began to roar in her ears and behind her forehead.

"I'll recapitulate once more for Comrade Nalder what Gerhard Wenzel said: the Comrade-in-charge isn't the only one who has noticed your arrogance. Even Gerhard, who hasn't been with us very long, has often been puzzled by your unreasonableness, what he calls autocratic behavior. You were also talking about her work discipline, weren't you, Gerhard?"

Gerhard Wenzel nodded. The deep wrinkles, which divided his brow into three oblique bulges and always lent Wenzel's face an expression of extraordinary tension, came even closer together. "Quite right, comrades. I certainly don't want to cast aspersions on anyone here, but in the house journal we couldn't have done that, coming in an hour late every morning or leaving an hour early. The colleagues in the lobby watched us like hawks. Would have been unfair to the others, too. Something else: it says in the letter, if I understand right, that the worker in B. was supposed to write this letter—can't remember the name just now—but you know already that he's dead now. So I don't know. You can take it from me, I know the workers, I was in a factory for four years, but a worker would never have said something as autocratic as that,

156

much less without his collective."

"It's curious, Josefa," Elli Meseke said. "You write so many good things about workers. Didn't you ever stop and think that you might be able to learn a few things from them? Discipline, for example? Or modesty?"

The roar in Josefa's ears was growing louder. The sky, unaffected by her desires, had turned into a dark, pleasant evening. Günter Rassow stood up quietly and turned on a light, which twisted blue-white in the neon tube before it shattered the last gentleness left in the meeting with its garish and merciless brilliance. "Wouldn't it be advisable after all," he said, "to talk about the point under discussion? Surely Josefa wasn't summoned here for lack of work discipline, but on account of a letter that I have to admit is rather naive..."

"Well, I understand something completely different by naive," Ulrike Kuwiak said.

"It doesn't have to mean anything. In my eyes the letter is proof of naiveté rather than malice."

"Maybe then you should tell us, Hans, what you mean by naiveté," Elli Meseke said and smiled forgivingly.

Hans Schütz took the pipe out of his mouth for the first time since he had been taking part in the discussion and sat up straight. "By naiveté I mean precisely what the word means in Meyer's *Lexikon*, but I would be willing to define it again for a few people should that be necessary..."

Strutzer tapped loudly with his pencil on the table top. "Comrades, I really must ask you to stop quarreling. Our time is precious, think of Lenin, economy of time. The matter is too serious for such a spat. So please, back to the subject."

Elli Meseke signalled Strutzer that she had something to say. Strutzer let her have the floor.

Elli smoothed her rosy face with a sigh and folded her hands. "Yes, comrades, what's the best way to put it. I think that the letter does concern Josefa's attitude towards her colleagues and towards discipline. Now, whether we call it autocratic like Gerhard or arrogance like the Comrade-in-charge, it's the same thing in the end that gives us pause. And if we want to help Josefa, and that, after all, is why we are sitting here, we can't get around this question. You know, Josefa, please don't take what I'm about to say personally, it's meant as constructive criticism. But when I see you rushing through the hallway half an hour after work begins in the morning with boots and cape and your head held high, I often ask myself: "Come, come, wherever does that girl get all that confidence?"

"Right," Ulrike Kuwiak said and giggled quietly. Gerhard Wenzel gave a satisfied nod. "The description hits the nail right on the head, as they say," he said. The secretary of the Letters to the Editor department, who never said anything, sat pale and thin in her chair and smiled. Then she hesitantly raised her arm.

"I, too, think that Comrade Nadler ought to think over the charges made here. For example, her relations with the technical personnel. I wrote three letters for her a while ago while I was very busy, although, as everybody knows, I'm not responsible for the national politics department. But I've never gotten a word of thanks. This may be just a quibble, but I don't think it's right."

Up until this point in the deliberations Josefa remembered every word exactly; she could reconstruct every gesture, voice and intonation as if she had heard them from a tape recorder. Her brain recorded everything after that as a mere confusion of stimuli that stood out hard and sharp from the roaring that swallowed the rest of what happened. She remembered talking. Hans Schütz later told her that she had made a calm, almost cool impression at the beginning. She reacted with unexpected humility to the accusations, Hans Schütz said, to an extent that he had thought that the whole business might still turn out all right. But then, and he didn't want to believe his own ears, she had tried to explain how the letter had come into being, speaking the whole time with a somnolent calm: the black limousine, the dead bird, the quiet—it was spooky, he said.

Josefa remembered Strutzer. He had leaned back in his chair and listened to her in a victor's pose. And, although Josefa couldn't see his feet, she remembered seeing all of Strutzer sitting up straight with his left arm on the armrest of the chair, more ornament than support, his right hand on his upper thigh, his left foot placed slightly forward: King Strutzer in his pose as ruler. Then the sentence that Josefa didn't know whether she had understood correctly or whether she knew it only from Hans Schütz' account: "Comrade Nadler has just given us her own best proof of her pathological overestimation of herself."

She remembered the mad commotion she couldn't control; it got hold of her; her body lost all sensation and all resistance. She stood on the edge of the abyss. Half a meter separated her from the sharp drop between earth and the imponderable thing into which she threatened to fall if she didn't defend herself from the creatures leaping around her, striking her with long, pointed lances on legs, breasts and stomach, and she, blindly trying to drive them off her crag where she belonged despite everything. She was grateful to her body for having given up its right to feel and suffer so that she could throw herself against the lances with wild shrieks to scare off her pursuers. There were too many for Josefa to weigh her blows. She turned on her own axis and swung her right to exist like a club, to exist on this crag, stunned her attackers with the force of her blows and fled, wounded and limping, into a cave on the edge of the cliff that could be reached only by the steep wall, unattainable for those who shrink back in horror from the sight of the depths.

Three weeks later the imponderable had lost its terrors for Josefa. It had lost its inscrutability, lodged between roof and floor and dizzy with the calm that had held her for a few days. All became comprehensible, possible, emanating from the thought of escaping from the availability she had lived with since childhood. She could now turn away from all the plans others had for her. There was the suspicion, which was more like a hope, that this would be the way to kill her restlessness, which had condemned all her actions to be wrong; and the prospect that she could then finally find out by herself what was the essential thing she was looking for, which she and only she had to do in the years she had left to live. These thoughts cheered her. Josefa understood then for the first time what people meant when they talked about their private lives. She hadn't understood until then where the mysterious boundary between a private and another life was supposed to run, where the one began or ended, which life was nobody's concern and no one talked about. My husband, your wife, my business, your affair, a particular sort of life that only possessive pronouns could describe: Private Property, No Trespassing, Beware of Dog. Josefa had been unable to see her marriage or her child as something divisible from her life with Luise or Hodriwitzka or Strutzer.

She began then to understand the double life of others, wanted it herself in order to separate carefully the life she chose from the one that was forced on her. When she walked up the stairs to her apartment in the evening, her child in one hand, shopping net in the other, she felt that she had achieved her goal for the day. She had been on the hunt from the morning onwards for these last hours before going to sleep. Now she brought her plunder into her cave in which she and her boy were safe from unwelcome intruders. This is the reason she had answered pointless letters to the editor, put up with having to look at Günter Rassow's thin back, let Strutzer's triumphant smile roll off her back defenseless. What began now belonged to her alone, remained unattainable to all the Strutzers. If she wanted to she could paint all the walls of her apartment black or red or lilac. She could walk all day long on all fours and bark like a dog. She could be vulgar and yell abuse about anyone who just happened to pop into her head. It was nobody's business and she didn't have to talk about it. She was surprised and amused when she took note of the fact that the endlessly derided sayings "Small but mine" and "My home is my castle" began to make sense to her, and she didn't try to prevent it.

Some days the three of them ate supper together. Josefa brewed tea, put candles on the table, passed out napkins—something new in her housekeeping that Christian noted with mockery. She talked less about the *Illustrated Weekly*, generally avoided subjects she feared could create tensions or simply uneasiness. Christian had accepted her sudden change with as much relief as puzzlement. He was happy not to have to examine every sentence by Strutzer inside and out until he was revealed in his utter insidiousness, which probably existed only in Josefa's imagination, especially since the thought depressed Christian that he was in part to blame for Josefa's situation. All the same, the tip to write two texts on one subject had come from him. He was happy at the prospect of less excited days in which he could take care of his own work, which he had been neglecting. Josefa made a balanced, almost happy impression on him, even if her calm sometimes seemed suspicious. He suppressed the thought that this serenity could be feigned, because as long as he had known Josefa she had been uncontrolled and hot-tempered, so she would be more likely to tear Strutzer apart in infinite variations while he slept next to his fat wife than to munch quietly in her chair while waiting for the detective series to come on.

He often felt her caress or gently kiss him while he was half-asleep at night, but he was too tired to wake up again or to stretch his arm out to her. The lust that had kept them awake into the morning hours during the first weeks was sated. So was the fear gone that there would be no night to follow this one. Josefa lay alone with her dreams, bloodthirsty fantasies played out by horrible ghouls and devils that tortured her and kept at it when she opened her eyes and looked out into the empty lantern light behind the windows. Then she wanted to hold on to Christian, his warm skin, his rising and falling breast, a living being next to her. Sooner or later she would fall asleep.

In the morning when they had breakfast together she told him her dreams, not all of them, just the important ones. She remembered an especially frightening dream quite clearly. She had waked up sometime between night and dawn, long before she had to get up. There was only a streetcar, which rattled noisily as it sped untrammeled through the stillness, and Josefa thought that she could tell it was empty by the sound it produced. She went into the kitchen, drank ice-cold soda water, thought about what she wanted to eat, took two bites from a sour pickle and went back to bed. Christian was fast asleep with his face to the wall. Josefa leaned her head against his back. He moved away from her without waking up. Josefa turned over on her other side so that they lay back to back. Maybe she could fall asleep in this position. When she closed her eyes she saw two people in a room: a man and a woman, who looked like people she knew, although Josefa couldn't remember ever having seen them. The man and woman looked past each other across a bare table.

I want to go to the ocean, the woman said, I believe in the superhumanly large, in the unseen, I believe in the ocean.

It is too late, the man said, we have to go.

Yes, the woman said.

The white light of the lamp hanging above their heads blinded the man. He smashed the lamp with his bare hands.

I can't see you any more, the woman said. There was fear in the woman's voice.

The man stood up. He had only one leg. He hopped on the one leg to the window, got the candle and put it on the table. I don't have any matches, he said.

Use the flints.

The man hopped to the oven, picked up the flints and made fire. The candle light fell across the woman's eyes. Her eyes looked as if they would burn.

Why don't you come along, the woman said.

The man sat stiffly in his chair. He did not look at the woman. I can't go that far, he said.

Because you're too lazy. And too cowardly. Because you're too lazy and too cowardly. The woman had screamed.

The man pulled in his head at the woman's shrill voice. His mouth was twisted as if he wanted to speak, but nothing came out except a suppressed rattling in his throat.

The candle flame rose up to the ceiling. The man leaped out on his leg into the corner of the room and croaked roughly: You want to kill me.

The woman took a glass out of the cupboard, filled it with water and took it to the man in the corner. That isn't me, it's the wind. It's blowing from the ocean today.

The man trembled. He couldn't hold his glass. The woman brought it to his mouth.

The man drank hastily, the water glugged loudly down his throat. Don't gulp so loud, the woman said, that's disgusting. She took the water away from the man's mouth.

Don't go away, the man said.

No, the woman said.

162

Take off your clothes, the man said, jumping into bed. The woman got undressed. A red mark shone on her round stomach.

Are you pregnant? the man said.

Yes, she said, it will be a special child, this is the mark.

She lay down on the bed. Be careful, she said, or you'll break it.

The man lay down next to the woman. The woman stroked the man's red scarred leg stump.

I don't want to, she said.

The man hit the woman in the face with his fist. Blood flowed from her eyes.

I should have gone after all, she said. The woman felt her way to the faucet and washed her face carefully with a wet towel. She groaned.

The man sat up on the bed and cried. He had pulled the bedspread over his stump. You can't forget that, can you, he said.

No, I can't look at it any more. I can't see anything any more.

The man laughed insanely. She can't look at it any more, he screamed, jumped up at the woman, picked her up in his arms and jumped back into bed with her. She can't look at it any more, he gasped. She can't look at it any more.

The woman lay still on the bed. The man pulled apart her legs. Here's your ocean, the man screamed, pushing himself deep into her. The woman groaned. The man made love to her. He turned her over on her back, on her stomach, on her side. The bedcovers were red with the blood from the woman's eyes. Then the man got off her. Without looking at her, he asked: was it good? The woman didn't answer. The man grabbed hold of her with his heavy hands. She was dead.

Christian hadn't gotten enough sleep that night and was in a bad mood. He had already complained the last few days that he couldn't sleep with her for long in one bed because he felt afterwards as if he had been broken on the wheel and cut to pieces. Besides, he would get rheumatism if he spent many more nights next to the cold wall under a drafty window. Josefa suggested they change places. She was used to sleeping by the wall. Christian paced nervously up and down the room, felt along book shelves, couch and table looking for his glasses. "Your apartment is also much too small for three,'' he said, 'I don't come here to work, don't read any more. Just the newspaper. It'll do for that. Haven't you seen my glasses?''

Josefa pulled her feet up on to the chair as if she would bother his search less that way. No, she hadn't seen his glasses. Christian rummaged under a pile of old papers. "You might get rid of these sometime, you know." He found his glasses in his jacket pocket. Josefa laughed. "You laugh at every fucking thing," Christian said, poured himself some coffee and reached for the newspaper. Josefa looked at him as he leafed through the paper, practised as he was in finding the essential news, passed over bold-faced print, gave only a passing glance at the business page, lingered longer at foreign affairs and the arts, turned past sports, concluded with the death notices.

"I had a strange dream," she said. She told the story, with a distinct enjoyment of the bloody details.

Christian looked up at her perplexed, folded the newspaper and put it down on the floor next to the chair. "Where do you get all this anger?" he asked.

"Don't know," Josefa said. Christian's question took a while to sink into her brain with its full weight.

This anger. This. Not any one but a definite one that he knew and whose secret he thought he had found. And now he was shocked because she knew something about it. Sometimes when she lost herself in his arms from one second to the next, because he had forgotten who belonged to the body that he held in his arms. When she felt that he was fighting her, no, not her, not that exactly, only her body, which he had secretly stolen from her and fought it until he had defeated it, subdued it; until it belonged to him alone and Christian remembered Josefa again. He secretly gave her body back to her, as he had stolen it, kissed her face in repentance.

"Did you ever feel this anger against me?" she asked.

Christian took off his glasses. He usually took off his glasses before he said something unpleasant. Josefa couldn't remember that she had ever noticed the connection before. She had only known this hesitant gesture for a short while: the reaching for the temples, the leisurely, time-consuming folding of the bows and the half-blind glance at her in which she underwent a transformation into a blurred, dissolved Josefa not only without a body but without a soul as well. This way he could speak out of her reach, taking shelter behind a fog that only her voice penetrated: no smile, no fear in her eyes.

"Different than you might think. It may be that you always have it, but it is most often asleep and you don't perceive it. And then sometimes it's suddenly there. It isn't really anger at you, it's more against me, a very gross and vulgar anger against me and I don't even know where it comes from. And as long as you fight it, you won't get rid of it. You have to accept it and pass it on. I feel bad about it after the fact. Sex murderers must have feelings like this, worse of course, with the simple difference: they kill and others don't."

Christian stopped talking, opened up the bows of his glasses, put them back on again. "Don't look at me so shocked, I'm not going to kill you. Are you sure that women feel different? Perhaps not as physically, at least not against men, because they are usually stronger. But what do you think women feel when they beat up their children because they fell in a puddle or simply asked an annoying question? Or when they pester their husbands because they shuffle their feet or smell bad or scratch their beards. Isn't that almost the same thing? Wives have always poisoned their husbands instead of slaughtering them."

Josefa pulled her legs up even closer to her body, rested her chin on her knees. It was cold in her room in the morning and the furnace wasn't giving off any heat yet. Maybe that's the way it was. They had all this anger, men and women, she too. She thought of her divorce. She didn't like to think about it. They had buried five years in abuse, mutual guilt, disgust. The fight over the books, furniture, in the end over a kitchen knife costing two Marks thirty. She had lain in wait for half a year so as not to miss the instant when the other forgot his guard and was left vulnerable. Since then she knew her capacity for anger, for primitive vulgarity, and was afraid of it. "Isn't it in both our interests to refrain from being angry, you and me? At least for a person who wants to be mine, whom you want to be his, even if you can't manage that

165

for everyone?"

"That would be great," Christian said and Josefa saw that he furtively glanced at his watch as he said it. "I'm just afraid that the temptation to choose the most vulnerable and the most defenceless is simply too great. It lessens the cost, it's even fun you know; I think it's as awful as you do. But that's the way it is for most people."

"For you too?" she asked softly.

"It happens," Chrisitian said evasively. He was in a hurry, he also pressed Josefa, "Hurry up or we'll get there late."

They didn't talk much on the way there; the old car's motor screeched simultaneously in all registers and they would have had to scream to understand each other. Christian called up in the evening to say that he would be coming late, that she shouldn't wait up for him. Josefa forgot what they had been talking about.

She had wanted to forget it. She didn't want to admit the threat she felt lingering as a result of their conversation. Now that there was no longer any plan that applied to her, none by the others and none of her own, she thought of it again: she remembered every sentence and every scene of her dream, and she was surprised at how exactly she could have known as early as a few weeks ago what would happen with her and Christian. But even when Christian came less often to—as he said—work on his dissertation, which was long overdue, she didn't admit any thoughts about their conversation. It never occurred to her that he owed her an answer that she was afraid of.

What could she have done two weeks ago with the answer she knew in the meantime, without Christian having told her? What other path was left that would have led past this day, which she had spent in bed because she didn't care about anything any more or because no one cared about her any more.

She thought of the desolate evenings without Christian when Strutzer and the *Illustrated Weekly* were the only things that made up her day. Strutzer when she quit work and Strutzer the next morning when she began. Nothing in between. Only her bad conscience with her son, whose shrill voice she couldn't stand, whom she often yelled at, sent away when he wanted to sing her a song he had just learned, or didn't tell him a story as he was used to hearing before going to bed, under the pretext of a headache. She put him to bed earlier than usual, and when it was finally quiet she leafed indifferently through a book, switched listlessly from one TV channel to the next. She reproached herself for being impatient with her child, who had meanwhile fallen asleep and whom she would have liked to have made up with on the spot.

She sat in her chair, her legs outstretched, her chin resting on her knees dreaming, waiting for the phone to ring or for a knock on her apartment door. When it did ring she was startled only to fall back into the same uneasiness because the caller wasn't Christian. Until the excitement and the pointless waiting for the evening to be over became unbearable, when she took two tablets from a glass tube labelled "non-barbiturate sleeping pills".

She didn't like the stuff. She had a funny feeling about the interference with her brain. She found her every movement strange, as if her arms and legs didn't belong to her. And she felt the very second in which she fell asleep. A sudden fall into dizzying depths, waking up each time with a fast heartbeat because she thought she was going to die. Memories of the green towels and the black mask, the injection. Dead. But not dead. She calmed down. It was only the pills. Anesthetized brain cells, she would wake up again tomorrow. Finally grey, warm indifference tightening up around her. So what, what about it, she wouldn't feel it. Only the child…

Although she found the stupor disgusting and it scared her, she ended almost every evening without Christian this way, when the minutes fell on her like raindrops, regular and dull.

She had trouble getting up in the morning. The numbness in her limbs and head lasted longer than the manufacturer promised on the slip included in the box. Josefa came to herself slowly only after a cold shower and strong coffee. She perceived the first hours of the day only superficially, like the landscape from a moving train. The time until noon, fortunately, went by faster than usual.

Jauer watched her with special interest on such days and Luise asked if she was sick, she had such feverish eyes. Josefa went straight to the washroom and looked at her eyes in the mirror. They were right: they were shining feverishly, and her pupils were opened wide like Jauer's before they had treated him. Josefa was startled but calmed down with the thought that, after all, Jauer had swallowed the stuff for many years and in large doses, not just occasionally as she did. As soon as her trouble with Strutzer was over or as soon as Christian had more time for her again, she would be able to get along without it too. Just another two or three weeks and it would all be over.

Christian phoned on a Sunday morning he and Josefa had planned to spend together. He couldn't come, he said. He had to hand in his theses for his dissertation on Monday; not only did he have to, but he wanted to as well. He simply couldn't make it and Josefa would have to understand.

She had cooked. It wasn't spaghetti with tomato sauce this time but a proper meal: lamb with green beans and dumplings. She had stood in line at the butcher's on Friday, which seemed too much for her, squeezed-in between strange stomachs and behinds. But she had put up with it, hadn't gone to the canned goods counter to put one or two cans of lamb goulash into her shopping net, although she and the boy never ate anything on weekends except canned meat. She had had Luise, who was considered an excellent cook, write her out a recipe for potato dumplings, had been standing in the kitchen for an hour grating potatoes and basting the lamb.

"But you are coming to eat," she said.

"There's no point," Christian said, "once I'm there I'll stay over, you know that."

"Then you just won't stay," Josefa said. She knew that all her efforts to talk him into it were pointless, said curtly: "all right, then you won't," hung up, turned off the oven and the hot water for the dumplings, cooked fried eggs for the child, ate nothing herself, took two tablets out of the tube and lay down.

She told her child, who had sat down beside her with a picture book, to turn on the TV in case he woke up before she did. The tapping of the rain on the windows melted into a dull roar. Josefa rolled over right next to her child, whose gentle wheezing from chronic bronchitis, comforted her strangely. She put her hand on his breast to calm his nervous cough. "It'll be spring soon," she

168

said, "the cough will go away then."

"Are you going to hide Easter eggs in the park again?" the child asked.

"Sure thing. And let's go to sleep now."

The child quickly fell asleep and Josefa looked at him for a long time, the way he lay next to her, his head to one side with his chin stuck out willfully, his loose fists on either side of his head. Napoleon, she thought, a man too. And one day he'll be sleeping with women and he'll tell one of them on the phone that she's gone to the trouble of cooking for him for nothing.

Gradually a sleepy numbness spread over Josefa. Only the sound of the rain grew menacingly louder, swallowed up the Rickert's vacuum cleaner and her child's breathing. It was a single note from the ground: dull and booming, an army in measured tread. Josefa remembered a scene: she, ten years old, her bed was next to the window then as well. Outside the window a tram stop, people waiting in the rain, which stood like a wall between heaven and earth. The people were standing bent over by the rain and the cold. Some had umbrellas that the wind got under and turned inside out again and again. Josefa was kneeling in bed, securely wrapped in a blanket, looking at the shivering people until she fell onto the pillow exhausted, overwhelmed by the awareness that she wasn't shivering. It was only at the sight of people on the street drenched to the bone and shivering that she knew what warmth was. She sometimes hoped for rain or a snowstorm for this feeling she never enjoyed except secretly and with a bad conscience.

Later, when she had grown up, she tried a few times to repeat the game, had watched shivering people, wrapped herself up in a warm blanket and had invoked a feeling of comfortable security as she did it. But she no longer felt anything more than the satisfied and very practical discovery that she wasn't standing in the rain or in the cold, but the sensation was gone that she had managed to flee in time into her cave. The scene had lost its mystical quality.

On this day, while noises and feelings grotesquely distorted Josefa's numbed head, the thudding of the rain only seemed menacing, a tireless assault on the thin building walls, behind which she had sought shelter. Outside, the deluge and everyone hoping

169

for his ark. A thousand arks, three thousand, ten thousand, a civilization of arks, a person in every ark, lost, condemned to extinction.

Christian came in the afternoon.

The child sat on Josefa's stomach, alternately held her nose shut and pulled at her eyelids with his small fingers. "Wake up," he crowed, "wake up. Christian's here. You have to cook now."

Josefa didn't know why her child was already dressed this early in the morning and why she had to cook now.

"What time is it?" she asked.

"Four thirty."

Christian looked at her askance. She was probably babbling like a drunk. Awful stuff. She gradually remembered the lamb and dumplings and the phone call. She was too tired to get angry, rolled over with her face to the wall and fell back to sleep.

"Come on, get up," Christian said.

"I'm not getting up," Josefa stammered, "I'm never getting up again when it's raining; when it's raining I stay in bed."

She pulled the covers over her head. Talking wore her out. She only came to herself again in the evening; the powerful smell of lamb and savory had woken her up. Her son set the table and repeated two phrases over and over again: Be nice and quiet. Or else Mommy will wake up. Be nice and quiet. Or Mommy will wake up.

Josefa got up, walked quietly across the hallway into the bathroom so as not to attract Christian's attention. She looked at herself in the mirror: dull eyes swollen from the long sleep, light yellow sallow skin. She held the shower head to her face. The cold water ran across her mouth and eyes. Her skin regained its sense of feeling. Josefa thought about what she should tell Christian. Might be better to say nothing at all. She simply slept during the day, was already at it. She got dressed, tried to put her face in order with the help of all sorts of cosmetic junk. When she finished she smiled at herself in the mirror, smiling would be the best thing to get rid of the sleepy flaccidity.

Christian had made the bed and opened the window wide. It wasn't raining any more and cool clear air streamed into the room.

Christian spoke only to the child as they ate, and Josefa was happy at the time she had gained to think of an explanation, because Christian would ask her later and she couldn't get around giving him a plausible answer. She could say that she had a headache or a toothache and had confused the pain tablets with the sleeping pills. That sounded credible. Or she could say that she hadn't been able to sleep at night... no, then she wouldn't have needed any pills during the day. She even considered telling him what really happened: that she could no longer bear to wait for him and that she sometimes wished she was dead, not to die, she was afraid of that, but to be dead, not to have lived at all, not to have to leave anything behind because she knew nothing. She had quickly abandoned the thought again without knowing why she couldn't dare to tell him the truth. But the vague suspicion that her feelings would shock him had made her hold back. Josefa remembered the smell of the lamb she had chewed on without interest, she smelled the cool, sweet air of that evening, once again felt her tired solitude. Didn't know why she hadn't already understood this evening, why he had had to say this sentence to her only a few days later: Decide only for yourself. Don't rely on me.

Christian didn't ask the expected question after the meal either. They watched a silly western Josefa had already seen, but she didn't say so because she was afraid that Christian had already seen it too. They would have had to turn off the set and talk to each other. Or, what would have been worse, remain silent. Josefa was glad not to have to answer questions. Nevertheless, she was irritated by Christian's lack of interest. She had stood in line at the butcher's on his account, grated potatoes, cooked. She killed the days for his sake, poisoned them furtively with little white pills, and he acted as if all this didn't concern him. She felt now and then that he was watching her. But as soon as she turned around to him, he was looking straight ahead, into the TV set. Then finally: sentimental-heroic music. The sheriff laughs. The deputy polishes his sheriff's badge with awkward pride. The End. Josefa pushed the Off button, lit another cigarette, stood a long while at the window.

"I know a psychiatrist," Christian said.

Josefa turned around slowly and looked at Christian with incomprehension. "Yes, what of it?"

Christian took off his glasses, rubbed his eyes, looked at Josefa with his half-blind glance. "He might be able to help you," he said. "You shouldn't play around with these things, Josefa. I found the empty bottles in the kitchen cabinet just now." Christian stopped talking, opened the bows of his glasses and closed them again. Josefa stood in front of an open window, stared sceptically at Christian's mouth.

"It can happen to anybody," Christian said, "but you have to do something about it in time. You're a mess now, not that it's any wonder after this whole farce. If you can't pull yourself out of the hole by yourself, you'll just have to get some help. He can help you for sure."

"You can help me," Josefa said. "I don't need any psychiatrist to come back one day like Jauer, with thick red cheeks and dull eyes, simply adjusted to another scale, slower or faster, like an alarm clock. What would someone like that be able to do with me? Can he throw the Strutzers out or build power plants, or can he make you come here more often? All he can do is to make sure that I don't notice all that any more. A therapy like that would be a great success: I think Strutzer is charming; B. a town like any other; I stop loving you because I can't love any longer. I won't even miss you. I'm cured. The Rickert vacuum cleaner won't bother me anymore because I'm half-deaf, all my senses dulled. I don't get excited any more, don't yell any more; on the other hand I find pulled-down pants incredibly funny and can sleep at night. Learn to accept the world as it is; come to terms with things; find peace within yourself. And in the end I'm a happy person because I've become stupid. Why then didn't we just stay in the trees as happy apes without the wrongs of civilization? Next to the atomic bomb, the most horrible and cunning threat to mankind are the psychiatrists." Josefa was talking loudly. Christian closed the window, tried to embrace her. "Please, don't get so excited, you've misunderstood me."

Josefa pushed Christian's arm off her shoulder roughly. "Did you say: go to the psychiatrist or didn't you? Well, why not? Even

172

children need psychiatrists nowadays. Because they can't sit still eight hours a day, because their parents stare at the TV all day long and don't say anything to them except: wash up, go to bed, don't be so loud. And when the children have a tantrum and go into screaming fits one day, they send them to the psychiatrist, to anyone whose title begins with *psy-*. He puts the screaming and kicking legs somewhere and somehow or other amputates that young head filled with questions.''

Christian gave up trying to calm her down. He sat down in the chair next to the furnace, supported his head with his hands in a meditative or simply patient way, in any case calmly, which sent Josefa into a rage.

"Are you even listening to me?'' she asked a little softer. "Do you know what I think? They stuff us full of pills until nothing bothers us any more, we don't want to do anything, until we're tired and content and don't want to change anything because we've forgotten how to feel what has to be changed. Psychiatrists block progress. And you want to send me to one of them because it's so simple, much simpler than saying: 'I, Christian, will help you.''

It was only when she had stopped talking and her last sentence stopped short in the unexpected stillness that it seemed to her that she had gotten rid of all her despair. She would have liked to yell, but she was too exhausted. She let herself fall into a chair and remain motionless until Christian knelt down on the floor in front of her, caressed her like a child and spoke cautiously to her.

"It was just an idea I had. Please just forget it. I don't want to sneak off, either, no way. I want to help you.'' He warmed her cold hands and slowly loosened the painful cramp in her neck and finally she was able to cry, because she had a tiny bit of hope.

They made love that night unlike all the other nights. They had back then—back then, she thought, it was ten days ago—she couldn't find the word for it back then. Now she thought of "melancholy''. And "self-denial'', a word she never used normally. She remembered the salty taste of that night, which had come from Christian's tears or from her own.

173

III

The next morning the sky was blue as an ocean on a map, and you could have gotten the impression that the world was standing on its head. Blue, still water hung weightless in the room, the buildings stood firmly on their gables and the pedestrians looked the way children usually imagine people from the southern hemisphere: connected to the ground by their feet alone and yet mysteriously not falling. Josefa stuck her hand out the window, felt the gentle, soft air and decided not to put on a coat, although she knew that she would be shivering when she came home in the evening and although she could already sense the embarrassment of being the only one standing in the subway without a coat or jacket, followed by the indulgent smiles of those less careless than she.

She remembered that she had heard or read about a drink called violet water as a child. Ever since, she considered violet water the best-tasting drink she could think of. It had to be light blue and crystal clear and have a lasting sweet taste; more than anything else the first unexpected spring breeze came closest to her idea of violet water: a lake filled with violet water she could bathe in. Josefa stood on the curb and waited for a gap between the oncoming cars until a rust-colored monster huffed and puffed to a halt. A boy with curly blonde locks, wearing a small red t-shirt at least two sizes too small on his naked chest, waved generously from the open window: please, ma'am, he called. A line of small colorful cars waited patiently behind him until Josefa had reached the middle of the roadway and called out another greeting to the boy. He laughed, stepped firmly on the accelerator so that the monster screeched, shook and leaped ahead as if it belonged to a circus and not to the city sanitation department. Josefa thought that a government that could make the weather must have an easy time of governing. Nice weather for price increases, bad weather for outdoor pop concerts or for summer vacation sales, healthy weather for receiving heads of state—not too hot or too cold—the same for demonstrations, average weather for Children's Day so that they could visit museums and exhibits. Variations were useful even within the same day. Warm and sunny until 8:00, after that violent storms and gusts: anyone who arrived late at work got wet. Gloomy and cool during the day to raise work morale. It would be nice and cloudless again for holidays to promote the recreation of the work force. There would, of course, be differences between industrial and administrative areas. Special adjustments would have to be found for industrial regions, for example, specially programed storm equipment for every shop floor in order to take normal, day, late and night shifts equally into account.

The open-plan office was almost empty, although Josefa had arrived twenty minutes late. Günter Rassow was the only one present from the national politics department; his desk was perfectly ordered as always. Josefa was irritated by the fact that, unlike her absent colleagues, she hadn't been able to wrangle two or three hours under the pretext of a long drawn out appointment in a library or a delayed interview at a press agency in order to take a walk and go for a cup of coffee at an espresso bar. There were tulips on Günter's desk. Every time Josefa saw tulips she had the desire to eat them. One time she hadn't been able to control herself and bit off a piece of a fat blood-red tulip. It tasted bitter and Josefa had spat it out.

Günter Rassow looked behind him at the electric clock over the door. "Well, get enough sleep?" he said and smiled with disapproval. "You know," he said, "it's none of my business, I mean it doesn't matter to me if you come in late. But I think that it really isn't too good for you just now. Couldn't you just try a little harder for a few weeks?"

"Sure, *I* could," Josefa said, "but my kid is so tired in the morning. And when I try to speed him up he screams. And I'm probably not the last one to get to work."

"Other kids are tired too and their parents don't come in late every day. You really ought to have more understanding in your situation."

Josefa waved him off. "Would you please stop with this fucking punctuality? You don't ask either how I manage with a kid and without a husband when I spend the whole week on the road or write on weekends or at night. Just leave me alone with your

175

bullshit for a change."

Günter shrugged his shoulders, turned back to his newspaper and underlined a paragraph with a ruler and red pencil line by line.

"Do you want to come along for some coffee?" Josefa asked.

Günter looked at the clock again, this time at his watch too, took a sandwich bag out of his briefcase and got up without a word.

"Did you watch it last night?" Rassow asked between spoonfuls of cottage cheese.

"What?"

"Well, what else—Frankenstein."

"Damn, I forgot! Was it good?"

"Nice and gruesome. My mother was visiting me. She didn't dare leave the house."

The only woman Rassow ever talked about was his mother. He had just turned forty and it was unlikely that there had never been a woman in his life. But he simply answered all questions on the subject with a bland smile and avoided any elucidating information.

"I stayed in the basement until Saturday evening," Rassow said, "I need a new shelf. No way you can buy one."

"I slept."

Günter sighed. "I'd like to do that myself sometime."

"Well, then go ahead."

"I can't sleep during the day. I've never been able to, not even in the hospital. Dumb habit. Or upbringing. My mother always used to say: 'Only a good-for-nothing sleeps in the daytime.' That sticks with you. You can't shake it off."

"Parents are pretty bad."

"You might have a different opinion when your son talks that way about you someday."

"Who knows?"

Günter scraped what was left of his cottage cheese out of the glass bowl, carefully licked his spoon clean and pushed the bowl in front of him. "By the way," he said and wiped his lips and fingertips clean with a handkerchief, "I didn't tell you about being punctual just now for no reason." He looked urgently at Josefa, just waited for her question in order to be able to tell her something important.

176

"I see what's going on," Josefa said impatiently, "but cut it out. The weather is so nice."

"It hardly makes any difference whether I cut it out or not," Rassow said *sotto voce*. He lowered his head and continued talking at the table top so that no one nearby could read his lips: "Strutzer still has all sorts of things planned for you."

"So what," Josefa said brusquely. Rassow's tendency of blowing every bagatelle into a state secret got on her nerves. "What do you mean? Is there something new?" she asked all the same, while Rassow kept stirring his coffee in silence.

"I'm not really not allowed to talk about it." He almost whispered and edged a bit closer to Josefa. "Strutzer wants to discuss your conduct in front of the Party leadership at the members' assembly. The Party leadership has agreed. But Josefa, I beg of you...not a word. Not even to Luise."

Josefa felt the fright in her stomach as a hot, sharp stabbing sensation slowly spreading to her legs, into her arms. Her hands should begin to tremble. She looked at her fingers until her anxiety had reached them.

"But why?" she asked.

Rassow didn't answer.

"Why, for crying out loud?"

"Not so loud," Rassow said and put his hand on Josefa's arm. "Just don't get excited. I shouldn't have told you. My God, I'm in a real mess if you talk about it."

"All right," Josefa said without looking at Rassow. His fear was embarrassing her. "I won't say anything—And why aren't I permitted to know about it?"

"You'll get an invitation—in writing."

As usual, Josefa thought, the same thing again only bigger, all this crap about violet water and circus mares from the sanitation department: spring didn't make the slightest impression on Strutzer.

"Were you in favor too?" she asked.

"What do you mean: in favor?" Rassow said. "I wasn't in favor. It was just hard to be against it; you've acted rather foolishly, not to mention provocatively. If Strutzer wants to discuss it at the members' assembly there's hardly any way to object. If he had only wanted to pull out the letter again that would have been different, but this way..."

"And Schütz?"

"Was opposed at first. Well."

Rassow suddenly had a strange cough and Josefa saw Jauer, who was standing next to their table with a cup in his hand.

"Sit down, isn't taken," Rassow said, relieved that he could get off the subject.

Jauer told them about the weekend walks he had been taking on the city outskirts since he had been in the hospital. Every Sunday he drove to a lake and ran around it. That was part of his therapy, he said. Being alone, the natural bond to the countryside and the definite goal, too, just to run once around the lake, his joy in the functioning of his body evoked a whole new feeling of self-importance. Jauer had noticeably changed his terminology in the past few weeks. He no longer felt at ease, certain or uncertain, but had more or less a feeling of his own worth. He was also no longer mad or depressed, but decompensated. He no longer talked about his desire, or lack of desire, to work, but about his motivation. Right now he was tremendously motivated, he said, and it seemed that Jauer was talking about his psyche or his physis as if they were things unknown, existing independent of him, but of whose genesis he had an amazed and pedantic awareness.

Jauer's story touched Josefa's thoughts, crossed them and left blanks in them, which Josefa recorded as being unpleasant and annoying without exactly knowing what sort of associations Jauer was trying to urge on her. She imagined the days and weeks awaiting her now, the good bits of advice and the fear and Strutzer, always Strutzer, over and over. Jauer looked at her with his dull eyes. "Training," he said, "you can train the psyche like a muscle." Jauer ran around the lake without thinking of anything except the lake and the trees and the smell of the forest. You can learn that. Jauer already knew how. If only she knew how long the red line had been running across his forehead. But she would have an easier time than Jauer. She wouldn't be alone. To remain who she was for one person. He had often reached incredibly creative states during his walks, Jauer said with a voice that was no longer

178

uncertain. She didn't need a psychiatrist. Her heart beat faster and harder for a moment. No, she would still have Christian. Since yesterday she knew that he would stay. She wouldn't have to endure lonely, sleepless nights like Jauer.

"I have that kind of mood," Rassow said, "I get my best ideas in the summer when I'm fishing. I never go fishing without pencil and paper."

Jauer nodded. "Although," he said, "I don't write anything down. You have to let it sink into you; let it sink deep into your subconscious; that steadies you incredibly."

"What do you let sink in," Josefa asked, "your creativity?"

"The thoughts, so to speak," Jauer said, "the reflected consciousness in the subconscious. You don't suppress it but you make it completely your own, you nourish yourself from them, so to speak, and the subconscious is a sort of digestive organ. It constantly guards the balance between you and your thoughts which, if you don't express them, can never return to you in their original form, but can only be processed through your subconscious."

"And it works?"

"Training," Jauer said, "just training."

Rassow said that he definitely wanted to try it; he wanted to start this summer while fishing.

"The most important thing is: don't express your thoughts, let yourself be nourished by them instead. If you can manage that the rest comes of itself."

Josefa got up. "I have to make a phone call." She was bored by Jauer's breakfast course on psychotherapeutic experiments. Sometimes she thought he was crazy. He was fatter, could sleep, his hands didn't tremble any more, but he was crazy.

She thought over where she should go, seesawed slowly down the stairs one by one. She stopped on the landing, leaned her forehead against the cold, glass wall, then her whole body. It it breaks I'll fall, she thought without feeling any fear. Through the glass she smelled the dusty air drawn by the sun from the streets, she heard the tiny people below laughing and talking. It's been a long while since I've flown, she thought. She wanted to test the wind direction on the flag that was waving on one of the tall buildings. But the flag hung loose and flabby on the pole. Restless longings rose in Josefa. She closed her eyes, looked for an image but it stayed black behind her eyelids. She took a deep breath to suppress her restlessness. Love, she thought, I want love. A love different from the one she had for Christian and for her child. Not a love that was exhausted, constantly tired, one you could live in. I want to love everyone and everyone ought to love me.

When she pulled herself back from the glass wall, she had the feeling that she was in a cage: massive walls left and right, you could look in from the front, retreat was possible only backwards and down the stairs. She went on, further, past the *Illustrated Weekly*, step by step, slowly, because she still didn't know where she wanted to go. Now don't be sentimental, she thought, love for everyone, that existed already as Love Thy Neighbor. And she didn't mean that. What she meant was simpler, very simple really: she had left her apartment building. A blonde boy in a monster had blocked the street for her and had waved to her. She had waved back. It was spring and she had to think about violet water. Then she came into this building, had found out something about Strutzer from Rassow. In addition, she had let Jauer's lecture go in one ear and out the other and had forgotten about the boy and the warm day and that it would soon be summer, too. And she hadn't wanted to forget that. It was that easy.

It was this day that she had thought for the first time of simply leaving the earthquake-proof building once and for all, to run down the sixteen floors; if she was going for good she would run, she thought. She could write a letter, politely stating her decision in it and just as politely ask for the remittance of her file. She had also thought of doing it on the same day, which she considered suitable for weighty decisions. On the third floor she went into the library and asked for an illustrated book on Africa.

The librarian was puzzled. Everyone wanted to read books about Africa; what was it all about, she asked. Josefa had taken the elevator to the sixteenth floor without having thought once about wanting to leave the building. She spent a lot of time leafing through the book, examined every detail of the glossy color pictures as though she had to convince herself that there was something in

180

the world that had nothing to do with the *Illustrated Weekly*, with Strutzer or with the hunk of concrete she spent her days in. Bald young girls with large rings in their ears, who didn't take them off at night, as the caption in the book said, looked with curiosity through the camera into Josefa's eyes. A woman with a child with a bloated stomach on her large hanging breasts. Who knows how many children the woman had given birth to and how many of them were still alive and what the others died of? A child, his face full of flies. Pictures that Josefa knew, which looked like that or something like it. Everyone seen with European eyes, shot with precision cameras, performing strange ceremonies; seldom something familiar and then only by accident. Josefa felt herself close to the mothers. All mothers resembled one another. They have the same hands when they hold their children: loose hands, fingers slightly spread apart to cover the small body. Josefa thought over who she would have been in a photo book about Europe, what thoughts unfamiliar foreigners would have when they looked at her picture. But how could they have taken her picture for that purpose? Josefa with child. Or Josefa at her desk, her child on her lap. That would be closest to the truth, but it would give the wrong idea about working conditions in an industrialized society. Josefa decided on a picture with child, black and white, on non-gloss paper. How would she look next to the mother with the resigned expression? Happier or unhappier; different or similar? The rich relations who unfortunately have tuberculosis. The king's little daughter, protected from the sun in a dark cell, who looks longingly across her nicely trimmed part to the street where the poor children in rags are playing hide-and-seek.

When she looked at the pictures the same envy overwhelmed her, she admitted grudgingly, that she had felt as a child for her grandmother Josefa when her mother had told her about her difficult childhood and Josefa had wanted to be on a green meadow among yellow buttercups, barefoot, a cow next to her and the sleeping twins. Something in the pictures aroused her envy or her longing, which Josefa at the same time dismissed as thoughtless sentimentality. As if she knew nothing about famine, protein deficiency, amoebae, infant mortality, contagion. Yet, there was

181

something in the girl's look, in her bent-over back, in the way she bore her naked breasts that belied all the pretentiousness of civilization and that fed Josefa's suspicion that this bald girl with the rings was happier than she was. She found a green note on her desk at noon informing her officially of Rassow's state secret: "The Party leadership sees itself compelled to bring up your conduct at the assembly of members."

"It's your own fault," Luise said. And when Josefa met Rudi Goldammer in the white hallway, he put his arms on her shoulders, bowed his head and sighed: "yoy-yoy". Josefa thought that Rudi looked like a pale, sad clown with the corners of his mouth and eyes hanging down. "You've really gotten us into a pretty pickle this time," he said.

"I'm sorry," Josefa said.

"Uh huh," Rudi said, pressing his hand firmly on Josefa's shoulder, "oh well, it'll be all right." Then he let his arms slip off Josefa almost casually. "It'll be all right," smiled faintly and went into his office.

For the second time today Josefa felt like simply leaving and not coming back any more. The hallway seemed artificial and ridiculous with the clatter of typewriters and the ringing of telephones behind the doors, the shiny polished floor, the "Caution! Wet Wax" sign: a film set which was monstrous and at the same time pitiful. The walls of *papier maché*, noise from a tape recorder. And what was she supposed to feel sorry about, she thought. She wasn't sorry at all, but those were her lines in this film. When Rudi looked like a tragic clown she had to say: I'm sorry. Sometime or other they must have agreed on their roles in the play, must have accepted them as final.

Why else would she have had to say, I'm sorry?

IV

She no longer had to say she was sorry. Rudi's sad face didn't concern her any more. He had to find himself a new one that everyone had to feel sorry for. They needed to find someone for the role, if only for the others, for Jauer and Rassow and Schütz, who could find out this way that they didn't have to regret anything, that they didn't have to feel sorry about anything. But at least once, in an hour, today, Josefa wanted them to feel what they were losing. She would have to do without the comforting feeling that she was better, more conscientious about her duty, more reasonable than they were. They could yell the phrase "She has to be sorry" against all four walls until they were hoarse; all they would hear would be an empty and unconfirmed echo.

But she had stayed on this day, which had begun with the boy in the red t-shirt in the monster and her appetite for Günter Rassow's tulips. She had also come back on the next day and the day after that. She had looked at documents and filed them, made phone calls and sat at conference tables.

She had to think of Brommel with his thick tomcat's head, when he had looked for the germ of doubt in her, his eyes squinted together to narrow slits, when he had said: "Perhaps you haven't belonged to them for a long time now and simply don't want to admit it." How long ago was that: six weeks or less. It had seemed impossible to her back then to lead that sort of cunning life, to conclude a phony peace with Strutzer, to put her better knowledge to paper in secret so that it could be read at some time or other or be forgotten. There were moments in between when she had longed for the peace that such a life would have offered her, in which she could finally demote Strutzer to indifference. She would join the ranks of the silent ones, the ones seemingly without a brain, who waited for the end of reports and discussions with empty faces, would place her uncontroversial manuscripts with a harmless smile on Strutzer's desk, and only in the evening would she have Christian confirm that she was still her old self in spite of it all. She would have to hear the sentences spoken again that she had said before, and she would have to know that there was one person who heard them besides herself. Evening after evening she would have to line up for a certification of authenticity in order not to forget who she was.

She had told that to Christian two days after the violet water morning, two days after she had found the bright green invitation on her desk. And then, stuttering, tortured, having demanded certainty from him that he was there for her, the "decide only for yourself; don't count on me."

Her mind wasn't ready to accept the contents of the sentence. It played dead, unconscious like a body subjected to unbearable pain.

"I have to explain something to you," Christian said.

"No."

"Please, just listen to me for five minutes."

"No," she said, this time louder.

He pushed his chair in front of her, sat down, his forearms propped on his upper thighs, his hands folded between his knees, sat as if determined to persist in this guilty look, which was at the same time forgiving, until Josefa thought of another one.

"I don't feel good about this business," he said softly. "I feel very awful, rotten."

"This isn't necessary."

She had whispered and Christian hadn't understood her.

"Sorry?" he said.

"This isn't necessary," she said.

"But there is something like this," he spoke timidly, walked on his words as if they were eggs, millimeter by millimeter, in order to tell at the right moment if they were going to break. "But you can want something, really want it, imagine it over and over again until you are quite sure that you want it. And then when it comes, the way you've really and truly wanted it to be, it's different. That is possible, after all."

"No."

"But that's the way it is."

"That's how you see it. Then you just haven't really and truly wished for it. Then you simply wanted it that way, simply that way because you didn't have it. And for fifteen years. You yourself don't believe that's what it is."

"You used to be different."

"It seems that way to you because it didn't affect you."

"No, you were different, you were more confident, stronger. That was it, that's why I liked you."

184

"Then you simply made a mistake."

"Or you began to love me because you couldn't cope by yourself. Josefa, if you didn't think of that in fifteen years, why now of all times? You wanted to sound a retreat. When the ground began to shake under your feet, you wanted to have at least one foot on solid ground. I understood that, I wanted that too. But I can't do that when you stop being yourself. These pills, these accusations, your constant waiting, the fear. When was the last time you had a good laugh?"

"What should I laugh about," she said distracted. A weak attempt at protest, pointless, not meant seriously. Something had been coming over her for weeks, quietly and unavoidably, and she hadn't looked, probably felt that something was secretly moving, had pretended to be blind, deaf and dumb.

"And now?" she asked.

He took off his glasses; ah ha, she thought, so this is it. "Dunno", he said: he does know, she heard. "Somthinsgottachange," he said, tried to spare her, why go on, "alrightthen," she said, kept staring at the tiny coffee spot on the tablecloth, "wellthen," she said.

"I wouldn't have talked about it now," he said.

"Pleasestopit."

Silence.

Jump up, she thought, hold onto him, scream, yell, plead, don't go, don't do that, I can't, please, stay, grab his hair, hold tight, ears, neck, real tight. Please stay.

"So go then," she said, "go now," looked at the tiny brown spot.

"Believemeitisnteasyforme," he said.

"Scram," she said.

He got up, put on his glasses clumsily, didn't look at Josefa, she leaned on him at the door. "No, wait a bit, just a little," she cried, he stroked her head, "lemmego," she screamed. Then they didn't talk for two hours. She didn't see him to the door when he left. "I'll give you a call," he said as he buttoned his jacket. She looked after him, listened incredulously as he quietly opened the lock on the door. She remained seated in her chair and waited for the despair she knew would set in now she was alone and began to understand why she was alone. But the emptiness in her remained painless and cool. She looked strangely at the pictures on the walls, the oval mirror, the ceiling black with cigarette smoke: her child was sleeping in the next room—she was between all that, as before, like a year ago, or like two years ago. But something had ended and there was no despair over it. It will come, she thought, when I wake up and begin to move, it will break loose as soon as I get up. She remained still in the chair. Whatever you do, don't mix up your head, upset the rigid order your thoughts were moving in right now.

I have to do something, she thought. Get angry and scream, maybe it would help, she thought, if she went into a rage. Furious at his betrayal. Who was the betrayer? Christian? Herself? Both? Neither?

When Grandfather Pawel was deported from Germany, Grandmother Josefa, who was a Baptist, was advised to get a divorce and stay in Berlin with her children. Her grandmother had first packed her own things and then her grandfather's. She hadn't emigrated with him to America and not to Russia, and she had forbidden Grandfather Pawel from taking to the road. Later on, however, she wanted to go with him to the ghetto. They didn't allow her to do that. Her grandmother hadn't tried to falsify her life or to run away from it. Faith, love til death us do part. In the meantime that had been stricken from the list of approved words. Protected from abuse. From being used, as well. Consequently there was no betrayal in Josefa's case. There was no betrayal possible where there was nothing to betray. No, there was no anger in Josefa, not against Christian and not against herself. More surprise at what had to happen finally happening. We react precisely, as in the laws of physics, with fatal predictability.

He is right, she thought, he is right.

The next day she asked Luise for a few days off.

The buds on the still bare linden trees in front of the window glistened sticky in the sun; another two or three weeks and the bright green leaves would roll out of their husks. Two or three weeks later and the dust from the street would turn them grey and dull. That's how long spring lasted. A thrush crossed the sky. It glided to earth with outspread wings, then back up again. There was something white between its wings. When the bird came closer, Josefa recognized the doll. The doll wore a white lace-trimmed dress and its plastic fingers were delicately spread apart. A white veil covered its face. Fly the bride, black bird. The heavenly trumpets sound from the funnels of the watering can. The last notes are poured out with the water. Don't cast off the bride, black bird. But look how her veil blows longingly in the wind beneath the sparse myrtle and how its rigid fingers are already beginning to stir. Bring the bride to her bridegroom so they can wed. She opens wide her sleepy doll's eyes and blows the veil from her face. Where did she get these eyes and this mouth? They belong to me. You greedy black sneaky bastard, don't open wide your yellow beak, this bride won't do you any good. She has poison in her veins and glowing coals in her breast. Bring her to her bridegroom so he will die from her poison and turn to ashes in her fire. Fly faster, bird of death, fly with the wind. Look out, she's moving her legs, now her arms. It's her artificial head beneath her artificial hair that is creaking here. She's moving. You've lost if she's alive. She takes her veil from her head and holds it to the wind. The wind tears her veil from her hand. She wants to get off now. Fly faster, bird. She jumps. Don't flail after her, or she will crash. She spreads her rigid arms as if she wanted to swim, she lays into the wind and flies. Get her back. She wants to fly high into the icy sky where the poison in her veins freezes and the flame in her breast smoulders.

The bird circled the linden tree in front of the window, came down on an outer branch and cleaned its feathers. A white spot shone on its back between its wings. Josefa had never seen a thrush with a white spot on its back before. Perhaps it had flow over a construction site and the apprentices had thrown a paint brush at it. The alarm clock stood straddle-legged on the carpet, ticking. It would ring in half an hour. In half an hour Strutzer would open the large assembly hall to let in those waiting. She could still get up, get dressed, she could still make it in a taxi. Josefa reached for the phone, quickly dialled: Mr. Grellmann, please.

Colleague Grellmann is eating, maybe in another half hour.

Josefa dialled again.

"Luise? Josefa here."

"I'll call back," Luise said.

Strutzer or Rudi Goldammer were probably there with her right now if Rudi didn't have a toothache today.

Josefa stuck one leg out of the covers, let it hang out over a side of the bed. Her leg rested on the carpet. Josefa then took an arm out of bed. It swung lazily above the floor. I'll get up in ten minutes, she thought, a taxi won't be of any use in ten minutes. She ran into the kitchen, put on the hot water, ran back into bed, thought over whether she should drink coffee or tea. She decided on tea.

When she finally wanted to get up Luise called. Was something the matter, she asked, or had Josefa thought things over again.

"It's all right," Josefa said, "I'm sticking to it. Tell them that I'm not coming, that I'll never be coming again."

The thrush on the linden tree was still preening its feathers, and it seemed to Josefa that the white spot between its wings had gotten smaller.

V

On the same day that the comrades of the *Illustrated Weekly* had come to the conclusion that it should be considered whether Comrade Nadler was worthy of remaining in their Party, the embodied unity of idea and discipline, the Supreme Council, decided in an afternoon session that the old power plant in B. had to be shut down in consideration of the health of the citizens of B. and in disregard for short-term economic gains.